DEMON MARKED

SHADOW CITY: DARK ANGEL

JEN L. GREY

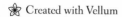 Created with Vellum

CHAPTER ONE

LEVI'S leftover sweet peony scent on the sheets mocked me. My lungs wouldn't work. I couldn't believe that fate had made such a huge mistake by putting the two of us together. Now I was stuck because we'd completed the preordained bond...and he'd *left* me.

His words from last night flashed into my mind. He'd said he would have to do things I wouldn't like, but he couldn't have meant *this*. Telling your preordained mate you were going to Hell but you'd be back was bad, but leaving her like she was a piece of trash was unforgivable.

I'd never understood what *broken* felt like. Before Levi had evoked my emotions, I'd thought people who had meltdowns were unbalanced. How could one person mean so much to an individual that they couldn't function?

Unfortunately, I now understood far too well.

Numbness surrounded me, but it didn't penetrate where I needed it most—my heart.

My heart fractured, the sharp pain worse than my wound from the dagger that had stabbed me ten hours earlier. The outer numbness made my inner agony more intense, and my chest heaved as a sob racked my body.

"Rosemary?" Annie's soft voice called through the bedroom door. "What's wrong?"

I didn't have the strength to respond. All I could focus on was the falling, choking sensation of loss inside me and the sharp sting of betrayal. It literally felt like I'd been stabbed in the back—and here I'd always thought the saying was a cliché.

The same question repeated in my mind over and over. How could he have done this to me? To us?

I'd surrendered my heart, body, and soul to him, and within hours, he'd abandoned me.

Like I was worthless.

A casual screw.

But he couldn't have faked his feelings—the bond was intact. We could no longer hide our emotions from each other. Why put me through this pain?

Footsteps pounded toward the room, followed by a loud banging on the door. Killian's deep voice sounded worried as he asked, "Are you two okay in there?"

His assumption that Levi was still here with me made the situation more real. But why wouldn't he assume it? We'd all been such fools.

I needed to respond, but I had no energy. My body heaved as I held in my sobs.

"She didn't answer me, either," Annie murmured. "I'm worried. She's *crying*, Killian. That's why I linked with Sterlyn."

"You did the right thing," he assured her, then yelled, "Rosemary! If one of you doesn't open this door in two seconds, I *will* come in there. I don't care what I walk in on. Do you understand?"

No. I didn't want him to find me like this. I had to gather my wits.

But no matter how hard I tried, I couldn't find the strength to tell him I was fine. Not that it would matter; he'd know I was lying. The sulfuric stench would hit his nose within seconds.

I wished wolf shifters didn't have such a keen sense of smell.

I was *not* fine. The newly connected half of my soul was gone. The connection was not deathly cold but cool, reminding me he'd left to go back to his home dimension.

Hell.

Levi had left me for the underworld.

As if turning his back on me hadn't been enough, he'd chosen the princes of Hell over us.

He had seemed so sincere last night, risking his life to save mine, and when we'd connected...

I couldn't think back to that event without part of me dying.

Shattered didn't adequately describe my heart.

Obliterated.

Annihilated.

My heart raced. I wasn't sure I would ever recover.

The door splintered, and Killian stormed inside.

I buried my head under my pillow, not wanting him to see me like this, but I could feel his towering six-foot-four-inch frame hovering over me.

"Rosemary?" he asked in confusion.

No one had ever seen me cry since infancy. I'd cried less than a handful of times in my life, and those occasions had been because of *him*, too. Levi—no, *the demon* had too much influence over me.

Killian's musky sandalwood scent mixed with Levi's,

and I wanted to scream at the alpha wolf to leave. This might be my last chance to remember Levi's scent, and I didn't need Killian's intermingling, diluting it faster.

Oh, gods. My emotions were on par with a mortal's, and I yearned for the one-dimensional state of being I used to have.

Emotions were overrated, especially the negative kind.

Killian sighed. "Where's Levi?"

There it was—the inevitable question I'd have to answer multiple times but couldn't. Not yet. Instead, I sobbed even harder.

"I'm going to *kill* him," Killian growled, and the bed dipped as he sat next to me.

Not if I get to him first. I grimaced at the thought, unable to harness the anger I needed to believe those words.

Oh, how I wished I could. Anger would be a welcome distraction from the devastation swirling inside me.

Strong arms wrapped around me, but not the ones I desperately desired. Having Killian in bed with me felt wrong, despite it being innocent. There was only *one* person meant to be in bed with me, and he'd left me like I was replaceable. As if I meant nothing.

I wrapped the covers tightly around me, since I was wearing only the shirt Levi had given me after we'd bathed together last night, and I forced myself to move to the couch positioned under the bedroom window. My clothes had been torn from the injuries I'd sustained yesterday in the battle against the demons.

"Hey, what's wrong?" Killian sounded hurt.

My heart twinged. I hadn't meant to upset him. "It doesn't feel right being in bed with you. Not when—"

He moved next to me on the couch and pulled me into his arms. "I'm here. You don't need to hide."

His tenderness added to my heartbreak. He was one of the *best* friends I had, but I still felt abandoned.

Levi should have been here, not Killian.

Unable to do anything else, I buried my face in Killian's muscular chest. His skin ran hotter than Levi's because of the animal inside him, and I cherished the difference.

He didn't say anything as I broke down further. I wasn't sure what would be left if I ever stopped crying. My soul had splintered, and I'd never feel whole again.

My eyes burned like they were on fire, and eventually, I had no more tears to cry. The debilitating pain remained, but everything inside me had dried up.

There was no telling how long he and I sat like this.

I sniffed, and Killian murmured, "I hate to ask, but what happened? Did he *do* something to you? I've never seen you like this before."

No one had. If anyone but Killian had seen me now, I'd be even more embarrassed. At least the first person I told would be him. It would give me some practice.

"He...left." Whispering those two words was the hardest thing I'd ever done, and that was truly saying something.

He leaned back. "Left?"

My vision cleared slightly, enough to take in the circles under Killian's dark chocolate brown eyes. His cappuccino hair was messier than usual because of the insane situation we'd had with a demon prisoner.

The demon prisoner who'd fooled us into thinking he was on our side. With whom I'd stupidly completed my preordained bond, a connection similar to what wolves called fated mates and vampires called soulmates.

Levi was the other half of my soul, and though we'd bonded not even ten hours ago, he'd already left me behind.

That shouldn't have been possible.

Would he have left if we hadn't bonded? Or had he stayed only until we had?

The questions stung, but I had to be pragmatic. My heart screamed that the timing was purely coincidental. If only I could trust it.

From what I'd seen with Sterlyn, Ronnie, and Annie, giving in to their connection with their other half had solidified their relationship. Griffin, Alex, and Cyrus hadn't *abandoned* them like Levi had abandoned me.

Not that I was jealous. I wasn't. Those three women were some of the best people I'd known in my entire millennium of life, but it *hurt* that Levi had left within hours of us completing our bond.

Mumbles from downstairs informed me that everyone was up. I could even detect Griffin's and Sterlyn's voices from here, though my mind couldn't focus enough to hear what they said.

That was enough for something other than turmoil to rise inside me. "Is something wrong?"

"Everything is as good as it can be, given the circumstances." Killian's body relaxed marginally at the change in topic. "We buried the dead and slept for a few hours next door. Annie connected with Sterlyn when she heard you..."

He didn't have to finish. I'd heard the conversation at the door even when the grief had overwhelmed me. "I did something stupid. I completed—" My chest shook again.

Apparently, my body had had a long enough break, and the tears were ready to fall again.

"You don't have to tell me." Killian sniffed and tightened his hold on me again. "I can smell it."

Between the stench of sex and the comingled smell of our souls combining, he'd know what we'd done. When two souls connected, their scents merged, and Killian could, no doubt, sense Levi's peony scent on me. It wasn't only because he'd been in bed with me not even an hour ago.

I couldn't keep falling apart. We had a lot going on. Here I was, mourning my preordained partner's abandonment when Sterlyn's pack was grieving the deaths of two of their silver wolves. Now there were only fifteen of their kind in existence. There might be sixteen, once Annie and Cyrus's baby was born, but we couldn't be sure about the heritage of their child.

Annie was a demon wolf, and Cyrus was a silver. Never had offspring resulted by forming a union like theirs. When a silver wolf mated with a regular wolf, their children were fully silver with no dilution. We'd learned it was the same for demon wolves. But while there was uncertainty around what to expect with their unique offspring, I was certain of one thing: their child would grow up to be a strong, good person like both of its parents.

The urge to stay wrapped in Killian's arms was all too tempting, but the longer I wallowed, the harder it would be to get up. If I wasn't careful, I could spend eternity lying in bed, mourning the love of my life.

I *refused* to allow him to have that much control over me.

I pulled away and wiped my eyes, then inhaled deeply to remind my lungs how to move. They were frozen as if they'd forgotten that although I was immortal, I needed oxygen.

"Let's go downstairs." Shifting my mind to something other than Levi should lessen the pain slightly. Something had to. It was too much to live with.

Killian's brows furrowed. "We don't have to. Let's stay—"

"I need to." My heart screamed, *No, don't do it*, but I couldn't lie here and let the world fall apart. My mother needed me back in Shadow City, and I had no reason to not return.

At least, not now.

Getting away from a room that smelled and reminded me of *him* would be good for me. I didn't want to leave, which told me I should.

"Okay, but maybe you should take a shower first." He bit his bottom lip. "I'll run next door to get you some clothes of your own and leave them in front of the bathroom door."

How did he know? I glanced down and realized the covers were thin, and though he hadn't seen anything unmentionable, I was clearly wearing a man's shirt that was four times too big for me. "Sounds good."

He slowly stood and paused. He tilted his head, his hunter green cotton shirt making his olive complexion glow despite the exhaustion on his face. "Are you sure you're—"

"Yes. Please stop asking." A lump formed in my throat, and my bottom lip quivered. If he kept showing me such kindness, I'd break down all over again. I didn't want to be rude, but I needed to move before heartbreak swallowed me once more.

Frowning, he nodded and headed for the stairs. He didn't bother shutting the door since it now hung crooked off the frame.

I scanned the room. The walls were beige, just like every other room in this house. The queen bed was centered against one wall, and the long cloth couch I was sitting on rested under the window, which faced the front of the house. The fluffy, forest-brown comforter had fallen on the ground when I'd wrapped myself in the sheet, and the four large pillows were scattered on the bed.

Everything looked the same. The world still turned, despite my devastation. How could things continue as they always had when I was destroyed?

I stood, and my chest tightened as I pulled down Levi's shirt, covering as much of my legs as possible. My jeans lay on the ground, but they were filthy, and this shirt was longer than some of my dresses.

As I stepped into the hallway, I glanced to the left, down the stairs, then toward the other two rooms catty-corner from this one. Killian had taken the one across from this room, and Ronnie and Alex were staying in the large master bedroom to the right.

The bathroom was between the other two bedrooms, and I rushed in, needing a reprieve.

I hadn't expected the torrent of emotions that surged through me when I closed the door. Memories of the night before, when Levi had taken care of me and gone as far as to bathe me, flashed through my mind.

I wished I could go back and change my decision...but my heart called me a liar.

Pushing away the memories, I padded over the cool red oak–colored tile and turned on the shower. I removed the shirt, and as I went to toss it on the ground, the strangest urge overcame me—I didn't want to wash it or get it dirty.

Unable to ignore the instinct, I placed the shirt gently on the marble countertop and bent over to get a clean towel from under the sink. When I rose again, I caught my reflection in the mirror.

I almost didn't recognize myself.

My normally straight mahogany hair hung lifelessly. My usually fair skin seemed ghostly, and the purple in my stardust-colored eyes didn't shimmer. My face looked gaunt in a way I'd never seen before.

All the stupid movies Sierra had made us watch painted love as something that made you timeless, but my reflection told a different story—one that had aged me.

The old Rosemary would have told me to get my act together. That one person didn't define you, and if you succumbed to misery, it would prove you weren't a warrior. She would've been right, but...this Rosemary saw things in a different light.

Sometimes, just standing in place wasn't only a battle— it was the entire war.

I would know, because all I wanted to do was curl into a ball.

I forced myself to turn away from my ghost and step into the tub. Even the hot water didn't soothe me.

A faint knock echoed in the bathroom, and Killian's voice filled the air. "I've put your clothes here."

"Thank you. I'll hurry." Even as I made the promise, I realized it would be hard to carry through. My arms felt like five-hundred-pound weights, and my breathing was ragged from scrubbing my hair.

"Don't rush. We're down here talking." Killian cleared his throat. "Kira is on her way, so you've got time."

Kira.

Levi's "Red."

Jealousy burned through my chest, but I pushed it away. He wasn't here, so none of that mattered.

I quickened my pace, enjoying the sting and burn of moving my arms. It distracted me from my inner pain.

Finally, I got out and grabbed the jeans and fresh burnt orange sweater Killian had provided. A faint smile teased my lips as I appreciated how well he knew me and my favorite color.

I dressed and made my way back to Levi's room.

Though my head told me I was being ridiculous, I laid his shirt on the bed, unable to get rid of it. I had a feeling that if I did, I'd regret it.

Suddenly, Kira yelped outside, and my heart began to pound.

Had the demons returned?

CHAPTER TWO

MY WINGS EXPLODED from my back through the slits built into my sweater as I raced to the window. I looked out and hurriedly opened it, my chest tight.

What if the demons had caught Levi and were using him as leverage? My stomach soured at the thought, and I focused on our lukewarm bond.

He wasn't here. He was still in Hell.

The trunk of Kira's blue sedan was raised, and Kira's poppy-red head was bent over it, searching for something.

No demons.

I wasn't sure if that was better. Considering how frantic she appeared, something was wrong. I needed to get out there.

I surveyed Shadow Terrace, making sure no dangers were looming that I couldn't see. The sun was rising, and I glanced around the immediate area.

The houses we were staying in were the farthest from the center of town. They were spread out much like the layout of Killian's pack neighborhood in which each house had a yard, though these front doors all opened right onto the cobblestone road. The houses were two stories high with backyards that abutted woods filled with redbuds, oaks, and cypresses, their leaves having turned the various shades of fall—reds, oranges, and yellows.

I noted that along with Kira's car, Griffin and Sterlyn's black Navigator and Alex and Ronnie's Mercedes SUV were parked on the street. Nothing seemed out of place around the burned house to the left or the house to my right where more of us were staying.

The homes had the same old-fashioned feel as the rest of the town. All the buildings were painted white with red roofs. The only things that varied were style and proximity. As you got closer to the heart of downtown, the buildings were connected with no room in between. Signature antique gaslights lined the concrete sidewalks that tourists traversed.

One building varied from the rest: a stone cathedral with a dome on top. It sat in the center of town, across from what had been the main vampire bar. The cathedral had been built about a hundred years ago as a way to lure humans to the vampires' feeding grounds. We'd learned that latter part recently, and it was connected to how Alex had become king of the vampires after his older brother had been killed.

Flying would have been ideal, but I couldn't risk a human seeing me, so I rushed downstairs and outside to the cobblestone road. Though I was still drained from the battle we'd fought not too long ago, I ran quickly. Physical movement didn't require magic. Anything that was natural for an angel, like walking, flying, or breathing, didn't require additional energy.

Kira probably couldn't stay long. As the leader of the police force in Shadow City, she had a demanding job and came here only to talk to us freely, without the risk of prying ears.

The closer I got to her, the more frantic she became. She kept opening a weapons box, feeling around inside, and closing it.

That *wasn't* normal.

The front door of the house I'd exited opened, and my friends ran outside. I could hear each one's footsteps clearly behind me: Sterlyn, Griffin, Killian, Sierra, Alex, Ronnie, Annie, and Cyrus.

Kira stilled and straightened while keeping her focus downward.

Red flags prevailed, and I took slow, steady breaths to calm my frazzled nerves. She was acting guilty, and my gut said a certain demon who'd left me brokenhearted was involved.

What had he done now?

Sterlyn stepped up beside me. She was close to my height, slightly under six feet tall. The long, light silver hair identifying her as the silver wolf pack's alpha was pulled into a messy bun, which wasn't her usual style. Her light purple-silver eyes were darker than usual, too, evidence of stress, mourning, and sleep deprivation. Her olive complexion was a smidge pale, emphasized by her black shirt, but if I hadn't known her, she would've looked put together. She could remain poised even in the midst of a crisis. "What's wrong, Kira?"

The fox shifter flinched, and her emerald eyes locked on Sterlyn. She bit her bottom lip. "I may have made a mistake."

My mouth dried. Kira was confident and cunning. For her to say that meant the situation was likely worse than I expected.

A loud sigh left Griffin, Sterlyn's mate, as he appeared beside her. His honey brown hair wasn't gelled like usual but rather messy, making the blond highlights that matched the scruff on his face stand out. He was muscular, almost on par with Cyrus, and the alpha of Shadow City. He had at least half a foot on Sterlyn and was the tallest person here. "Just tell us what happened."

"Drag it out," Sierra smart-mouthed. "Trust me."

The overwhelming urge to smack her rooted inside me. I spun around, my gaze landing on her, and my foot involuntarily took a step in her direction.

She lifted her hands in front of her face and blinked her gray eyes. A breeze lifted the sandy blonde ponytail she always wore. She was a few inches shorter than me, but her personality made up for it. She scoffed, "Geez, I'm sorry, but this is why I told her to hold out. You guys don't know how to let things go."

I would let things *go*, all right...

I froze and reminded myself that harming Sierra wouldn't accomplish anything. When rational Rosemary reappeared, I'd be ashamed that my emotions had gotten the best of me. Again.

Those *damn* emotions.

Despite Sierra annoying me, I was already on edge because of Levi, and it wasn't fair to take my frustration and hurt out on her. Being emotional was a huge pain in the rump. I'd always suspected it would be, but living it was worse than I'd imagined. Sustaining a rational headspace was *hard*.

"Sometimes, silence is the best solution," Alex murmured in his slight accent, which sounded faintly British. The paleness of his skin was normal, but his light blue eyes held fatigue. He stood beside Ronnie, his wife, who shielded Sierra from him. He was only a few inches taller than me but emanated a regal authority from growing up as vampire royalty. "You should work on that."

Ronnie cut her bright emerald eyes to her husband and shook her head. The sun glinted off her copper hair. Unlike her husband, she seemed nearly human since she'd grown up in the world outside of Shadow City and its surrounding areas, and though she was his vampire queen, you wouldn't know that from her down-to-earth demeanor. "You're just as bad as Sierra. You take every opportunity to chastise her."

"That's very true," Annie agreed. She placed a hand on her small baby bump and laid her head on her mate's shoulder. Her long brown hair cascaded down her back, and her brown eyes appeared sunken. Exhaustion wasn't good for a pregnant woman. Her body was already working overtime without the added stress and drama.

Her features contrasted with Cyrus's as he placed a hand securely around his mate's waist. His hair was a darker silver than his twin sister's, revealing he was also a silver wolf alpha's son but that Sterlyn was the true heir. Only silver wolf alpha children had silver hair. The rest of the silver wolves sported all different shades, though their fur was always silver in wolf form. Cyrus's eyes were pure silver, and right now, they bore dark circles underneath. He'd fought in the recent battle, and though Sterlyn was technically the silver wolf alpha, she and Griffin would be focused on cleaning up the corruption in Shadow City for some time, so Cyrus was acting alpha in her place. The role had made the loss of several silver wolves in the battle harder on him.

Seeing the couples' affection toward each other ripped open the wound in my heart. They all deserved happiness, but what I wouldn't give to have Levi here beside me...

My hands fisted, and my fingernails cut into my palms.

No. I wouldn't allow myself to miss someone who'd left me without explanation. I was better—

I couldn't bring myself to finish that sentence.

A sharp pain shot through my chest, and my vision blurred once more. Ugh, I had to lock this down before I fell apart in front of everyone.

"Kira, what's wrong?" I landed a tense stare on the fox shifter. She had to see that I wouldn't let this go.

Kira closed her eyes and ran her hands through her hair.

If she didn't start talking, I'd make her. My jaw ached from clenching, and I forced it to relax.

"For the love of the gods, Kira," Griffin growled.

Kira straightened her shoulders but avoided our gazes. "Well, the flat tire wasn't the only reason I left my car here last night."

This confirmed that her mistake had *everything* to do with Levi.

My pulse pounded so hard that my ears rang. What had *he* done?

If he'd screwed us over, we needed to know the situation we were in. We were already at a *huge* disadvantage with our small number of fighters compared to the demons, especially after losing two more silver wolves just hours ago.

"There was a reason Levi was in Shadow City the other night." Kira wiped her hands down the front of her jeans.

That, I'd figured. He'd been so careful with his explanation, like he'd been choosing his words to ensure he didn't inadvertently lie. If he had lied, we all would've known and called him out on it, so he must have truly been curious about the city. But he'd taken a huge risk by sneaking in there, and curiosity hadn't been his only reason.

"Which was...?" Sterlyn said encouragingly. Unlike her

mate, she was understanding and trying to prod Kira along. That was what made her the best leader of the bunch. She naturally understood how to make people feel safe and not judged. Being gruff with Kira would only make her clam up.

However, *I* didn't have the patience for it. With all the emotions surging inside me, my natural inclination was to be like Griffin, or worse. I wanted her to inform us, and every additional second she took made me more frustrated.

"Okay, I take it back." Sierra huffed. "Don't drag it out. Just say it. I *need* to know."

Alex groaned.

"What did you do?" I demanded. If no one would be direct, I would.

Surprising me, Kira met my eyes and murmured, "I gave him a sword."

There had to be more to it. She knew that demons already had weapons and wouldn't be acting this guilty over a mundane weapon. She hadn't told us everything...*yet.* "What *kind* of sword?"

Her lips smashed into a line. "Damn angel," I could've sworn she mumbled, but before I could respond, she continued, "It was a demon box, but it's empty. It looks like a sword was in it, but I couldn't check because the box wouldn't open for me. Levi had to have gotten into it."

My stomach hardened. I *must* have misheard her. She couldn't have handed over a *demon weapon* to a *demon.* This had to be a sick joke—one of the stupid pranks mortals played that never made sense to me. However, the air was devoid of sulfur. The only sounds were the murmurs of the humans in the town square a few miles away, the trickling of the river, and the cardinals and mockingbirds calling to each other as they flitted through the trees, enjoying the cool fall morning.

I moved to look inside the box and noticed the outline of a weapon...a sword. I reached my hand inside it, but all I touched was air. "It *is* gone."

"That's what I said." She waved her hand. "It's empty."

I closed the box, and the sign of a double-barred cross with an infinity symbol that connected at the bottom stared back at me. It was a demon symbol. "I checked because I wanted to make sure the sword wasn't invisible," I said. "Ronnie's dagger can be, but if I touch Ronnie's in its invisible form, it's uncomfortable."

"He got a demon sword," Sterlyn said slowly with no inflection.

She was trying hard to keep her wits, but the hurt inside me was shifting to anger.

"Why in the *world* would you provide a demon with a strong weapon?" Alex asked Kira through gritted teeth.

One piece of information Levi had shared with us was that the demons knew about Ronnie. Obviously, they needed this weapon, and I worried that Wrath would use the sword to take vengeance against the person who'd bonded with his dagger.

I was glad I wasn't the one who'd asked the question. At least Alex and Griffin were on the same page as me.

I was also at a loss. Kira was a smart woman. She might be young, close to Sterlyn's age, but from my perspective, this whole group was nascent—except for Alex and me—and they didn't make horrible mistakes like this.

"He said he needed to protect not only his father but all the residents of Shadow City and the surrounding towns. That if he wasn't the one to retrieve the box that belonged to his mother, another demon could use it to destroy everything I *love* and *protect*. He swore he was the only one who could ensure it would never fall into the wrong hands." Kira hung her head. "I mean, he *saved* me, and he seemed like a good guy. He wasn't lying. The box was sealed, so I couldn't check, but I didn't realize it was a weapon until I opened the trunk and saw this open."

My ears roared. Could that be why he'd saved her? But how could he have known she was the police officer responsible for guarding the artifact building? Kira rarely left Shadow City, so she wasn't widely known outside the high city walls. Maybe he'd saved her in hopes that she would divulge information, but I'd shown up before she could?

There were so many possibilities that my head spun.

The one time we let our guard down, Levi sneaked away with a weapon.

Finally, my mind landed on one thought, and it made me sick. He'd confided in his *Red* that something huge could happen, but he'd never told me.

I understood why he hadn't at first, but after we'd completed our bond, things had changed. He would've felt it. Why hadn't he trusted me? What was so special about her that he would risk everything in the hope that she would help him?

He'd told me that he refused to let his father remain in Hell, but that didn't mean taking a powerful sword where my enemy could easily get their hands on it. Why did he need it to get his father? None of this made sense, and my stomach soured.

And here I'd been hoping that he had a plan and hadn't just abandoned me. He couldn't have faked the emotions I'd sensed from him last night.

Could he?

Kira's face fell. "He couldn't have lied, right? I would've smelled it."

"I don't think he meant to lie, *if* he did." Ronnie ran a hand down her face. "If Levi is connected with the sword and doesn't die, no one will be able to use it but him. That's what he had to mean."

"How did you even get it out?" I demanded. This whole situation was surreal, but Levi appeared to have goodness in him. If his actions were somehow a way to keep the balance, then he was doing what he *thought* was right, no matter how misguided he might be.

Kira exhaled. "I told them I needed to be the one to inventory the room where the most guarded weapons are kept. A small shipment came in, and the other guards went to unload and catalog it. It was dark and late, so I took the box to the car, not realizing it was a weapon or what he meant to do with it."

She hadn't meant harm, but intention didn't matter.

My body shuddered as my blood ran cold. The princes of Hell would be desperate for that kind of power. Even hurt and infuriated, I didn't want Levi to *die*.

Maybe I shouldn't have completed the bond.

Flashes of our kisses, of Levi washing the blood of battle off me in the shower, of the way we'd moved together—of how, for a brief moment, all had felt right in the world—made the truth apparent, even if I didn't want to face it.

All the pain in the world was worth it.

Gods.

Oh, how I'd fallen.

"Fine, he might not be planning to give the damn sword to the princes of Hell, but plans don't always go accordingly." Killian crossed his arms. "What are we going to do?"

The answer was simple. "We focus on the problems in

Shadow City, since they appear to be escalating," I replied. "We can't risk closing the portal in case Levi comes back with the weapon, and we don't know anything about Hell. The last time we closed a portal, it reopened. At least now we know it's close by." A throbbing pain ran through my veins.

I hated the thought of deserting him, but he'd made his choice...whatever it was.

"Agreed." Sterlyn moved so she could face us. "Kira made a mistake, but if Levi holds true to his word, we won't have a problem. Until we learn otherwise, we deal with the things we can influence. The four shifters who attacked Yelahiah and Kira will be in jail until the inventory at the artifact building is complete."

The news got worse and worse. "Azbogah is up to something." The angel and council member never stopped scheming.

"Why would you say that?" Sierra's brows furrowed. "They're in jail. That's a good thing."

Alex shook his head and waved at the empty trunk. "At least one artifact is missing, and Azbogah will swear their attack was justified since the building was broken into and things were stolen. They'll get off."

Not if we had anything to say about it. I hated to do it, but the time had come to confide in my mother. She always knew what to do.

But before I could suggest as much, Griffin's eyes glowed. "We've got to go back to Shadow City. There's been a horrible accident."

CHAPTER THREE

GRIFFIN'S normally strong composure crumbled. "We've got to go. Kira, the police need you." He pivoted and raced toward the Navigator.

My body became heavy. Griffin was beside himself, and I'd seen him like this only when Sterlyn was at risk. I had a strong suspicion about what was happening.

His mother was in danger.

Taking a hurried step after her mate, Sterlyn called over her shoulder, "There's a fire at the Elite Wolves' Den, and Ulva and several other shifters are trapped in their condos."

My instinct had been right. No wonder Griffin was panicked. Ulva was his last surviving parent.

"Holy shit," Kira grumbled, and slammed the trunk. Her phone rang, and I suspected it was the police force, searching for their leader. She answered the phone as she raced to the driver's-side door. "I'm on my way. I just heard. Until I get there, I need you to handle it. Reach out to some angels to see if they can help get the trapped residents out."

There was no doubt in my mind about what I needed to

do, especially since finding angels to assist might be difficult. I would bet money that Azbogah was behind the fire and had most of the angels occupied with whatever plan he'd concocted, and the other angels would be training or doing their day jobs.

As Kira shut her door, the Navigator spun out and raced back toward the city. Kira wasn't far behind them, leaving the rest of us standing in the driveway, stunned.

"Us, too," Ronnie said as she and Alex blurred to their Mercedes, and within seconds, their vehicle was running.

I was born to take action, not stand here like a knot in a log. "I'm going to help."

"Are you sure that's a good idea with you—" Killian began, but my glare stopped him.

I wouldn't allow Levi to affect me so much that I lost sight of who I was, even if the pain was overwhelming. I was still the angel who wanted to help every good person, regardless of supernatural race, because that's what was truly just.

Ulva definitely fit that description.

Sierra sighed dramatically. "That's how *not* to talk to a woman. It's no wonder you haven't found your fated mate— you aren't ready. You'd run her off saying misguided crap like that."

"You haven't found yours, either," Killian grumbled.

Needing to go, I reassured them, "I'll be fine. I *need* to help."

Annie and Cyrus nodded with understanding. They'd gone through hard times and were sympathetic to the fact I needed something other than Levi to focus on.

Levi.

My eyes burned, and I took off into the air, refusing to let them see me cry. As quickly as possible, I raced across the sky. I needed to get high enough that humans would think I was a bird. My wings flapped hard, and the exhaustion inside me twinged. Even though flying didn't use magic, I was halfway drained of energy after the intense fighting, healing last night, and most of all, my mate being in a different dimension. The aching void swirled from all the emotions inside.

The air was cooler this high up, even with the sun shining down on me. The sensation helped clear my head, but despite the freedom and peace that flying brought, Levi stayed way too present in my thoughts.

I had a feeling he always would. I'd have to figure out how to survive it because living with this intense pain forever would be worse than a prison sentence.

My throat constricted, making it difficult to swallow. I was spiraling, and Ulva needed my help. I couldn't stand still and lick my wounds, even though I had mortal feelings now.

Humans frequently said that fate had a sense of humor, and I'd always found the saying odd. Fate wasn't a living, breathing thing, but rather the universe holding the knowledge of how to balance the world. Each event, even the horrible ones, happened for a reason, and the end justified the means. Fate didn't decide who was evil but rather knew *what* they would make and how to rectify the consequences.

An angel being preordained with a demon was nonsensical. It would only cause more strife between angel and demon. Then add in that the demon had *left* the angel, and it had to be some cruel joke.

A flock of birds rose about fifty miles away, though they appeared closer. Being in the sky made it hard to judge distance if you hadn't learned to do it correctly. I'd taken a geography class at Shadow Ridge University to learn about the world outside our closed-off little area, and they'd explained a similar phenomenon when someone walked along the ocean. Apparently, where the land was flat around the shoreline, something that looked close could be several miles away.

I'd never seen the ocean before, and I yearned to. I needed an experience separate from Levi. He'd ruined Shadow City and Shadow Terrace for me, and even Shadow Ridge would bear a touch of his memory because of the silver wolves we'd lost in the demon attack.

As I approached the gigantic bridge that connected Shadow Terrace to Shadow City, I gradually flew lower. Once I reached the bridge, the humans wouldn't be able to see me. The Shadow City witches had cast a constant cloaking spell over the bridge and the enormous dome-shaped city. The spell also created the illusion that the Tennessee River was significantly narrower than it actually was, and if any humans on boats drew too close to the Shadow City island, they felt an overwhelming urge to leave the area, protecting it from discovery.

The connecting bridge looked identical to its sister bridge on the Shadow Ridge side. Sterlyn had compared its immense towers, which jutted high into the sky, to some bridge in California. The bridge was magnificent, and I couldn't fathom that humans had designed something similar to this, but Ronnie had shown me pictures on the internet that proved this Golden Gate Bridge had a similar grace in its suspension to these two. Supernaturals must have been involved in its making. That was the only conclusion I could draw.

Massive, concrete-like walls surrounded the city, standing well over one hundred stories high. The city's emblem—the skyline of Shadow City with a paw print hovering between the two tallest skyscrapers—was carved on the outer wall over and over again. After the death of Mother's brother, Ophaniel, the father of the silver wolves, she had insisted the paw print be included to represent him and the silver wolves whom he'd helped to escape before his untimely death. Because of Ophaniel's sacrifice, the wolves had avoided the same brutal future, but they'd left their home behind. She'd wanted a stark reminder of the tainted past Azbogah had created.

Angel glass covered the top of the dome, which prevented anyone from coming or leaving through the air. The only ways in or out were the two gateways on either side of the city. Both bridges could also be raised from inside if needed, preventing anyone on foot or in vehicles from getting to the sturdy gates.

I descended onto the Shadow Terrace bridge and heard Griffin's Navigator quickly approaching. That was one nice aspect about flying—I could travel faster than cars.

Even though the vampire guards on this side didn't know me well, they knew all angels lived within Shadow City, so there was no question about whether I should be allowed inside.

As if confirming my suspicions, I heard the crank turning as Griffin sped across the bridge toward me. At least the gate would be raised so he could drive through without pausing.

Since Alex and Ronnie had taken over the throne, all supernatural races except demons had finally been allowed into Shadow Terrace, though most non-vampires still shied away. This area was old, and supernaturals were set in their ways. Change took time to truly take effect, and even with other vampires knowing we'd fought alongside them, I and other non-vampire visitors to the town still got strange glances thrown our way.

I could only imagine what everyone would think if Levi had been beside me right now.

My heart became so heavy that it skipped a beat. The agony was so overwhelming that I wasn't sure if I would ever get back to who I'd been before I met him.

When the gate was high enough, I barreled inside, desperate to reach the Elite Wolves' Den. The beautiful colors swirled around me, and my magic began to recharge. With the sun shining on the dome, the colors were bright, and my breathing evened out. I immediately felt at home.

Angel glass was the best source for angels to recharge their magic, as the lights it created reflected the angel magic inside us. Shadow City was similar to Heaven, where a few angels had stayed. Most angels had come to Earth to support humans, but intentions had become convoluted along the way, and some angels had decided they wanted us to rule the world. Enough angels had disagreed with that sentiment, so Azbogah had decided that angels should rule *this* city instead. The city was meant to be a haven for all supernaturals, but angels had distorted that goal and turned the place into an exclusive haven for the most powerful. If you ruled over the most powerful, you essentially ruled over the world.

I sped over the city's vampire section and headed toward the shifter area. On the way, I passed Alex and Ronnie's mansion. The royal family, which included Alex's sister, Gwen, inhabited the four-story Neo-Renaissance-style building, which was different from the other buildings around it. Several of their household employees lived there, too, and guards ensured that the king, queen, and princess were safe in their home at all times. Shadow City could be more ruthless than the world outside with four very different supernatural races living so close together in a space only a select few were allowed to leave.

I pushed onward, and my wings grew stronger as my magic reenergized. When the white capitol building came into view, I knew I was approximately halfway through the city, which meant I would be at the Elite Wolves' Den in a minute or two. Similar to Alex and Ronnie's mansion, the capitol building took up an entire block, a giant white rectangle with a cathedral-like roof. The colors of the air reflected off the building, giving it an iridescent glow.

I skimmed over the downtown area and its modern buildings. They had a similar aesthetic to downtown Shadow Ridge. When Killian's pack settled in Shadow Ridge after the silver wolves left, the pack built the town to mirror what had been their home, and now the injustice of their situation sank like lead in my stomach. Over time, their pack had been cut off from the city as if their sacrifice had been meaningless. Yet they still patrolled their bank and kept watch over the city's borders as well as Shadow Ridge University.

My favorite building, a stucco-sided structure with a purple stained glass dome on top, came into view. The only thing that would've made the capitol building prettier would be if the glass had been orange, but the purple had been selected for its association with archangels.

Sweat beaded on my forehead as I flew toward the smoke billowing from the golden-colored Elite Wolves' Den. It blew into the top of the city's glass dome, the stench already filtering into the area around the capitol building.

This was worse than I'd expected.

Shadow City had never had a fire before, and I'd assumed the blaze would be on a much smaller scale. From here, it looked like twenty out of the forty floors were engulfed. The fire started midway up the building, making the top half the target—the residences of the most prominent wolf shifters in the city.

Bile burned the back of my throat. My gut said Azbogah was behind it, even though we probably couldn't prove it. If it was him, he had gone too far. He wanted to ensure that he had a say as to who got the third seat on the shifter side of the council, but this kind of devastation was unacceptable. Sterlyn and Griffin weren't even considering anyone inside Shadow City for the position, but rather Killian on the outside. They hadn't brought him up yet since Azbogah would fly off the handle at the idea of the representative coming from outside our city, and the plan was to calm matters on the shifter side before they nominated Killian. They didn't want to give Azbogah more ammunition when things were already stacked against them.

Griffin had wanted to go all in, but Sterlyn knew that wasn't smart. As partners did in a good, supportive relationship, the two of them had discussed the matter, and he'd agreed to wait to move forward with Killian until the four shifter attackers were in jail and the artifact situation was handled.

Now was not the time for my mind to circle back to Levi.

Forcing him from my thoughts, I soared toward the building. The police and guards were at the bottom. A few of them were attempting to scale the building with no luck. Flames licked upward from the outside stairwell, preventing anyone from making it up or down. Anyone on the top floors was trapped.

My lungs burned in the acrid air, and I worried there might already be casualties from smoke inhalation. I wasn't sure what to do. Ulva lived with Griffin and Sterlyn on the top floor. If the building collapsed, she'd be in the most disastrous situation, but the people on the lower floors were in direct contact with the flames.

Going with my gut, I flew down to the wolf guards and police officers on the ground. Conferring frantically, their faces strained, they stood there as if they didn't know what to do.

"Call the witches. They should be able to extinguish the fire," I said. They probably wouldn't like an angel telling them what to do, but they were clueless. "Find Breena—she'll help."

Out of the three witch council members, Breena had a pure soul. If I could count on any of them offering to help, it was her. I wouldn't waste time trying to chase down Erin and Diana. Knowing them, they'd be wherever Azbogah was, expecting someone to be looking for them and not Breena.

Surprisingly, they all seemed relieved. "Okay, got it." A guard nodded and ran off to the side, pulling out his phone.

Tires squealing, Griffin and Sterlyn skidded to a stop in front of the building, and Griffin jumped out of the car. Veins protruded from his neck, and his eyes opened so wide that white showed around the irises. He stumbled toward me, placing a hand on my shoulder, and pleaded, "I know it's dangerous, and I don't want you to put your life in jeopardy, but you're the only one who can get her. Will you please save her?"

That was it.

My friend had asked for help, and he was here to direct others so more lives could be saved.

Sterlyn said, "Grab a bucket, hose, bowls, whatever you

can get, and throw it on the building. We have to contain the fire."

Good, she was taking control. That made it easier to leave. "I'll get her."

I shot toward the top floor just as an explosion shook the building.

CHAPTER FOUR

THE LOUDEST NOISE I'd ever heard rang in my ears as heat engulfed my body. I faced the building as a section of the angel glass wall sailed toward me. The framing had fractured from the explosion, and the wall barreled down.

Angel glass was unbreakable, and I had a whole freaking wall seconds away from hitting me.

I tried to fly out of the way, but my body didn't respond quickly enough. The glass slammed into me, and my skin screamed in pain from the heat and heavy weight. I attempted to flap my wings harder, but it only slowed my descent marginally.

I was *still* falling.

Everything within yelled at me to clutch my ears and curl into a ball. I'd never had the urge to do that before, but even the wind hurt me.

An angel dying like this would be ironic. We were meant to stay in the air, not die from a *fall*.

"Rosem—!" Sterlyn called frantically from below "... help...please!"

The ringing in my ears magnified, cutting off some of

her words. My head pounded, and nausea churned in my stomach.

The little bit I could hear didn't sound like the Sterlyn I knew, which reinforced my unfavorable situation.

Gritting my teeth, I forced my wings to flap harder to slow the drop. Within seconds, I'd slam into the ground, and this glass would crush me if I didn't do something about it pronto. "Everyone move!" I shouted, then strained...or I thought I did. With the ear-splitting noise growing louder, I couldn't even hear my voice inside my head.

"Move!" Sterlyn commanded. "She's...drop...glass."

Thank the gods for shifter hearing. I doubted even Sterlyn would have heard me if I'd managed to speak.

Straining and pushing through the pain, my head felt light. How the hell was I supposed to save people like this? Every second I struggled with this blasted thing meant fewer people I'd be able to rescue, and I couldn't even hear anymore.

A faint floral scent filled my nose, and warmth spread through my chest. It was the smell of angels. Could a few of them have finally arrived to provide assistance?

I hoped it wasn't a situation where the mind played tricks on the brain, but I had to trust my instincts. They'd never let me down before.

"Someone...Rosemary!" Azbogah's commanding voice sounded like an army general in battle.

Acid roiled in my stomach. Of course he'd show up here like a knight in shining armor. This would not only make it appear like he hadn't had a hand in the fire but that he'd arrived in the nick of time to help the *shifters*. The surviving wolves would feel allegiance to him.

I refused to let him take all the glory.

I clamped on to my anger, and it helped reenergize me.

Adrenaline pumped through my body, assisting me in ignoring the pain. My wings flapped harder, but they didn't have the same hold as normal.

"Ro...ry," Mother said from close by, and then the glass began to lighten.

I wasn't arrogant enough to believe that I'd suddenly gotten that much stronger. I glanced to my right and saw Mother flying next to me. Her forest green eyes were narrowed, and her amber hair was dulled by the smoke. Her blood red lips were mashed into a line as she lifted her side of the angel glass, her huge black wings flapping hard.

To my left was my father. He was the opposite of Mother in many ways but mainly in appearance. Where she was all dark, he was light, with stark white feathers and piercing blue eyes. Even his butterscotch-blond hair was more white than yellow, and he wore his favored white suit. The dark smoke swirling around us somehow made him seem more angelic.

The two of them lifted the glass off me, and the pressure on my body released. I hadn't realized just how heavy it was. No wonder I'd been struggling.

Mother's lips moved, but I couldn't hear her. The deafening noise had taken over, and my head pounded.

I had to get Ulva. Azbogah would save her last so that Griffin would be hurt and torn apart.

The flames continued to climb, but I noted Breena's waist-length brown hair below. Her coffee-colored eyes squinted up as she and a few other witches chanted a spell.

Good. That should help things tremendously, though the full coven would've been better. I'd seen Breena with those girls below, and they were the weaker members of the coven. I assumed they were the members willing to brave Erin's wrath by befriending the black sheep of her family.

Water coalesced in the air, forming rain clouds, which began to pour over the building. The residents here had never experienced rain before, and a few people ran under the awning next door to hide.

That might have been me if I didn't leave Shadow City so often, but now I treasured the water from the sky.

Racing toward the top of the building, I flew past Azbogah. He hovered, watching his followers do his bidding. His seven-foot frame towered as the water slicked down his black suit. His caramel hair wasn't in its usual spikes, having been flattened by the rain that filled the sky. His large midnight black wings flapped proudly behind him, blending with the smoke, but the most troubling thing was the way his haunting winter-gray eyes scanned me. He said something, but I couldn't hear it. He pointed to his ears.

Instinctively, I reached up to my ears, mirroring his motions, and felt warm liquid dripping down my fingers.

My eardrums.

They'd been destroyed.

Another problem for another time.

Acid inched up my throat as incredible pain seared through my head, body, and heart, but I refused to succumb to the injuries.

I was a fucking warrior, and I wouldn't let fate break me.

Renewed vigor charged through me, mixing with the agony. I'd behead any enemy who got in my way, though I might sob uncontrollably while I did it.

I'd still do it because that was who *I* was.

I landed on top of the large balcony in front of the living room of Griffin's condominium. My feet touched the dark platinum tile that ran through the entire house. The cement-like material on the roof shook and fractured under an intense heat that should've been impossible in the climate-controlled environment of Shadow City.

The material sagged, and the two large gold chandeliers hanging over the black lounge chairs next to the black stone bar top fell and shattered.

Ulva stood at the glass door, desperately trying to open it. Her ash blonde hair was covered with soot, and her sapphire eyes were wide with terror. The angel cement must have buckled, and the door couldn't budge.

I rushed toward her, and her bottom lip quivered when she saw me. She said words I couldn't hear. If I had to guess, they were, *Go. Leave before you get hurt.*

If I left, no one else would come to help her get out. Normally, I would've rolled my eyes, but I kept my negative thoughts to myself, despite thinking she was an idiot for not wanting assistance. My heart also warmed—she would rather die than have me risk my life. Not many people would feel that way, and it proved how selfless she was.

"Move back," I said, though I wasn't sure how loudly or softly I'd said it.

Ulva shook her head and pointed behind me.

That was all that I needed.

As soon as she released the door, I grabbed the outside handle and strained. My body screamed, and I bit my tongue, focusing the pain anywhere but where I needed my body to be strong.

My hands slipped, and I glanced down to find them coated in blood. What the—

Blood oozed from my skin. It was red from third-degree burns. Oh, gods. I was in worse shape than I'd realized.

The rain wasn't hitting here, blocked by the overhang of the balcony, and the smoke inside the condominium thickened. Ulva had moments before she'd suffocate.

Throwing caution to the wind, I flipped my wings to the sharp, spiky side, then realized that half of my feathers were fried as well. No wonder I couldn't move easily.

Not pausing, I struck the side of the cement. The material was hot. I wasn't sure it would give, but I spun back and forth and kept up the assault, ignoring that more and more of my feathers were flaking off.

Ulva's head hit the glass as her body sagged to the floor. I couldn't see the living room's white leather couches—that was how thick the smoke was inside.

Her face landed by the glass, and her eyes grew heavy.

She was fading fast.

As I jammed my wings as hard as possible into the wall, Azbogah's smell overwhelmed me. That had to be my imagination; he would *never* risk his life, especially not for a shifter.

Two strong hands grabbed my waist and pulled me away from the door. I spun around and came face to face with the dark angel.

He said something, but I didn't bother to watch his lips. Ulva's life was at stake. I couldn't let someone else die on my watch. I couldn't let Griffin down. And I needed to prove to myself that I was still the same angel. Maybe a little more mortal, but the same angel who did everything in her power to do what was right, even when it was hard.

I could feel Azbogah's hovering presence, and I let my hatred spew from somewhere deep within. "I *won't* let her die. Not on my watch. So either help me or go the *fuck* away."

I rarely cursed. But if ever there was a time for loose lips, it was now.

Azbogah's eyes narrowed, and when I limped past him, he grabbed me again and tossed me aside.

Landing on my feet, I got ready to sprint toward him, but I paused as he used his wings to create a large enough hole between the cement and the door for it to open. He slid the door open and turned to me.

Ulva fell onto the balcony floor as smoke poured from the opening into the sky. Azbogah didn't look at her. That action I'd expected from the dark angel, but I didn't understand why he'd helped me.

He walked over to me, his hands glowing. He cupped my ears, and I felt his power mix with mine. The sensation was faintly familiar, but it had to be an illusion from the pain and the void inside me. After a few seconds, I could hear faint sounds around me as he healed my busted eardrums. He dropped his hands and whispered in my ear, "Don't tell anyone, Little One."

Little One.

Why did he always call me that when we were alone?

Just as quickly as he'd come, he vanished, flying back to his post out in front to watch his troops fight his war.

Though he hadn't fixed my ears completely, I could now hear the surrounding noises.

The fire crackled, but it sounded as if it had died down some, which could be because my hearing wasn't back to normal.

I rushed to Ulva and gently picked her up, cradling her in my arms. The pain from the burns on my body overwhelmed me, and I began to see black spots. Between that and being so damn tired, I wasn't sure how much longer I could stand.

But I had to make it down to the ground.

Her breathing was shallow. Getting her out of the burning condo might not have been enough to save her. Each moment I delayed put her life at risk.

"Rosemary!" Mother called frantically as she landed on the balcony. She glanced behind me, and then at the woman in my arms. "This was stupid! You could—"

"Please take her," I begged. "She needs to be healed quickly." After the blast, my magic had been depleted, and with the city lights hidden by the smoke, the charge I'd felt when I'd arrived was gone.

Mother nodded. She took Ulva and glanced at me. "Can you make it down?"

I wasn't sure, and I didn't want to lie. "Hurry, please."

"Go on, Yelahiah," Father said as he landed beside me. "I'll stay close to her."

His honeysuckle scent wafted around me, and his presence calmed me.

Nodding, Mother took off, leaving the two of us alone.

"Let me—" Father started.

I lifted a finger. I needed to fly on my own, but I also wanted him beside me in case I fell. This was the weakest I'd ever been. My heart was shattered, my body was tortured, and my mind wasn't what it should have been due to fatigue. I was willing to admit I might need somebody, and gods, I wished it could be Levi.

I'd heard the phrase *rock bottom* before, but I'd never understood the magnitude of it until now. With being unable to stand up to a horde of demons, the silver wolves nearly being annihilated, bonding with Levi only for him to leave me behind, and now being physically beaten and not able to help the shifters in Shadow City, I felt as if I couldn't fall much farther.

Tears burned my eyes at the desperate longing inside me. I'd give almost anything to see him again, but I couldn't focus on that.

Not here. Not now.

"Just stay close, okay?" I said, biting my bottom lip. I'd never been so vulnerable before, and I wasn't sure how he'd respond.

His blue eyes sparkled, and he stepped toward me, careful not to touch my burned body. "Always."

The rain poured, and the two of us jumped off the balcony. I let myself fall.

The cool water pelted my hot skin, and some of the sharp throbbing ebbed. I needed to get back to my home and heal myself, but I had to make sure Ulva was all right first and find out if other residents were harmed.

As I flew past the burning stories, I saw that the flames were dying. Erin and Diana had joined the other coven members below and were casting a spell to douse the fire.

When the buildings were constructed, no one had considered needing things like water sprinklers—not with a coven close by, and not when the natural elements weren't severe. The witches controlled the climate inside the city dome, and it was always comfortable.

Most of the angels were here now, flying into the building to save the trapped wolves. Luckily, the disaster had occurred during the day, so at least half of the wolves would've been out tending to business.

Another political move I assumed Azbogah had employed.

Police officers and guards were helping people get medical attention, and vampires were healing the most severely injured shifters. Angels and vampires didn't usually heal others—it was frowned upon. If the angels found out I'd been helping shifters heal during battles over the past few days, they would ostracize me.

Clearly, Alex and Ronnie didn't care about perception. Ronnie stood over Ulva, blood trickling from her wrist into the shifter's mouth, as Griffin and Sterlyn hovered beside her. The wolves didn't bother trying to fight drinking the vampires' blood; their conditions were that bad.

Erin ran around to check on people as if she cared. She couldn't hide the vileness of her soul from me or any other angel, but only people of angelic descent could sense it.

"Rosemary..." Sterlyn sighed as her gaze landed on me. "Are you okay?"

I couldn't speak. I swayed on my feet and nearly stumbled.

Father gently placed his hands on my shoulders.

"Clearly, she's not," Azbogah scoffed, and lowered himself beside me. "And neither is your building or your people."

No, he didn't get to start. Now wasn't the time. I spun around, ready to take him on.

CHAPTER FIVE

"NOBODY WAS *TALKING* TO YOU." I was at my wits' end, and my tolerance for bullshit had been met. I usually kept my mouth shut when dealing with all things Azbogah because arguing with him was like trying not to lose a feather: pointless.

I was usually the one giving Sterlyn or Ronnie the eye, wanting them to stay under his radar.

Why cause unnecessary drama? was what I used to think, but I was beginning to see things differently. My emotions were hindering my logic—or perhaps the burning condo had pushed me too far—but I was done pretending to be complaisant.

Mother's mouth dropped, and I couldn't blame her. I never shied away from confrontation, but I didn't seek it out, either.

Running a hand through his hair, Father bit his bottom lip.

Azbogah's jaw twitched. "What did you say to me?"

Still holding her wrist to Ulva's mouth, Ronnie glanced at the dark angel. "You heard her. Sterlyn was asking *Rose-*

mary how she was doing. Last I checked, she could speak just fine on her own."

Azbogah's nostrils flared. "The fact that the *silver* wolf needed to ask when the answer is so apparent speaks volumes about her intelligence."

This was why I usually remained silent. Azbogah refused to be topped.

"It's a mortal's nice way of checking on someone." I'd explain it in a manner that he might be able to relate to. "She knows I'm hurt, but she doesn't want to say I look like I could die at any second. That was her way of gauging whether I'm injured as badly as she suspects."

His head tilted.

A shiver ran down my spine. Azbogah helping me with Ulva didn't make any sense, but I didn't have the energy to consider his motives. Even though I was exhausted and my magic was close to depleted, there was so much to do. "How can I help?" I asked. I might be able to heal someone who was severely injured enough to hold them until Alex or Ronnie could get to them.

"You've done more than enough," Sterlyn said as she left Ulva's side and made her way to me. "You need to go home and rest. The fire is under control, Alex and Ronnie are healing the injured shifters, and the witches are working on extinguishing the flames completely. There's nothing more you can do."

Even though she hadn't meant to make me feel useless, the sensation washed over me. I struggled to take a deep breath. "I'm sure there's something—"

"Rosemary, you need to listen to them." Mother frowned. "Pahaliah, tell your *daughter* we all should head home. We need to heal her, and she needs to recharge."

Azbogah stiffened. "Fine, but first thing tomorrow

morning, we need to hold an emergency council meeting to discuss what happened here."

His words gave me pause. Was he actually putting the meeting off until tomorrow when he could have demanded one for tonight? Why would he do that...unless he had a plan he needed to follow through on? That had to be it.

Instead of arguing, I surveyed the area. Ronnie had moved on to another injured shifter, and I noted that Gwen, Alex's sister, was among those healing the wounded as well. Even in a state of duress, the princess, like her brother, maintained a regal air. She strutted through the scene in her black four-inch heels, her shoulder-length ivory hair pulled into a haphazard ponytail and her chestnut eyes showing a touch of crimson in the irises as she dedicated herself to helping the shifters. She and Alex proved people could change. They'd grown up jaded and selfish, but Ronnie had opened their eyes to a better way.

Every preordained partnership I'd seen had changed not only the lives of the two connected souls but also the lives of those around them for the better.

Well, everyone's but mine.

There wasn't much I could do. At least fifty angels were rescuing people, and most of the floors appeared to be clear. I sighed, trying to work past the burning ache in my throat. "Okay."

Even if I tried to fly, it would be a struggle in this state, and I didn't want my mother or father draining themselves to heal me in front of Azbogah. His watchful gaze made me feel vulnerable enough.

Ronnie removed her wrist from Ulva's mouth, and the alpha's mother turned her eyes to me. Soot marred her face, but her olive complexion had returned to normal, and her breathing was steady. "Thank you, Rosemary. If it weren't for you..." Her voice grew thick with emotion.

I wasn't the one who'd saved her, but I didn't need to look at Azbogah to know he was staring at me. I could feel his gaze deep in my core.

I thought he would want Griffin to know his mother was safe because of him and have some sort of perceived leverage over the family, but he was smart enough to know that wouldn't make Griffin fold. Griffin had morals and ethics, and he didn't just look at what was right for the wolf shifters. He considered their well-being but counted everyone else's as well. What was best for the shifters wasn't necessarily best for the world, and a negatively balanced world would impact the shifters negatively, too.

Azbogah should've learned that when he tried to take control of Shadow City the first time. Obviously, he hadn't learned a thing, since he was back at his political games.

"I didn't do anything special." That was the safest thing I could say without informing them of what Azbogah had done.

Her voice softened. "You have an instinct for helping people in need. It's a rare trait, and I'm proud to call you a friend."

Friend.

Even though I was old enough to be their distant ancestor, they viewed me as their equal. At one point, I would've abhorred the thought, but not anymore. I was honored that they considered me one of them. I bit the inside of my cheek to prevent my eyes from glistening. The last thing I needed was for Azbogah or another angel to see that I was highly emotional.

Unsure how to respond, I said the first thing that came

to my mind. "Rest. Even with vampire blood, you should take it easy until you're back at full strength."

"Let's go." Mother inhaled and held her breath. "We need to tend to you."

"The quicker she heals and rests, the better." Azbogah clucked his tongue. "The meeting will be scheduled for first thing tomorrow morning."

Wanting to remove myself from his watchful gaze, I headed toward the woods that separated the shifter neighborhood from our own.

"Rosemary, wait," Griffin called desperately.

I turned around as he rushed toward me. When he reached my side, he nibbled on his bottom lip and murmured, "Thank you. I shouldn't have—"

"It's fine." Even if he hadn't asked, I would've done everything I could to save his mother. Ulva had always been kind to me.

"No, it's not." Griffin moved as if to place his hands on my shoulders but stopped short.

Thank the gods. My skin still throbbed like it was on fire. I detested showing weakness, and if he touched me, there was a huge chance I would whimper. I didn't want anyone to witness that, especially Azbogah.

He rubbed his neck and said gruffly, "It wasn't *right* for me to ask that. You mean a lot to me, and the fact I put you at risk, along with—"

"You were desperate. I understand, and I'm not upset. There is *nothing* for you to apologize for." My eyes stung. If he kept talking, tears would inevitably fall. However, I didn't want to cut him off and hurt his feelings. I placed a hand on his shoulder, since he wasn't injured, and attempted to smile, but my skin felt as if it were cracking.

Smiling was officially not an option. The truth was that

him asking me to help Ulva had flattered me. He'd trusted my instincts and believed that out of everyone here, I'd been the person most capable of saving his mother. "That was one of the most honorable requests anyone could ask of an angel, and we're friends."

Even though the smoke still hung thick in the air, a shifter would be able to pick up the scent of sulfur that came with any type of lie.

His face smoothed, and some tension left his body. "Uh, okay, but never do that again. You're part of my family, too."

Wow. This whole situation had affected Griffin. He wasn't usually this emotional unless it involved Sterlyn. My scalp prickled. I wasn't sure how to respond. Did I thank him? Nod? I was pretty sure walking away wasn't an option because that would be rude. My emotions weren't helping me—I was quite certain they were intensifying my discomfort. My heart raced as I tried to figure out an appropriate response.

Azbogah cleared his throat loudly, ruining the moment.

For the first time in a millennium, I was somewhat tempted to hug him. Still, I wouldn't have avoided the encounter with Griffin even if I could. He was right. We *were* family.

I dropped my hand and turned back to my parents. Mother was glaring at Azbogah, while Father's forehead was lined with concern.

Thick smoke floated toward the top of the dome, the surreal darkness of the city skyline broken only by glowing embers, reminding me of demons in shadow form.

My heart panged.

Levi.

Would he haunt my thoughts eternally? I was certain I knew the answer, and it wasn't one I liked.

"Get some rest," Sterlyn said as she took Griffin's hand, pulling him back toward Ulva. "Call us later?"

I nodded. Now that the immediate threat was over, my skin was screaming in pain, and my ears were still ringing, though not as intensely. My heart...well, that was shattered beyond repair. However, these moments with my friends had given me a sense of peace I'd never had before. Although there were times when I didn't feel like I fit in since I wasn't from their era, they'd never made me feel excluded. Not even when I didn't understand their vernacular or their humor, or why Sierra sometimes chastised me for being rude.

"We'll be at the council meeting in the morning," Mother said stiffly as she and Father flanked me.

As I pushed my wings out to take off, my body protested. I was slower to ascend than when I'd been a little angel learning how to fly.

Mother *tsk*ed from below, both feet still on the ground. "We can walk, or if you want me to heal you now..."

Part of me didn't want to be healed, but if something were to happen, I needed to be able to fight. "Fine," I murmured.

My feet touched the ground once more, and Mother's hands glowed brightly as she tapped into her angel magic. When she laid her hands gently on my ears, I almost whimpered.

Her pure white essence flowed into mine, and the magic swirled inside, immediately syncing with my familiar essence and going to work.

My hearing cleared further. Now I could hear the faint murmurs of the people still at the Elite Wolves' Den. They would probably be there for hours, trying to clean up the mess, determine the cause of the fire, and remove the smoke from the air.

I listened closely to ensure no one stumbled upon us. Even though Mother wasn't doing anything wrong, angels didn't like to be seen as weak, and I was no exception. Though needing help wasn't a weakness, it was perceived that way, especially for a woman. I didn't want Mother to use too much of her power on me, either. Azbogah knew that at least one of them would heal me, and he could try to capitalize on it somehow.

I didn't trust the man.

"I'm good." I would be back to normal by morning. I would be able to handle a fight with little issue.

Ignoring me, she continued to push her magic inside me until Father touched her shoulder. "You heard her, dear."

Mother's lips mashed together, and she dropped her hands. "Fine. Then let's hurry home. There's much to discuss."

My heart dropped. I had hoped we would put off that conversation until morning. I could ask, but that wouldn't be fair, especially since I was almost physically healed. Mother had been asking me for days to come back and help navigate the political arena. I'd turned her down every time, telling her there was something I was handling.

And boy, had I messed that up terribly. She deserved to know what had happened. It would inevitably blow back on us since the shifters had accused her of stealing from the artifact building.

She took off, and Father smiled sadly at me. I used to think he was slightly odd when he gave me this expression, but not now. He just felt things more deeply because of the special skill given to him in Heaven.

Not wanting him to read me, I took off after my mother. I needed a few minutes to ground myself.

As we passed over the artifact building, I purposely looked anywhere but at the lot behind the building, afraid that if I glanced at it, I would imagine Levi. He'd almost kissed me there, and I'd foolishly almost let him.

But despite my determination, my gaze kept drifting toward the place where we'd stood.

Soon, we reached the oaks, cedars, and redbuds that made up the Shadow City forest. We flew close to the tree-tops to avoid the worst of the smoke. Usually, at this time of day, I'd glimpse fox, wolf, cougar, or falcon shifters in the area, but today, the forest was barren—yet another reminder of the horrible events that had led up to this moment.

The smoke was still thick around us, and I hoped the witches figured out a way to dissipate it quickly. My lungs burned from breathing it in.

Our gigantic glass condominium high-rise came into view, and I sighed. Being able to sleep in my room with no reminders of Levi would deliver the closest sense of peace I'd have for a while.

The Elite Wolves' Den had been modeled on the angel residences, but unlike the shifters, we didn't use cement in our buildings. Our walls were all glass, which would've been useful for the wolves if they had followed our design completely. A fire was nearly impossible, although there wasn't quite as much privacy.

Our condo was on the top floor, like Griffin and Sterlyn's. Since housing was limited in the city, children born after the border had closed had to live with their parents until they agreed upon a union with another angel for reproductive purposes. Then those two angels would wait for a place to open up or find temporary housing in the city to live together, even if they weren't exclusive, to hopefully be blessed by fate and raise a child together.

My feet landed on the glass floor, which was frosted so we couldn't see our neighbors below. In the center of the area sat four wicker lounge chairs, each large enough that an angel could sprawl out with their wings surrounding them.

Mother glided to the sliding glass door, opened it, and waved me inside.

There was no point in putting off this conversation any longer. I walked in.

Father followed a few steps behind as if to ensure I didn't try to escape.

My stomach roiled. The fact that they might consider it a possibility bothered me, but could I blame them? Mother had repeatedly asked me to come home, and I'd turned them down without explanation.

I strolled into the mostly bare living room. Facing each other around the room's center were two dark charcoal couches that almost matched my wings.

From this spot in the house, I could see the kitchen to the left. Everything was glass, including the cabinets. The only solid thing was a round, glass-topped table with large white wing-shaped legs supporting it. Four chairs in the form of black wings surrounded the table where we sat and ate together on rare occasions.

Since angels had limited emotions, our houses were pretty bare, and we didn't hold gatherings unless we were celebrating a graduating warrior class or the like. Looking at it through my new lenses, the place didn't even feel like a home.

My room was to the left, and frosted glass prevented anyone from seeing inside. The same was true of my parents' room on the right.

Too tired to stand, I made my way to one of the couches and sat. I placed my hands in my lap, waiting for Mother or Father to begin the inquisition.

Father settled on the couch across from me. He licked his lips as he mirrored my stance and said softly, "It's nice to have you home again."

As usual, he was the peacemaker. Mother and I were similar and usually got along very well. We were close by angel standards, and when we fought, it was over something we fundamentally didn't agree on. Usually, my mother supported me and my decisions. The last time we'd disagreed was when I'd decided to have a casual relationship with Ingram. She'd warned me that he had ulterior motives, and I'd discounted her concerns.

But Ingram was a younger version of Azbogah, so I should've realized I couldn't trust him.

"Yes, it's about time you came home." Mother pivoted toward me, scowling. "Now tell me what was so important that you couldn't be here when a civil war is looming. And why do you smell different? I swear there's a touch of a new sweet floral scent mixed with yours. Even the smoke couldn't hide that."

A civil war.

Of course she didn't want to discuss that over cell phone.

No doubt I'd hear all about that tomorrow in the council meeting, but the information I had to share couldn't leave this room. The best approach was to start with the worst news.

Even as I tried to justify my decision, I knew it was a horrible one, but the words left my mouth before I could reconsider my strategy. "I found my preordained other half."

"What?" Father's mouth dropped open. "That's not possible. Who is he?" He scanned the room as if he were waiting for an angel to walk in and stand beside me.

"And why wasn't he helping you at the fire?" Mother added.

If they thought this was bad, wait until they heard the kicker. "Because he's a demon, and he left me."

Mother turned as still as a statue. Father's eyes widened in terror. However, this was just the calm before the storm.

CHAPTER SIX

I WRAPPED my arms around myself, trying to hide my shaking hands. My leg wanted to bounce with all the nervous energy bubbling inside me, and the urge to rush to get the rest of the story out almost overwhelmed me. I forced my leg to remain still, not wanting them to see I was affected. They already knew something was off, and they needed time to process this information without distractions.

When dealing with my mother, I'd learned early not to throw a huge issue with multiple problems lumped together at her all at once, but rather let her process the information bit by bit. I'd been torn on what to inform her of first: being paired with a demon or that a demon sword was missing. I figured the latter would find its way into whatever discussion she desired to have with me, so the most pressing issue was my heart.

She clasped her hands in front of her chest. "And you *completed* the pairing?"

My throat constricted. She didn't need to make it sound as if it was the worst thing that could have ever happened. I understood it wasn't ideal. I'd fought the bond, but when Levi had risked his life for mine...well, I'd thought we both were in this forever. I didn't realize he'd leave me the next day.

"Would we be having this conversation otherwise?" I arched a brow.

"You're focusing on the wrong thing, dear." Father cleared his throat. "She found her *preordained*. That hasn't happened in over a millennium."

Mother waved her long black fingernail. "We're *not* acting as if this is a good thing. The last preordained pair was the ultimate disaster. You *know* that."

For a moment, I felt like I used to with Sterlyn and her friends: confused. Normally, I was at least relatively on the same page as my parents. "What are you referring to?"

"None of your business," Mother snapped.

Her unease made my skin crawl. Maybe I had miscalculated and should've discussed the sword first, but the damage was done. "I understand you're upset, but I won't tolerate you talking to me that way. You're not the one with a connection to a demon. You just have to deal with the shame of your daughter having one."

"Is *that* what you think this is about?" Her eyes tightened. "This has nothing to do with my reaction."

"Then *please* tell me what the problem is." My voice grew louder, and I hated that emotions were leaking through. My blood was boiling, and I tried to take deep breaths to keep myself from becoming irrational.

Her brows furrowed as she examined me. "Because having a preordained changes you, and it's not always for the better."

My gut ached as if I'd been punched. "How do you know that?" I hadn't yet been alive when other preordained mates had existed. Angels used to find them often, but then something changed. No one knew how or why.

"We've been around longer than even you can fathom." Father reached over and patted my hand. "But that's irrelevant. What I'm concerned about is that not only did you find your preordained half, but you also completed the bond with the..." He paused as if it was too hard to say.

"Demon?" I offered. His hand on mine had my vision blurring, but I blinked back the tears. If Mother saw them, it would upset her more. Though not ideal, it wasn't my fault. I hadn't chosen him. Fate had chosen us for each other.

Mother hissed like a vampire. "Don't say that word as if it were any other. You were *raised* better than that."

The instinct to protect Levi stole my breath. "He's *not* bad. He doesn't radiate negative energy. He didn't get to choose. He was *born* that way."

Mother threw up a hand, and I jerked back. She always remained so poised, even during the most caustic council meetings, due to a lot of self-restraint. Here, she wasn't worried about her image. "Yet he *left* you."

And the punches kept coming. My heart tore into shreds, which I hadn't thought possible.

She hadn't said anything untrue. She was stating facts, which I respected, but her motive felt cruel.

This must have been how I had come across to my friends every time Sierra had scolded me for my rudeness, and being on the receiving end made me want to hide my face.

I wanted to respond *he had to*, but I didn't know that. If he had left to save his father, I believed he would've told me. He'd made it clear that he wouldn't leave his father down there, and I respected him for that. That was what made him different from the other demons I'd heard about.

But he hadn't talked to me. To make matters worse, he'd taken a demon sword with him. To me, that screamed betrayal, not just a temporary leave of absence.

Pain rushed through my body, nearly toppling me over. I would survive, but I hoped the agony would recede with time. Forever would drag otherwise, and though I didn't enjoy the concept of death, it would be nice not to feel this kind of torture for that long.

"Yelah—" Father started.

"No, Pahaliah." She placed her hands on her hips and fluffed her feathers. "You don't get to be the nice guy here. She has to see facts."

"Believe me, I do." I wished I didn't and I could live in denial, pretending he'd come back any second. However, while I might have made a foolish decision, I wasn't an idiot. My distress proved I wasn't ignoring the real possibility that I had been betrayed.

My heart protested. I'd felt his emotions that night, and they ran as deep as my own.

But love couldn't withstand everything. No matter how much a person cared, they couldn't save something that was meant to be destroyed.

"A little too late." She sighed and pinched the bridge of her nose.

"I'm beating myself up enough for all of us. I don't need your assistance in the matter," I said curtly. She wasn't trying to hurt me or be cruel—I knew that—but that didn't change the fact that she was making me feel worse. "Believe me, I'm aware of the consequences."

"That's the thing." Her wings hung limply by her side. "I don't think you are. There's a reason I've repeatedly asked you to come home." Her chin dropped to her chest, and she cast her gaze downward. She looked defeated, and it shook me.

Stomach quivering, I steadied myself. "The civil war?"

Father nodded. "Azbogah is gaining followers. Yelahiah being attacked by shifters and then accused of having something to do with the artifact break-in has made her look guilty and unfit to lead."

Those had to be Azbogah's words. He was still the self-proclaimed judge, even though that title had officially ended when he'd come to live on Earth. "And my absence made it appear as though I wasn't supporting her, either." A chill racked my body.

I'd screwed up far more than I'd realized.

"You're here now." Yelahiah exhaled and walked slowly toward us. "That should mean something, though it would've been helpful days ago."

"I had a good reason for my absence." I wanted to hide my face. I'd let my parents down, the two people who'd always been there for me. They were more parental than most angels, showing concern and always being accessible. I hadn't truly understood that until now. "And for not attending the university as expected so I could train angels on how to integrate if the time ever arrived."

Mother sat next to Father and crossed her leg. "Because you were fornicating with a demon?"

Cheeks burning, I refused to lower my gaze. That would only give the illusion of guilt. Though I'd had sex with Levi, it hadn't been until a few hours ago. It wasn't like we'd been making hot, wild...

My heart ripped open once more, and I had to stop my thoughts. How could I miss someone so much when I'd known him for such a marginal amount of time compared to my long life?

"No, that's not why." I couldn't deny it. That would only cause a sulfuric stench to waft around me.

She waved a hand. "Then please, share." Her tone was condescending.

In a second, she'd wish being with Levi was why I hadn't come. "I was helping Annie and Sterlyn and the others to ensure that the demon didn't escape before he gave us information."

"Did you learn anything?" Mother folded her wings into her back and steepled her fingers.

Another angel might have added, *before having sex and binding your soul with his moments before he left you,* but not her. This again proved she cared in ways that other angels couldn't.

Could she experience human emotions as well?

"The princes of Hell know about Ronnie, and Wrath wants his dagger back." That was one of the biggest pieces of information we'd gained from Levi. Though we'd suspected that someone in Hell might eventually wonder who she was, we hadn't considered that Wrath might already know. "And all demons aren't evil. There are many who are truly undecided."

"What?" Father's brows furrowed. "That's impossible. They would still have wings if they hadn't fallen."

"I'm not saying that many didn't choose to go to Hell, but some didn't feel as if they had a choice, and some were born there." I should've pushed Levi for more information instead of trying to stay away from him. During those two days I'd avoided him, I could've learned so much more. I'd done it to protect my heart, but that hadn't helped. The fact that I was sitting here like this proved my efforts had been futile. "Not all have chosen to be malicious."

"Oh, Rosemary." Mother rubbed her forehead between

her eyes. "And you *believed* him? He could've chosen his words carefully to allow you to hear what you wanted, since you were"—she paused, searching for the right word —"*invested* in him."

I laughed. The word worked, but for some reason, the choice was funny.

Her head tilted as if she were staring at someone she didn't know.

That was fair. I had become a little more rounded. Or maybe *obtuse* would be the right word for an angel to understand.

"I think she's still injured," Mother murmured, as if she expected me to not hear her. "I must have miscalculated how much I healed her."

I rolled my eyes. I was ready to prove that Levi hadn't lied to me. "I'm fine. Did you notice anything strange that night I left the council meeting in a rush?"

"Of course I did, but you said you would explain later." She arched her brow. "I'm assuming now is the time."

"Levi—I mean, the demon sneaked inside the city, and not one angel was aware." If he were truly evil, we would've felt him, especially once he was inside. "He's the reason Kira didn't die when the shifters attacked her."

Father's eyes bulged. "A demon got into Shadow City?"

"Yes. He's *not* evil." At least, he hadn't been then.

Mother's fury left, replaced by concern. She stood and exploded her wings from her back. "That's not good. They must be sending demons with neutral energy to try to steal things for them. He must have been looking for something within the city."

"He was." It wasn't a secret. They were taking inventory of the artifact building, so this would have come out. "And he got it."

She stood so still, I wasn't sure she was breathing. Father leaned forward, placing his elbows on his knees.

I straightened my shoulders, bracing myself to tell them. My palms grew sweaty, but I ignored them. "He got hold of a demon sword."

Shaking her head slowly, she whispered, "That can't be. They're taking inventory. Your fox shifter *friend* is even leading the inventory."

Father held out both hands. "At least we're aware."

"How does that help us?" Mother scoffed. "They're going to try to pin that on me! Wait, did Azbogah know about the demon? Is that how he got in?"

I hadn't considered that, but I didn't think he had. If he knew we'd closed a demon portal, he would've put me and the others in prison. I was sure that would hinder whatever plans he had brewing. "No, the demon sneaked in under Sterlyn and Griffin's car when they came to the meeting."

Mother rubbed her temples. "I admire your dedication to Sterlyn and her pack and agree we should protect the silver wolves. They're family. But ever since they came here, they've caused disarray."

That was a true statement. Despite that, I was so glad they'd come. They'd made me believe in a mission and given me more purpose than ever before.

Father asked the question I'd been dreading. "How did you capture the demon?"

And I told them everything. I should've told them before now, but I'd stupidly thought I was protecting them. I should've known better after seeing what had happened with Eliza, Ronnie, and Annie. Secrets had a way of coming to light.

In a rush, I told them about the demon wolves and how they'd attacked us months ago, wanting to give Annie to a prince of Hell. That our only choice had been to get the witches to close the portal to Hell. I informed them about Eliza and her coven and how the strong older lady had been sucked into the portal seconds before the spell had sealed it permanently. I added that the princes of Hell were rumbling and more demons we couldn't feel were coming to Earth.

When I was done, I felt worse.

Mother pressed a hand to her abdomen. "You didn't think we should've been involved in every one of those decisions?"

She'd never been disappointed in me until today. The air sawed at my lungs. "I should've told you, but I knew Azbogah was giving you a hard time, and I wanted to handle it."

"This is going to look bad for our family." Mother lowered her head. "If you wanted to destroy us, then good job."

My vision blurred, but I refused to take it. I hadn't done anything wrong. "I did what anyone would do in that situation. I fought on the side of justice. Those women the demon wolves stole were mistreated, and the demon wolves were handing over their own daughters to demons for gods know what reason! I get that none of this is ideal, but strategy is rarely easy, and I *made* the best decisions I could in the moment. I'd make them again in a heartbeat." The truth settled over me, and I hadn't realized how strongly I felt. "The only regret I have is not informing you as the incidents occurred."

Mother opened her mouth, but Father reached over and took her hand. "That's enough. Rosemary is hurt, and we know she had the noblest of intentions. Let her rest, and we can continue this discussion later."

He was right. I needed sleep to think clearly. I hadn't gotten much, and despite my mother's healing efforts, my body was still injured from the fire. My magic was almost undetectable.

I nodded and headed to my room on the left side of the condo. I didn't have anything else to say; I was depleted emotionally, physically, and magically.

As I left, Mother murmured, "This sounds like something Eleanor would do. What has gotten into her?"

Eleanor.

The angel was only a few years older than me. Before I was born, Mother had taken her in because Eleanor's mother had chosen evil and fallen. The girl did anything she could for attention, even going as far as to sleep with Ingram while I was—like I even cared. I'd appreciated it because it had taken some of his focus off me.

When Mother became pregnant with me, she'd also been dealing with the loss of her brother. She'd found another angel couple to take Eleanor in during that overwhelming time. Of course, Eleanor blamed me for everything.

Not wanting to hear more, I ran my hand over the frosted glass wall. I enjoyed my privacy more than most angels, and I flopped onto the burnt orange comforter that graced my king-sized mattress. Tears spilled from my eyes as I let the torment of the last twenty-four hours take hold, and I fell asleep mid-sob.

SOMETHING POUNDED INSIDE ME, and I opened my eyes. I glanced around my room, taking in the charcoal dresser across from me and the matching end table to one side.

Discomfort throbbed in my chest, and I lifted my hands. My skin was completely smooth once more.

Then what was making me feel this way?

My hearing seemed fine, but when I focused inside, I sensed that my magic was less than half full. I'd expected to heal faster, although the smoke inhalation had done a number on me. Still, the sensations coursing through me didn't make sense.

Another sting pulled inside me, and I noted the center of the pain.

It was my connection with Levi.

Something was *wrong*.

CHAPTER SEVEN

EVERY CELL in my body screamed for me to go help Levi. Our connection pulsed with agony, even with him in another dimension. A cry lodged in my throat, but I swallowed it down.

With all the battles I'd trained for, never had I been prepared for this kind of war—the internal kind where I could do nothing to help the person in pain.

There was no way to reach him, and the desperation that burgeoned within suffocated me. I threw my legs over the bed and bolted upright as I gulped down oxygen. But no matter what I did, I couldn't catch my breath. Sitting here wasn't right. I needed to help him, but that was impossible.

The demons would feel me as soon as I crossed into their world. Then they'd descend, and even the best warrior couldn't compete against sheer numbers.

Something warm dripped onto my hands.

Was it blood?

The smell of salt informed me they were tears, and when I opened my eyes, I found clear liquid on my palm.

A month ago, this would not have been possible. I'd never cried like this. That had changed since I'd met *him*.

Much had changed because of him.

A soft knock on my door made me gasp. I jumped to my feet and gritted my teeth. I shouldn't have been able to be caught off guard. Levi was affecting me without even being here, and my blood boiled.

"Rosemary?" Mother asked. "Can I talk with you for a minute?"

Gods, I had to get myself together before the council meeting.

Inhaling deeply, I steadied my voice despite my soul shredding inside. "One second, please."

I raced into the attached bathroom on my left and slid the glass door closed behind me.

I went to the charcoal sink in one corner, close to the shower. The fogged shower door swung open to a huge rain shower. Angels did enjoy luxury. Although I didn't mind having the best, I didn't require it.

I placed my hands on the countertop and cringed at my reflection. I looked normal. My skin was back to its fair tone, and my purple-tinged mahogany hair was full. Only my eyes hinted at the turmoil inside, appearing a darker purple, the hint of twilight almost unnoticeable even to my supernatural sight. The only signs that I'd been injured were the bloodstained shirt and dirty jeans I still wore.

Gross.

I should've showered last night, but I'd lacked the energy. I'd have loved to say it was because I'd been injured, but it had everything to do with a sexy, dark-haired, mocha-eyed demon I missed more than anything in the entire universe. *Universe* was the only way to describe it because the world wasn't all-encompassing enough.

I couldn't let Mother see me like this. She'd be appalled.

After turning on the water, I stripped down and stepped into the shower. She'd be upset that I was making her wait, but I couldn't allow her to see me so disheveled. She'd think I was falling apart.

I submerged my body, wanting the water to wash away everything.

The pain.

The memories.

The grief.

But the crazy part was that I *didn't* actually want that.

What I truly wanted was for Levi to have never left. We should have been together, someplace where we could be ourselves without repercussions. Wherever that might be.

A loud knock pounded on my bathroom door.

Mother could be relentless.

"I *said* I wanted to discuss things with you," she said loudly. "That didn't mean take your time and get in the shower."

Annoyance flared inside me as I gritted my teeth. "And *I* said I needed a *second*."

She gasped, and I cringed.

I'd allowed my emotions to get the best of me, which was unexpected for an angel.

Taking a deep breath, I tried clamping down on my connection with Levi, but I couldn't.

I had to lock this down. If I didn't, the situation would only get worse.

After taking a few slow breaths, I found the strength to sound almost normal. "I'm sorry. I'm a little off this morning. I figured our conversation would take some time, and I wanted to jump in the shower quickly so we wouldn't be late for the council meeting. You know how Azbogah likes to get there early and begin his campaign."

"Yes, of course." Mother sighed with relief. "I'll be in the kitchen, waiting for you." Her heels clicked as she walked away.

The urge to stay in the shower was strong, but I *had* to ignore it. I had a feeling my mother was relieved that I'd sounded more like my old self, and I didn't want to ruin the little progress with her.

While I bathed, the preordained bond flickered. My skin crawled. Something was horribly wrong, and I could do nothing about it.

As a warrior, I always focused on a goal, but I didn't know what that was anymore. I wanted to risk everything to reach him. If he hadn't walked away, I wouldn't have hesitated to fight my way to him.

But he'd walked away from me without a goodbye.

I had to respect his decision...didn't I?

Fear paralyzed me.

What if he had chosen the other side? Could that be causing the discomfort—something going awry with our connection? Once someone turned the back on mankind, they could no longer have a preordained mate. Could our bond be dissolving?

My legs gave out, and I knelt as pain shot through my chest. The idea of losing our connection hurt worse than the thought of living without him.

How was that possible? I'd thought it would be easier that way, but my soul screamed inside.

My knees throbbed from hitting the tile floor, and my body shivered. I had to get it together. If he had made a choice, there wasn't a damn thing I could do about it, especially now.

I slowly stood, despite my lungs contracting in protest. My chest heaved, but I held back the sob. I'd already cried too much over him, and I hated that he had this much control over my mind and body.

This couldn't be healthy.

I used to believe that the Divine gave us too much to bear so we would have to rely on her and trust her completely, but I wasn't sure I could survive this pain much longer.

Could you die of a broken heart? The word *yes* rang in my ears, but that could have been wishful thinking. The thought of spending eternity feeling these emotions made the future seem bleak, but I wouldn't allow anyone or anything to take away my will to live.

I forced myself to rinse my hair and turned off the water. As cool air hit my body, the contrast in temperature reminded me of the night Levi and I had connected, and my heart panged as if it were being stabbed repeatedly by a dagger—or a stolen demon sword.

My eyes burned, but I finished in the bathroom and dressed in my favorite burnt orange long-sleeved shirt and a pair of jeans. Despite my parents dressing formally, I preferred more casual attire, mainly to be prepared for a fight at a moment's notice. Having a long, swirling skirt was a complication I'd rather not deal with. Mother used to give me a hard time about my outfit choices, but once I'd been allowed to attend Shadow Ridge University and learn how to blend in with the rest of the world, she had relinquished that battle.

When I was ready, I took a moment to brace myself for the conversation with my mother. The more I acted like the Rosemary she expected, the better the conversation would go.

The pain of the bond increased like a knife twisting inside my heart. I stupidly rubbed my chest as if that would help.

With shaking hands, I opened my bedroom door. That was the last moment of weakness I was allowed until after the council meeting.

Entering the kitchen, I found Mother brewing coffee in the ice-blue coffee pot beside the silver refrigerator at the edge of the glass cabinets. From the frosted glass cabinets over the counter, she removed two silver coffee mugs.

A cup of coffee was exactly what I needed.

After filling each mug, she glided to the kitchen table, feathers fluttering. She perched on a chair and placed the second mug in front of the vacant seat to her right.

"Please sit. We have a few minutes before we should leave." Mother pulled the seat out, making it clear she wanted me to sit beside her.

Attempting to ignore the agony raging inside, I slid onto the expected spot and was thankful she'd put only coffee out. I wasn't sure my stomach could handle food.

I took a sip of the bitter drink, and some of the tension in my head eased. Caffeine was the one vice mortals had that I'd understood even before becoming emotional.

Mother held my gaze. "I want to..." She trailed off and winced.

That was odd. Angels didn't usually say things that made them feel uncomfortable. Discomfort was rare when you saw facts with limited emotion. I remained silent instead of voicing my curiosity. I'd let her take her time. Eventually, she'd come out with it.

She crossed her legs and lifted her mug with one hand. "I'm sorry I was rather harsh with you last night."

My eyes widened. Mother rarely apologized. I could count on one hand the times I'd heard her say she was sorry in my entire existence. "I deserve it. I did complete—" I stopped.

Telling her last night had been hard enough. I didn't need to repeat the words, especially when my skin was crawling and I was barely hanging on to my sanity. "I did something questionable, but Mother, I *tried* to hold out. It's just—" Memories of Levi rushed into my mind, adding to the misery of the aching bond.

I had to stop talking about *him.*

"I understand somewhat." She blew out a breath and set the mug back on the table. "At one time, I had very intense feelings for someone, and it resulted in the *worst* mistake of my life. I just don't want you to experience what I did, and it frustrates me that I can't do anything to take this...discomfort away."

Discomfort.

She had *no clue* what I was going through. "I doubt you understand because that doesn't even come close to describing what I feel inside."

Mother's composure crumbled away. Lines of what could only be pain etched around her eyes. "Believe it or not, angels used to feel strong emotions. It's hard to believe since it was so long ago, but at one point in time, I cared for someone deeply."

"That's why you and Father are committed to each other." But their relationship wasn't hugely emotional. It was odd by angel standards, but they'd been together for so long that it didn't seem strange.

"It wasn't Pahaliah for whom I felt that, though I wish it had been. It would have made things so much easier."

She'd just revealed so much, but my mind locked on one

part. She'd had feelings for someone, and it was a horrible mistake.

Only one name popped into my mind, but it *couldn't* be him. "You aren't talking about Azbogah...right?"

I sucked in a breath. Mother was a good person, but she was jaded, mainly due to the death of her brother at Azbogah's command. She hadn't intervened to save my uncle Ophaniel, which had always puzzled me, but I'd never pushed the issue, knowing how deep her guilt ran—even for an angel. But I'd always wondered why she hadn't been able to stop Ophaniel's execution. If she'd *cared* for Azbogah, maybe she hadn't thought he would follow through, and so she hadn't stopped the execution in time.

"Yes, it was him. Angels don't dare discuss it because of the animosity that flows between the two of us now." Mother sighed and stared at the crystal glass ceiling. "I was so smitten with him, and then he started to change, and I was in denial. When he sentenced Ophaniel...things had already changed so much between us. He'd been growing cold and distant. Then, when he blatantly acted against my family—my brother and his children—it confirmed that whatever connection we had was fading.

"I didn't think that anyone would listen to Azbogah, but I was wrong. So wrong." Her eyes darkened as she traveled to a place inside her mind. "His relationship with me—an archangel—had elevated his status, at least temporarily, and my brother died before I realized that his life was truly at stake. That was when I realized *emotion* had blinded me and Azbogah had used me to gain more followers."

All of that was something I'd known, but I couldn't get past the preordained part. "Were you two—"

"There's nothing more to discuss about him." She shook her head firmly. "The feelings have turned cold, and he's turned into the angel he always wanted to become. I don't want to see your decisions cost you a similar price." She placed her hand on mine, her eyes lightening back to the color I'd always admired.

My frustration with her melted away, even though I doubted she truly understood the magnitude of what I felt for Levi. If I were in her place, I'd be concerned about me, too, especially after learning about her and Azbogah. "I can promise you one thing: I will *not* allow the demon to hurt anyone I have vowed to protect," I said. After graduating from warrior training, I'd promised her that I would always fight for justice, and just because I was bonded to someone didn't mean that would change. I was still my own person and had the same values.

"He already got away with a demon sword," she said bluntly, placing her hands on the table.

Her words were a slap. "I didn't know Kira was bringing a demon weapon over, or I would've carried the sword back to Shadow City. I would *never* have allowed him to take it, even if he is my preordained." Her past mistake wasn't even close to that. She'd known what Azbogah was trying to do. I'd had no clue Levi was using Kira to get what he needed. "Don't try to equate my mistake with yours." I wanted to say more, and maybe I would have before, but I didn't want to add to the burden she carried. I wanted to be considerate, but I wouldn't let her push me around. I needed to stand my ground and end this charade. "Don't push your bad choices and insecurities onto me. I'm *not* you, and I shouldn't have to pay for your regrets."

Her head tilted back as she surveyed me, and my stomach tensed.

"You're right." She stood and smoothed her dress with her hands. She nodded, her composure slipping back into place. "And it's time to go. The council meeting is due to start shortly, and we need to get there as soon as possible to see if we can decipher whatever Azbogah has planned."

"Is it time?" Father asked as he joined us in the kitchen.

He must have been listening to have timed his appearance so perfectly, but I wasn't surprised. He was probably the reason my mother had decided to talk with me.

"Yes, let's go." Mother marched into the living room and opened the sliding glass door to the outside.

I wanted to stay here and not deal with drama on top of the turmoil inside, but that would only make the situation worse.

I kept quiet and shut our balcony door, then flew beside my parents as we headed toward the capitol building.

The smoke was gone, only a trace left to be seen. The flickering lights weren't as strong as normal, which was probably why my magic hadn't fully recharged yet. No shifters were out, and I assumed they were resting after the trying night before. Though only the wolves had been affected, everyone had eventually shown up to help save the residents.

Even in the city, people weren't out like usual, leaving only a small trickle rushing toward some end destination. I'd never seen Shadow City so deserted, but we'd never had a fire, and the artifact building had never been broken into, either. Everyone was on edge, and rightfully so.

Mother led us the long way, heading toward the Elite Wolves' Den. When the building came into view, bile inched up my throat. It was no wonder the smoke hadn't fully dissipated. The once golden building was coated in ash and dirt and had collapsed in several spots, a stark reminder of the devastation.

The three of us didn't speak as we flew. There was nothing to say.

As we approached the white capitol building, my attention homed in on one person heading inside the large hunter green door. A person who shouldn't have been here.

CHAPTER EIGHT

I BLINKED IN DISBELIEF, but Grady Rosso's ruby hair was unmistakable as he waltzed into the capitol building.

My stomach churned more violently, as if fate were trying to see how far she could push me.

"What is *he* doing here?" I asked through clenched teeth. There was no reason for the fox shifter to join this meeting. Grady was a menace, and my friends and I suspected he was behind the shifter attacks against Mother and Kira.

Kira was the former fox leader's only child. Because Kira was female, Hank Rosso hadn't thought she was worthy to take over his role after he stepped down, and he had named Grady, his nephew, as his successor. But during a recent time of upheaval, Kira had helped us, leading Sterlyn and Griffin to use their council positions to back her in taking over the role. Kira was a better leader in every way, and it was only because of bias that her father hadn't supported her.

Father grunted. "I assume Azbogah asked him here for a reason none of us will like."

I pulled my cell phone from my pants pocket and typed a note to Sterlyn and Ronnie, informing them of our little visitor. Those two would inform their mates, so I didn't need to worry about including the men.

When the three of us reached the grassy lawn in front of the capitol building, I scanned the area. The unnatural quietness of the city unsettled me. Even in the middle of the night, the occasional nocturnal creature still scurried around. Nothing seemed out of sorts beyond the faint smell of smoke that tainted the air.

My phone vibrated with a text from Sterlyn: We're at the coffee kiosk, waiting on you.

She didn't need to say anything more. Her short response expressed her discomfort.

"I take it you alerted Sterlyn and her friends?" Mother asked as she stepped toward the door.

Obliging her, I replied, "Yes, but she must have known because they're already inside."

"Good." She nodded as her wings relaxed a millimeter.

If I hadn't known her so well, I wouldn't have noticed, but I'd learned at an early age that to truly understand my mother, I had to watch for subtle physical changes when she was out in public. She held tightly to her mask of indifference, believing if she let her guard down even the slightest bit, someone would use it to their advantage.

Now, I could imagine we had Azbogah to thank for that. He always tried to read her, and her seeming apathy must have given her a strategic advantage against him.

The three of us entered the huge, barren entryway. The yellowed walls needed a fresh coat of white paint, but Azbogah had demanded they remain as they were from the first day the doors to the hall had opened—a reminder of how long the council had reigned. His arrogance irritated me, but Mother often reminded me that wise people chose their battles, and these walls weren't a battle that should be had.

I found Sterlyn, Griffin, Ronnie, and Alex standing near the coffee shop in the corner of the room. All four were dressed casually, even Alex, which wasn't the norm for a council meeting. They looked rough, with dark circles under their eyes and soot streaking their faces. It was clear they hadn't rested all night and had been working to put out the fire and find shelter for the displaced wolves.

I shouldn't have left them.

Father touched my shoulder. "I'm assuming you'll meet us inside."

I nodded. The mixture of guilt, pain, and dread coursing through me was something I'd never experienced before. Each breath was a struggle, and the trauma from my connection with Levi was also growing more intense with every passing second. Every ounce of my energy was going into pretending I wasn't fracturing inside.

As I approached the four of them, the urge to avert my gaze coursed through me. I'd let them down by not staying to help longer.

Ronnie took a large bite of her cinnamon raisin bagel, the sweet scent filling my nose. Somehow, her normal action caused my throat to dry.

"I'm *so* sorry I left you all yesterday." My voice cracked.

Surprisingly, it was Griffin who stepped toward me. He rasped, "You have *nothing* to apologize for. You saved my mother and tried to help so many others when we couldn't do anything. If anything, *I'm* sorry you got hurt. You almost died trying to help us. That's a sacrifice few people would make."

My chest threatened to heave, but I held it back...barely.

"You're family." And they were. Even Griffin had weaseled his way into my heart. Oh, gods, I had to change the subject before I broke down. "Do you have any idea why Grady is here?"

"No. We've been relocating the wolves who couldn't find room in other shifter residences to the vampire section." Sterlyn sighed as she handed me an extra cup of coffee that I hadn't noticed until then. "The amazing king and queen of the vampires welcomed us into their section of the city with open arms and even provided several floors of various buildings for the wolves to stay until the Wolves' Den can be rebuilt."

Alex puffed out his chest and grinned. "*Amazing* is a humble way to describe those two royals, but I shall let it pass." He wrapped an arm around his wife.

My heart squeezed harder, envious that their relationship was so strong...unlike mine. I doubted mine could even be considered a relationship.

"Don't make his head bigger than it already is." Ronnie popped the rest of her bagel into her mouth. Unlike other vampires, she was half demon and required food as well as blood. "He toots his own horn all the time."

"There's only one person I want tooting my horn." Alex winked.

Normally, their sexual banter didn't faze me, but today, I wasn't in the right mind to handle it. "And you complain about Sierra not staying on point in a conversation," I snapped, and instantly regretted it, which disheartened me more.

Alex averted his gaze and scratched the back of his neck. "She's right. Sierra is a horrible influence."

I smiled to show I hadn't meant my harsh words. At

least Alex could handle criticism when it was warranted, but that didn't ease my guilt much.

"I don't think we'll have an answer until we get in there," Griffin said as he took Sterlyn's hand. "That's part of the power trip Azbogah enjoys."

"Let's go inside." Sterlyn's jaw twitched. "Everyone else already is. We were just waiting on you and your parents to arrive."

Without another word, the five of us marched through the inner hunter green door that led to the council meeting room.

As usual, Azbogah had taken one of the center seats at the large, U-shaped table in the middle of the room. Erin, the priestess of the Shadow City witch coven, sat next to him, her scarlet-streaked black hair waving down her arms as she batted her heavily lined, mist-gray eyes at the dark angel. There were twelve chairs in total, three each for the representatives of the four races, with six council members sitting along the middle section facing the door and three on each arm of the U. Naturally, there were several vacant chairs to the left of the doorway for me and select others where we could sit in and watch the proceedings.

My stomach revolted even more when I caught my mother glancing at Azbogah from the corner of her eye. So much had always brewed between them, but at least I now knew why.

Not wasting another moment, Sterlyn, Griffin, Ronnie, and Alex strolled toward the table and took four of the five vacant seats. Ronnie slid into the seat next to Erin as Sterlyn took the other seat next to Azbogah. Alex followed Sterlyn and sat between her and Breena, who was usually stuck in one of the side witch council seats, but not today.

Interesting.

Father sat perpendicular to Breena, his white wings seeming brighter in the dimly lit room, or maybe they contrasted with Griffin's dirty face and clothes.

A tight smile spread across Gwen's face while she scooted closer to the edge of the right side as Griffin sat between her and Father. Even though she wasn't dirty like the other four, her eyes bore the same dark circles. There was no doubt that Gwen had stayed beside the four of them, helping to find places for the wolves. Though she wasn't with the group often, she was definitely an asset and often stayed behind to take care of royal affairs so Alex and Ronnie could help us.

A loud chuckle left Diana from the end of the left side of the table, next to Mother and closest to me. She flipped her wavy maroon hair over her shoulder, and it hit Mother's arm. The witch's ebony eyes glinted with malice as she murmured loudly, "It's about time the four of them got here. It's so sad when council members can't be punctual."

Mother brushed Diana's hair off her arm, but her expression remained stoic. The only hint of her aggravation was the momentary tension around her eyes.

"We aren't late." Alex adjusted in his seat as he glared at the young witch. "Besides, we've been up all night helping find refuge for the fire victims."

"So was your sister, but she arrived here with the rest of us." Azbogah arched a brow.

I hated all the undermining that went on during these meetings, a constant stream of sniping. "Yet instead of addressing whatever topic you have in your pocket, you're wasting everyone's time with pointless criticism,." I said.

Cringing, I couldn't believe I'd spoken the words aloud. Even though I had no issue speaking my mind, I didn't usually actively attempt to antagonize anyone without reason. I left that tactic for Sierra. But my self-control was focused on appearing put together.

Mother closed her eyes for a moment, telling me she was disappointed. She'd taught me not to start battles when I didn't know the other person's plan. All that would accomplish was playing into their hand.

Erin smirked as she ran a long fingernail down Azbogah's arm and purred, "Even Yelahiah is losing control over her daughter. She couldn't get her to show up, and now this." She *tsk*ed.

I yearned to stab her with my wings. With the burning pain from my bond seeming to rip my body in half, having an outlet for my agony would be nice.

"I see why you needed me." Grady tugged on the oversize sleeves of his white button-down shirt. Even his brown slacks hung off his body, and I didn't understand how they managed to not fall. He looked like a joke, and it was asinine that Hank had thought the fox shifters would take him seriously.

Ronnie laughed. "We're good. You can leave now."

"You foolish girl," Azbogah sneered.

"I'd reconsider how you address a queen, and most importantly, my *wife*," Alex hissed as crimson bled through the blue of his eyes.

Things were about to escalate, but raw, unbridled pain surged through me. I sat in the chair against the wall and placed a hand on my chest.

"What is the point of this meeting, Azbogah?" Sterlyn asked. "We still have a lot to handle, and we need to move this along."

Azbogah nodded as an arrogant smile slipped into place. "Very well." He stood, using his tall frame to tower over everyone. "Sterlyn and Griffin have been losing control over the shifters for a while now. It began with attacks in Shadow Terrace and then escalated to an attack here at the capitol building. Let's not forget that the two of them—along with the now *king* of vampires—fought against our own Shadow City police when they tried to keep not only the current *queen* safe when she was still human but also our vampire residents, who were dying because they couldn't control their bloodlust."

"We're all aware of this," Griffin growled. "Is there a point to rehashing the past?"

The dark angel cut his gaze to Griffin. "I understand it must be hard to listen to your shortcomings, but there *is* a point to it all."

Sterlyn's eyes glowed faintly, and she said softly, "Please continue."

"Certainly." Azbogah rubbed his hands together. "Then we had yet another attack on not only an archangel," he said, gesturing to Mother as if we didn't know who he was discussing, "but on the very fox shifter Griffin and Sterlyn had put in charge—who, may I remind you, is also in charge of the police force that protects the artifact building, which was broken into on *her* watch. The shifters didn't trust the police force or the guards to handle the artifact building, so they took the matters into their own hands." He shook his head as he placed his hands behind his back. "Now the Elite Wolves' Den caught fire, which should have been impossible. Some might say it could be the flames of justice from a certain archangel herself trying to set up others for the fall." He stopped and glanced at Mother before pulling his gaze away to address the council. "Regardless, the longer these two are in charge, the worse things get. Even Ezra, who had been an outstanding council member, turned on these two."

Mother's face paled at his implication, but surprisingly, she stayed quiet. It was clear he was trying to point fingers at her for both the break-in and the fire, an astonishing act.

The worst part was that if I hadn't been present during the past few months, I might have seen some validity to his points, but there was no doubt in my mind that Azbogah was the culprit behind all the disasters and was framing Sterlyn and Griffin. My guess was that since Mother would adamantly fight against killing a silver wolf, Azbogah was using another strategy to remove Sterlyn from being involved in the city.

I glanced at Father, who had remained silent, as usual. He steepled his fingers and stared at Azbogah as if he could see how everything would play out. I wished there was a way I could speak to him telepathically.

"I move to have Grady stand in as the acting shifter council member until the inventory has been completed in the artifact building. Once we know the results, we can discuss the next steps." Azbogah gestured to Grady. "It seems only fair that this fine, outstanding fox shifter should take at least a temporary leadership role since the two wolf council members hastily removed the future he was entitled to. He would be free of biases in their favor, so a fair hearing can commence once all the information is available."

And there it was. Everything inside me screamed that he'd promised Grady the council position as a payoff for staging the shifter attack and potentially the fire.

Grady's back straightened. "The honor you're bestowing—"

"You can't be serious." Ronnie stood, not bothering to control her expression. "There's no way you'll have a majority vote for this."

"Let's see." Diana snickered, enjoying the drama. "I

know Breena, my priestess, Azbogah, and I agree. Let's ask the other council members in the room."

"Very well." Gwen nodded. "I do not support Azbogah's suggestion."

Ronnie, Alex, Griffin, and Sterlyn followed suit, leaving my parents to settle the matter.

Why did Azbogah think he would win this? I had to be missing something.

"Please, Yelahiah." Azbogah tilted his head as he regarded my mother. "You and *your husband* will make the final decision. I'm sure all the angels will be interested to see if you continue to support the wolf shifter representatives after refusing to act against your attackers."

Under normal circumstances, I'd have grown frustrated with him, but with the amount of pain raging through my body, all I could concentrate on was not slumping in my chair. I couldn't even sit upright, and I wasn't sure how much longer I could sit here. The overwhelming urge to leave grew with the intensity of the pain.

There was no question—I had to find Levi. No matter the cost.

Yelahiah inhaled sharply. "You're right."

I glanced up to see Father staring at her with concern as he said, "Yela—"

"No, Azbogah is right. Ever since the silver wolves showed up, there has been nothing but drama. I will oblige him and vote in favor of Grady *temporarily* acting as the third shifter council member representative."

Sterlyn nodded, not even batting an eye. She understood the position my mother was in, but Griffin frowned, not bothering to keep his emotions in check.

Father pinched the bridge of his nose as he conceded as well. "I will also agree with Azbogah's suggestion."

"Very well." Azbogah's wings fluttered in celebration.

My stomach roiled as a black haze filled my vision. There was no way I could stay. I stood on shaky legs and hurried through the entryway toward the main door, desperate to get out of there before anyone noticed the state I was in.

Moving more slowly than I'd have liked to admit, I reached the main door that led outside just as my heart and body seized. My body shook as stinging electricity coursed through my veins. As I desperately searched for the door, my legs gave out, and I crumpled to the ground.

CHAPTER NINE

A SPLIT SECOND before my face could hit the ground, an arm wrapped around my waist and pulled me upright. Ronnie's sweet scent filled my nose as she supported me against the wall next to the outer door.

Her eyes darkened to hunter green, and her forehead creased with worry. "Have you still not recovered from the fire?"

"I'm not sure what's wrong," I gritted out between my teeth.

If only it were that, then I would know how to proceed. I had no clue how to end the raging torment inside me. I wasn't even certain that finding Levi would improve things. If he was trying to end our connection, it could make things worse, although I wasn't sure it mattered. I was almost at the point of not caring about the consequences and forcing him to see me.

Across the vast entry hall, the door to the council room opened, and I forced myself to straighten despite the pain surging inside me. "I'm fine," I told Ronnie, desperate for her to drop her arm.

Understanding flashed in her eyes, and she took a step to the side, removing her hold on me.

I couldn't force myself to step away from the wall. I fisted my hands, my nails digging into my palms. Maybe if I forced some pain elsewhere, it would make the agony more bearable.

I soon realized that logic wasn't working out, but I was determined not to admit failure.

Alex stepped through the door first, which didn't surprise me, given his vampiric speed and Ronnie being with me. Sterlyn, Griffin, and my parents followed. No one else appeared immediately behind them. It was bad enough that this group was seeing me in this state, and I trusted each one of them.

"Rosemary, what's wrong?" Mother sounded concerned as she rushed to my side. She scanned me, her forehead lined with confusion.

The evidence of my pain was all internal, and gods, how I wished it were external. At least that way, I'd know how to explain the discomfort to her liking. "I..." I took a shaky breath, and my lungs protested the entire way. "Don't kn—" I gave up on talking. It took too much effort, and I didn't want to fall again, especially not in front of her.

Father pushed some of my hair behind my ear. "She can't stay here like this."

A rush of heat warmed my body as the connection between Levi and me sprang back to life, rising to a more natural level.

He was back on Earth.

My heart lightened with joy.

Levi? I connected, unable to ignore him. My rational side wanted to give him the silent treatment, but my concerned side needed to ensure he was all right.

Silence greeted me, making my blood chill. The pain inside formed into something ice cold...like impending death. Something was wrong with Levi.

He wasn't ignoring me—the other end of our bond was unresponsive, as if he were asleep...or at least this was how it had felt the one night we'd fallen asleep together after we'd connected. But it didn't make sense that he'd be sleeping since he'd just arrived back on Earth.

Something in my chest *yank*ed. The sensation was so strong, I couldn't ignore it, especially since it felt tethered to my heart. "I've got to get out of here."

"Yes, you do." Mother sighed. "Go back to the house."

I forced myself to control my voice, which took every ounce of training I'd received all those years ago. I wanted to act brashly, but that wouldn't get me far, especially with her. "No, Mother. I have to leave the city. He's here again."

Father was the only one who seemed confused as he rubbed his chin. "How could you know that?"

"Their mate bond," Sterlyn murmured cautiously in case there were listening ears.

Mother must have deduced that somehow because she nodded as if she had the final say. "Then you need to stay away from him."

I was no longer a young featherweight, and I could make decisions for myself. It also didn't help that my heart had so much pressure on it from the *tug* that I was afraid it would burst from my chest. "I can't." I grimaced at the raw vulnerability of that statement. I lowered my voice, ensuring that only this group could hear my next words. "He has the demon sword. I need to get it back so I can return it to the artifact building." Luckily, that was true.

"Can't someone else do it?" Mother sighed, but her

shoulders sagged in defeat. She knew the answer as well as I did.

Griffin crossed his arms. "She's the best person to find him, and if he shifts into shadow form, she's one of the few who can still see him."

I grimaced. Griffin was trying to help, but referencing my preordained mate's demon form was like stabbing an almost healed wound.

Shifting her weight, Ronnie glanced at her husband and said, "Alex and I can risk leaving since we aren't being targeted right now. Gwen loves overseeing the royal duties, and she's amazing at keeping us updated. I can stay with Rosemary the entire time since I can see him, too."

When Alex didn't agree quickly, Ronnie placed a hand on her hip and stared her mate down, no doubt using their soulmate connection to talk to him.

Every part of me wanted to turn and fly off, but I wasn't sure I had the strength to get to him. The suffering rolled through my body, and the pressure on my heart added more discomfort to the situation. I felt like a ticking time bomb ready to explode.

I had to leave.

Just as I opened my mouth to say so, Alex sighed and slumped. He grumbled, "She's right. We can take Rosemary and make sure nothing bad happens to her."

Mother scoffed. "It's a little late for that."

Fortunately, I had enough experience with her to know better than to waste energy on responding. Right now, my whole focus was on getting out of here and finding him.

For the weapon...of course.

"Come on, dear," Father said as he took Mother's hand. "Let's get back in there. There's no telling what's going on while we're out here."

Mother's wings fluttered, and she stared at me one more time. "Very well, but call us and let us know when you've retrieved it. Do you understand?"

She wanted to ensure I didn't do anything foolish, like trusting him again. The words burned, but I couldn't rebuke them. "I will." She deserved my loyalty. Because of Levi, the council would learn that an artifact was missing, and there was no telling what Azbogah would do. We needed to get the sword back before they finished taking inventory.

"I hate not going with you." Sterlyn took a step back toward the council room. She bit her bottom lip, clearly conflicted.

Her loyalty was rare and admirable in a person, but accompanying me would be a less than ideal decision. I reassured her, "We'll be fine. You have to stay here."

"If we need to go looking for him, we'll take a silver wolf. If we get into trouble, they can contact you immediately," Alex said as he moved toward the council room door.

Sterlyn's eyes glowed, and she moved closer to Griffin. At first, I thought she was linking with the silver wolf pack to inform them of our plan, but the unease flowing off her told a different story. She glanced at Griffin, then back at the rest of us. "Annie's feeling that strange sensation again. What if more demons are here to attack?"

The day kept getting better. "I don't feel any strong negative energy, so the princes of Hell aren't here, and I don't think they'd launch an attack on the city without coming in person."

Mother lifted her chin. "Rosemary is right. If the princes of Hell are planning to attack the city, they'll want to be part of its fall. I don't know the details of everything that happened because Azbogah negotiated their exit, but I do know there was no love lost."

"That seems to be a common theme where a certain angel is involved." Ronnie snorted, but her face was devoid of humor.

"You four should stay here while we assess the situation. We won't go into battle half-cocked, especially with our depleted numbers." Alex started back toward the council room. "I'll inform Gwen of what's going on and be right back."

His words stung. We'd lost so many lives. The silver wolves were down to fifteen, including two young silver wolves, Jewel and Emmy, who weren't with the pack right now. None of the regular wolves could see the demons in their shadow form, so Killian's pack was at a huge disadvantage. Of the vampires, only Ronnie could see the demons in that form since full vampires were only blessed with demonic powers and weren't actually part demon. "He's right," I said. "I promise not to do anything foolish, even if Levi is involved." Though I might be tempted, I'd fight the urge. My family was important, and I couldn't throw their safety and well-being away for a man who might not even want me. I refused to make the same mistake my mother had. These people had stood with me the entire time, and I'd return the favor.

Griffin sniffed, probably waiting to catch my lie. He understood the power of a mate bond and how the person on the other end meant more to each person in the pair than life itself.

Though I understood that power, I had to remember that actions spoke louder than words. Every chance Levi had been given, he'd shown he couldn't be trusted and that he didn't trust me. I wouldn't turn my back on the secure relationships I had for one made of just as many bad emotions as amazing ones. At some point, the rollercoaster had to level out, or I might lose my mind.

"You're one person whose bad side I'd never want to get on." Griffin shook his head and glanced at his mate. "I think she could kill him despite what he means to her. It's both badass and frightening."

I grimaced, my heart hurting at the possibility. It might come down to that, and I was sure Griffin overestimated my abilities.

The council room door opened, and Alex strode out. "We need to go, and you four"—he gestured to my parents, Griffin, and Sterlyn—"need to go back inside. Things are escalating, and you need to be involved." He breezed past me and opened the outer door.

"Be careful." Sterlyn rushed over and hugged Ronnie, then me.

Her freesia scent filled my nose, and I didn't feel quite as awkward in her arms. My heart warmed, giving me a brief reprieve from the overwhelming agony.

As she and Griffin headed back into the council room, Mother patted my arm and said, "Please be careful."

That was the closest any angel really came to saying *I love you*, a fact that resonated with me. We came across as cold and uncaring, but we *did* feel things.

I couldn't keep my feet stationary any longer. The hold on my heart jolted me forward, and I stumbled out the door, my hands quivering at my sides. "I'll meet you at Killian's," I said, and spread my wings, though I wasn't sure how well I could fly. My body still trembled with pain. The urge to find Levi was the only thing keeping me standing.

"Our car is here." Ronnie gestured to the slate gray Lexus SUV parked in the lot next to the building. "We've learned there's no telling when we'll need to leave quickly, so we always bring it now in case. Get your ass in the SUV, Rosemary, or you won't make it out of the city to find Levi."

She was right. Though the pain was better, anguish still coursed through me. If it overwhelmed me while I was in flight, I could get injured. "Fine, but the tug is coming more from Shadow Ridge instead of Terrace."

Pulling my wings into my back, I hurried into the back seat of the car, cramming my almost six-foot frame inside. Luckily, it was a luxury car and not as tight of a fit as some of the vehicles into which I'd been stuffed before.

Within seconds, Alex was in the driver's seat, and we were pulling out onto the main road that led to the Shadow Ridge–side city gate.

A few more people were strolling around the city, but for midmorning, the place was still quite bare.

The *yank*ing in my chest strengthened now that I was following it, which both appeased part of me and caused dread to bloom in my stomach. I wasn't sure what I would find, and that petrified me. Yet another new sensation to name, but *dread* was the only thing that could describe the heaviness in my stomach, the racing of my pulse, and my sweaty palms. Even when I faced trained warriors, I never experienced anything close to these horrible feelings.

My phone rang, and my shaky hands could barely remove it from my pants pocket. We pulled up at the gate right when I saw Annie's name flash across the screen.

Swiping quickly, I answered, "Hello?"

"Sterlyn says you're acting strange, so I'm guessing you're sensing this, too." Annie breathed quickly. "Why don't you meet us at the edge of the woods that lead to the old silver wolf family pack neighborhood so we can go in there immediately?"

I could get behind that plan. I had a feeling this *tug* would lead us to where we'd encountered the demons on that first day. Levi had blocked me from something, and I had a sneaking suspicion we were going to find out what. "Maybe you shouldn't go. If we're being pulled toward the same place, it's best if you don't risk your safety and the baby's."

"Not you, too," Annie growled. "Cyrus is after me, too, but this feels different. I don't know how to explain it, but it doesn't feel malicious like when we were attacked all those times. I...I need to go and see this through. I'm being tugged for a reason."

I understood all too well. If someone had asked me to stay back, I would have refused as well, but I didn't have a child growing in my womb. "But—"

"I promise," she said loudly, talking to both me and someone else, "if anything even hints at danger, I'll be the first one out of there. I won't allow anything to happen to my baby."

"It's not just the baby I'm worried about," Cyrus rasped loudly enough for me to hear him through the phone. "And even though your mother isn't as vocal, Midnight agrees."

Annie was right. She loved the child more than any of us. It was growing inside her. To be willing to go, she must have sensed it would be safe.

Ronnie turned to me from the passenger seat and said loudly, "Fine, but you'd better stay at the very back of our group, or I'll be picking your ass up and shadow-flying you out of there."

The city gate opened, and Alex drove through, pulling away from the prison city behind the wall. I'd never thought of it like that before, but Shadow City had changed in the past few years. It didn't feel like home anymore.

"You guys are impossible," Annie groaned, but there was warmth in her tone. "We'll see you there." And she hung up.

I didn't bother repeating the conversation because Alex and Ronnie had heard every word. Alex increased our speed, and the *tug* grew stronger with each passing moment.

I tried to control my breathing so I didn't hyperventilate. My lungs convulsed, fighting against the slowness, but I didn't let up.

We breezed through the two-lane streets of quaint downtown Shadow Ridge. People milled around the connected brick buildings, scurrying through the town and heading to work. The air wasn't smoky here, and the sun rose in a cloudless sky.

The town was small, so it wasn't long before Alex had driven us through and was turning onto the road that connected the two neighboring towns.

Oaks, cypresses, and redbuds were thick on the sides of the road as if they were protecting the traveling humans from catching sight of any supernatural creatures. When Alex turned left as if to head toward Shadow Terrace, he quickly pulled over onto a cutout on the side of the road and turned off his car.

I was reaching for the handle when the connection to Levi began to lose its warmth.

I froze. This cooling sensation wasn't due to Levi leaving Earth again for Hell—this could only be from near death.

I have to find him.

I flung the door open and jumped out, then let my wings explode from my back.

"Rosemary, what's wrong?" Ronnie called.

I didn't have time to explain. I had to find Levi. That had to be why our connection was tugging me so hard and why he wasn't responsive. "Levi's in trouble."

I took off into the sky as Alex yelled, "We need to wait for Annie and the others!"

"There's no time." I couldn't believe I'd been so stupid and stubborn and hadn't listened to our bond. No wonder I felt so much pain—he was *dying*.

All the times I'd wanted to kill him myself ran through my mind and added to the turmoil.

"Rosemary!" Ronnie screamed. "This could be a trap!"

Maybe, but if he died when I could have saved him, I wouldn't be able to live with myself.

I surrendered myself to the bond, letting it guide me. Even though I was determined to reach him, I wasn't ignorant; I kept an eye on the wildlife below me. The deer stepped leisurely through the woods, and birds flew all around, unperturbed, informing me that demons weren't close by.

The oranges and reds of fall didn't comfort me as I soared toward my preordained. Even though I was angry with him, I didn't want him to die. A life without him would be more miserable than one in which we were separated. Unfortunately, it had taken this moment for me to realize it.

Right before the former silver wolf pack neighborhood appeared on my right, the *tug* took me left, deeper into the woods. I flew lower, dodging the trees and pushing myself to get there...to him.

After a few minutes, a small cave appeared through the foliage.

Memories of the last demon portal we'd discovered replayed in my mind. That portal had also been located in a cave. This couldn't be a coincidence, and the *tug* was pulling me there.

The opening of the cave loomed closer, and my heart stopped as my eyes focused on a severely beaten Levi and the strange man hovering over him.

CHAPTER TEN

ALL I COULD DO WAS stare. Levi's skin was pale, not the light golden color I'd become familiar with. Blood soaked his tan shirt, and his face held a dark purple bruise with a large gash under his hairline. Dry flakes of blood coated his short espresso hair and clumped in his chestnut scruff.

He looked like death, and with the cooling of our bond, death was quickly descending.

The tall man had dragged him over by the stone wall the cave burrowed beneath. He leaned over Levi, his hands on my preordained mate's chest, no doubt ready to finish him off.

"No!" I screamed, wanting the man to pay attention to me instead of my gravely injured mate. "I'm going to *kill* you." And I had to do it quickly so I could heal Levi.

The man straightened and moved so that I could no longer see Levi. The sun shone on his dark coffee-brown hair and light golden skin. He narrowed his hickory eyes at me and ran a hand over his golden-brown beard. "We aren't bothering you. Leave us be."

I descended and landed a few steps away from the man between two cypresses, then spread my feathers out to make myself appear as threatening as possible.

The man was about the same height as Azbogah. He was muscular like Levi, but a hardness denoted that he'd not only lived in Hell but had been through it as well. Despite the maliciousness vacant from his stance, he could be a direct threat.

If the princes of Hell were using leverage to get undecided demons to turn, this could be this man's pivotal moment.

Not wanting to waste time by fighting, I lowered my head and stared the demon in the eyes. "Leave now, and I won't kill you." Under any other circumstances, I wouldn't have offered that, but I was desperate to save Levi. Everything inside me surged, ready to protect him and heal him the best I could. Though I was angry and hurt, him dying wasn't an option.

"I can't." The tall man gestured at Levi.

I came unglued. He would *not* be finishing that job.

I launched myself, dead set on eliminating him. Every second I fought this man, Levi came close to death. My heart ached, but my blood boiled as I readied to end the fight quickly.

Flipping my feathers to the sharp side, I spun around to behead the nuisance.

The man jumped back, and my feathers caught air.

He was smarter than the other demons I'd fought, which infuriated me. I didn't need a competent fighter right now.

The man shadowed into his demon form and charged. I'd expected him to pull out a weapon, but he didn't. I spun around in the nick of time as he blew past me. If I'd taken a split second longer to react, he would've nailed me.

I glanced at Levi. His chest was barely moving, and the bond was losing warmth.

Just as I glanced back at the demon, he slammed into me.

I stumbled but stayed on my feet, using my wings to keep myself upright. The demon reached for my neck, but I caught his shadow wrists and dug my fingernails into shadow made flesh. I couldn't move my wings in this position, and if I let go, his hands would clasp my neck.

Hoping that my strategy would work, I kneed the demon in what I thought was his stomach. In shadow form, it was hard to tell what body part I was aiming at.

The demon grunted, and his desperate reach for my neck went slack as his arms went partially limp. He blinked, his hickory eyes not red in the least. Maybe it would take Levi dying before his transition to evil occurred, but I wouldn't let that happen.

My ears pounded as I kicked the demon in the stomach again and dug my fingers deeper into his skin. Before I killed him, I wanted him to experience the same pain Levi was feeling. Warm blood puddled under my nails, but I ignored it.

I'd never enjoyed killing; it was merely a necessity, and this death was no different. I was simply more desperate, eager to save my dying other half. "Why didn't you just leave?" I gritted through clenched teeth as I released my hold on his arm and punched him in the face. "I don't have time for this."

He lurched back several feet, then slowly straightened. Crimson blood dripped from his shadow form.

Not the blue blood of the demons I'd fought before.

If he wasn't bad, why was he here, killing Levi?

"I can't take him back," the demon said dejectedly. "We have to stay here."

"*He* can stay." There was no way I'd allow Levi to leave again. He would be our prisoner once more, and we would force him to return the demon sword. If I was going to be miserable, I'd ensure he was just as despondent. The thick maliciousness of demons wafted from inside the cave. The portal had to be there. "*You* either die or go back. Make the choice now."

Ronnie's sugary scent drifted into the area, and within seconds, her shadowy form floated down to my other side. I didn't need to see her face to know she wasn't happy about me running off, but I had no regrets. I'd do it all over again if the situation reoccurred.

"Oh, my gods," Ronnie gasped. "Levi!"

The shadow paused. "You *know* him?"

I winced. The last thing we needed to do was inform the demon that we knew him. We couldn't let him go back to Hell alive now. Not that it had been an option, since the demon would have known he was leaving Levi with me, but this was different. We knew his name.

A blur charged toward us and slowed, and Alex materialized in front of me. A frown marred his face, and his usually pristine hair was in complete disarray, adding to the soot still coating his features. He and Ronnie hadn't rested, but here we were in yet another dire situation.

This time, I had only myself to blame since we hadn't waited for backup.

My connection with Levi cooled further. I didn't have another moment to spare. I had to kill the menace. "It doesn't matter if we know him—you're about to take your last breath."

"I'm not here to cause you trouble." The demon lifted his hands in surrender.

But I wasn't a buffoon. This had to be a trick—no demon would willingly hand himself over to an enemy that wanted to kill them. "And Shadow City is a safe haven." I sneered, ensuring everyone knew I didn't mean it so the air didn't reek of a lie. If anyone believed him, they would believe the lie that the city had been built on as well. "Do you think I'm an imbecile?"

"Rosemary, wait," Ronnie said.

Alex hissed, not liking Ronnie getting closer to the enemy.

She had a caring soul just like her foster sister, Annie. Ronnie had been raised in foster care, and though she was hardened, she gave people the benefit of the doubt. She likely believed that if this demon had been meant to fall, he would have before now.

I didn't believe that. I'd seen people change, and during the past few weeks, I had changed more than I had in a millennium. He could fall as easily today as he could five hundred years from now. Situations altered people, just like Azbogah had altered my mother. "I'm not waiting."

"I'm just saying that maybe we could get information from him. Hold him prisoner, seeing as he's here with Levi like *this*." Ronnie bit her lip as she stared at the man.

That was the problem with people seeing essences for the first time—they looked for goodness where there wasn't any.

"Because that went so *well* last time, love." Alex exhaled, clearly on the same page as me.

We didn't have time for this. Every second we wasted brought Levi closer to death. Everything inside me screamed to heal him. "Levi is dying. I have to save him."

"You're *Rosemary*," the demon stated as he transformed back into his human form. His eyes lightened, holding hope.

It wasn't a question. I rushed him, twisting my body around so my wings would slice his head from his body just as Levi linked, *No...Father.*

Despite my head protesting, I jerked my body to the side a millisecond before my wings would've severed the demon's head. The man who could be Levi's father let out a shaky breath and murmured, "Thank gods."

The demon hadn't bothered to move, as if he'd accepted death as his fate.

"Why did you pull back?" Alex asked, sounding confused.

I couldn't blame him. What I had done didn't make sense. For all I knew, Levi was dreaming about his father in his last moments. But what if this was his father? I couldn't hurt the man Levi wanted to protect. "I'm not sure we *should* kill him."

Our bond chilled until all the warmth had completely vanished.

There was no more time to waste. "You two keep an eye on him and the cave. The portal is in there, and more demons could come at any second. Let me know if you need me." I rushed to my mate, trusting Ronnie and Alex to handle the demon.

Levi's heart was barely beating. I clasped the cool, clammy skin of his arm and rolled him to place my hands directly over his heart. Wanting there to be no barrier, I grabbed his shirt collar and ripped the fabric open.

I placed far too shaky hands on his chest, hoping I had enough magic inside me to save him. I'd healed him once before when he'd taken a fatal shot meant for me, and it had required a substantial amount of my magic.

"What's she doing to him?" the demon rasped.

His concern couldn't easily be faked, but demons were excellent manipulators. After all, look at what Levi had done to Kira and me. The thought burned.

Ronnie sighed, at a loss as to what to say.

"She's healing him," Alex said. "There's no point in not telling him—he'll see for himself in a second."

Howls came from close by as Cyrus and the wolves drew closer. They must have been following Alex's scent to locate us.

Levi's eyes fluttered, but he didn't open them. He connected, *Sorry. I...*

No. We were *not* saying goodbye. He didn't get off that easily. "Shut up," I growled as I tapped into my core and funneled my magic toward him.

Warmth poured through my palms, and my hands glowed. I pushed the energy inside Levi, wanting the magic to work directly on his heart first. I needed it to reenergize and pump harder.

My warm magic collided with his cool power, the refreshing sensation reminding me of the mornings I flew high in the sky with the air brushing over my hot skin. My heart lightened now that we were together and touching, our magics merging in the way that preordained mates were meant to be together. The pain I'd felt had been from his injuries on top of the devastation of separation.

Our combined magics swirled underneath his skin, searching for the places that needed healing. In an ideal situation, I would focus on certain spots, but I had no clue where to aim, other than wanting to jump-start his heart. Clearly, his heart hadn't taken the brunt of the trauma and was overexerted. Not having a target caused me to utilize more of my magic than I wanted to, especially since I had yet to recharge fully, but my options were nil.

Padding paws neared, and birds chirped merrily in the sky. The world kept turning, even though the love of my eternity lay dying underneath me.

My magic spiraled, searching frantically within him. Shifting the directions of the energy inside, I pushed the magic toward his head, where most of the visible injuries were. I'd been searching in his chest, focusing on the larger arteries in case of internal bleeding, but all that had come back clear.

After a few seconds, my magic found his wounds. His neck was close to broken from the abuse inflicted—the kind of injury that resulted in a slow death rather than an instant one, which must have been the intent.

No wonder the pain had been overwhelming, and I'd only felt a fraction of what he'd gone through. My gaze skimmed his body, and I noted that the sword wasn't on him.

Maybe that was why the demons had tried to kill him. If the sword acted like Ronnie's dagger, then if it had connected with him, no one else could use it while he was alive. Did I dare hope that his sword could be called to him like Ronnie called her dagger to her? Where it materialized out of thin air? If that was the case, wouldn't Wrath have called his dagger eons ago?

Our connection flickered, fueling my determination despite the drain of magic on my body.

I'd do whatever it took to save him.

As I poured more of my essence into him, my magic began to heal the injuries. I couldn't heal him completely, but enough that he would survive.

Tears streamed down my cheeks as my chest convulsed. I'd come too close to losing him.

Feet shuffled toward us, but I couldn't risk tearing my concentration away from Levi.

"Stay back," Ronnie said, "or I'll kick your ass." I heard her move.

"Holy gods. You're the one Wrath has been talking about," he gasped.

Ronnie's demon blade must have appeared, and some of my unease dissipated. She was taking the threat seriously, even if he was Levi's father.

Levi's spine mended, but my magic was dangerously depleted. I didn't want to fall comatose around Levi and his father.

Our connection warmed once again, and the pain receded. That was a blessing, because I was depleting and wouldn't be able to heal him much more.

Gods, even in death, Rosey's scent surrounds me, Levi connected, and sadness poured into me.

I sagged as his voice and the fatigue hit me. Now that our connection was back to its normal temperature, I pulled the little bit of magic left back inside my core. *Death will be a blessing once I get done with you.* Even though the hurt still raged inside me, I couldn't muster the anger I'd intended.

He was here and alive, and it meant more to me than I'd ever thought possible.

His mocha eyes fluttered open, and though his face was bruised and painful looking, he no longer had a deathly pallor.

Rosey. The corners of his mouth tipped upward, but a grimace thwarted the smile, likely from pain. Warmth wafted toward me. *Is that really you?*

I frowned at him. Even though I was happy he was here with me, that didn't mean I'd forgiven him. I forced myself to stand and step back. My body tried to sway, but I planted my feet and remained upright, despite the twisting of my heart and the world spinning around me.

"Son, are you okay?" his father asked from a few feet away. Ronnie was holding out her demon dagger, preventing him from getting any closer.

"Father?" He slowly sat up and leaned against the cave wall, his face etched with pain. "How are you here?" His eyes flicked from his father to me. "Wait. Are you okay? I felt something awful through our connection, and..." He trailed off, and his forehead creased. "I was with the princes of Hell when I felt it, but I needed to get to you..."

My heart sank. He must have sensed my injuries from the fire...which led me back to the other pressing issue. "Where's the sword?"

He averted his eyes, telling me everything.

Two snarling silver wolves raced from between the trees. One stopped next to Ronnie, his hackles raised, as the second, who had to be Darrell, raced up to me. Both were on high alert and prepared to fight.

"Whoa." Levi waved a hand in front of his face and glanced at his body. "I swear, I'm not much of a threat right now. It's a struggle just to sit up."

"That's better than dying, which you came dangerously close to doing. Granted, you aren't out of the woods *yet*," I rasped, infuriated that he wasn't apologizing or explaining what he'd done and conflicted as to whether I wished I could heal him more or leave him worse off.

He winked at me but winced again. "But you couldn't let that happen." Happiness wafted into me from him.

Those were his first words to me? I fisted my hands, wanting to smack the smugness off him.

But before I could snap back at Levi, Cyrus charged into the clearing in human form, his silver hair wild as he scanned the area around us. "We need to get out of here. *Now.*"

CHAPTER ELEVEN

THE LAST THING I wanted to do was leave. I had a demon who needed to realize that his flirtiness would not remedy the issues between us, even though he was dead sexy. He had already hindered our precarious bond. We would have had enough struggles to make our relationship work without him abandoning me and stealing a demonic weapon. We already had most of the world against us.

"What's going on?" Ronnie asked, keeping her gaze locked on Levi's father.

Her ready pose struck me. She knew there was a threat and assumed it was coming from Levi's father, since he was the closest to us. For not having been raised in the supernatural world, she'd quickly become an excellent fighter. Her instincts hinted at her angelic heritage since most angels—and thus demons—had an aptitude for strategy and battle.

"Annie senses something strange like she did each time the demons appeared." A vein between Cyrus's eyes bulged. He was always serious, but ever since Annie had become pregnant, he rarely smiled unless it was directed at her. He'd been stolen from his family as an infant and raised by the enemy. They'd trained him for battle at a tender age, even for a silver wolf, and he'd grown up thinking his family had discarded him. Finding his fated mate had centered him, and Annie's pregnancy had made him more protective.

"The witch must not have been able to hold the spell. They've probably realized that Levi and I aren't in our cell." Levi's father glanced at the mouth of the cave. "We need to leave before they figure out we've left Hell. They want to kill Levi because he's bonded with his mother's sword, and no one but him can use it. Hiding us from the trackers will be hard enough, even with a head start."

My heart skipped. *Your mother's sword?*

Levi sighed. *She was the archangel of strength before she fell. Her sword is called the great equalizer because it neutralized whatever powerful being she fought. The demons want to use it to neutralize their negative energy so they can walk on Earth. They need a witch to perform the spell to destroy it, but it can't be bonded with a person when the spell occurs.*

Yet another thing he could've told me from the *very* beginning.

Ronnie's head snapped in his direction. "What witch?"

Levi's father tilted his head. "I'm not telling you anything more until we get out of here."

I huffed. This whole situation felt like déjà vu from when we'd first stumbled upon Levi. He'd pretty much said the same words.

Hissing, Ronnie stepped closer to the demon.

As much as I wanted to continue the conversation, I didn't want any of us to die. "We need to leave if they're coming through. Where's Annie?" If demons invaded, Annie couldn't shift while pregnant, putting her more at risk and making her a potential liability.

As expected, that question defused Ronnie enough for her to become more rational. I knew what she was hoping for, but we'd all seen Eliza get stabbed. It would take a miracle for someone to live through that.

Once things settled down, we'd talk to Circe, Eliza's daughter and the priestess of her former coven, to determine a way to close or impede this portal like we had the one near the demon wolf pack neighborhood. As of this moment, we didn't have the manpower to watch the threat and attack if someone crossed over. The silver wolf numbers had shrunk with each battle, and I couldn't alert the angels for so many reasons. We needed to devise a plan and come back here to shut down this plucking portal once and for all...after we got the sword back.

Yet another problem to address when we were out of immediate danger.

"She's with Midnight, about a mile away. We weren't sure what we would find, so she stayed back like she promised—kind of." Cyrus scowled.

He wasn't happy with her being this close, and I would wager that her mother, Midnight, had stayed with her for more reasons than being unable to see the demons in shadow form. Annie cared for their unborn child, but she also loved Cyrus. If he got into a precarious situation, it would be hard for her to not act.

We were wasting too much time, and we needed to move.

Exhaustion set in again, but I couldn't succumb to it.

"Didn't you hear me?" Levi's father groaned in frustration. "I didn't drag Levi here only to allow the demons to catch up and finish the job."

The wolf next to Ronnie growled, making it clear he didn't trust the demon.

I didn't trust him either, and this push for us to leave could be more manipulative than due to an actual threat. *Is he really your father?* I needed confirmation.

Yes. Why? Levi tried to stand, but he fell onto his side, scraping his head against the stone wall.

The pain inside me throbbed again, confirming we shared sensations through the bond. Without considering the consequences, I bent and wrapped my arm around his waist, then stood. My head spun, and I had to grip him hard to keep us both from falling again. My skin buzzed where we touched, making my head even fuzzier as our souls reached for each other.

Now wasn't the time or place. Even if it had been, I wouldn't be falling back into bed with him. Too many emotions were already involved. I wouldn't only be taking the edge off my sexual frustration but rather getting more invested in our relationship. In *feelings*.

And I refused to allow him to mistreat me further or abuse my fragile heart. I'd never been a pushover, and that wouldn't change for him.

Darrell leaned against my side, keeping me from falling. I hated that the wolf could see I needed help, but there wasn't much I could do about it.

Though the moon was barely less than half full, Darrell in wolf form was still slightly larger than a normal wolf, which helped to support my tall frame.

The size of silver wolves depended on the phase of the moon. At the full moon, or what they called the silver moon, they were as large as a horse, whereas on a new moon, they were the same size and strength as a regular wolf shifter. Ophaniel, my uncle, had been the guardian angel of the moon; thus, a silver wolf's angel half was tied to moon magic.

On the opposite side, demon wolves were tied to the new moon and were at their weakest during the full moon. Annie was the lone adult left of that supernatural race, the only other known demon wolves being a few young boys who had gone home to live with their mothers' packs after we'd eliminated the corrupt demon wolves, including Annie's father.

Levi shuffled and stumbled, nearly making him, Darrell, and me topple over.

"Isn't Levi okay? I thought you healed him." Alex arched an eyebrow.

His words irritated me under my fatigue and stress. "I couldn't recharge after the fire because the smoke hindered the city lights. *This* was the best I could do." I gestured at Levi, still pressed against me.

Levi took a ragged breath. "Don't make her feel inadequate. She did more than *you* could."

Stop. You don't have that right. He didn't get to come back and pretend to be a knight in shining armor.

I didn't require a knight. I could take care of myself, and he didn't get to act as if he cared. He'd *left* me. Anger-fueled adrenaline pumped through my body, burning off some of the fatigue, though not enough to make a significant difference.

Levi's head jerked in my direction, his disbelief flowing into me. *The right to side with you?*

Black spots blotted my vision, and it had nothing to do with exhaustion and everything to do with the white-hot fury coursing through my veins.

A response to his question would be more than he deserved, so I locked down my mind.

"I can help—" Levi's father started.

Cyrus cut him off. "I'll take him." His eyes darkened with a wild and desperate glint.

He wanted us to get out of here and ensure his mate and child stayed safe.

Needing distance from Levi, I nodded. His touch would soon weaken my defenses, and I had to remain strong. "Be careful. His spinal cord is still injured, and it wouldn't take much to put him in a bad state again. I don't have the strength to heal him again so soon."

My throat dried.

Inherently, I'd already known that, but saying the words out loud made them more of a reality—the kind I didn't want to face no matter how furious I was with him.

Cyrus hurried over. "I'll be careful."

When he reached Levi's side, he slowly picked him up, cradling him like a baby.

"Let me try to walk," Levi grumbled.

"You fell over while sitting, son." His father shook his head. "The longer you make us take to get to safety, the more at risk your preordained is to get hurt."

Without acknowledging Levi's complaint, Cyrus took off at a steady pace. He ran at a slower speed than usual, careful not to jar Levi too much.

Ronnie nodded in the direction Cyrus had gone and said to Levi's father, "Move. I'll be right behind you, so no funny business." She flicked her wrist, bringing the demon's attention back to her dagger.

Alex's jaw twitched, but he remained silent, though I was sure he wanted his wife to stop waving the dagger around, broadcasting what she had in her possession. If Levi's father couldn't be trusted, she was painting an even larger target on her back.

Levi's father exhaled but hurried after his son. Ronnie

and Alex followed, staying close enough to the demon to react if he tried something devious.

The remaining silver wolf looked at me, his grayish topaz eyes examining me.

Chad.

I should've realized it was him, but that was how focused I'd been on Levi. He was hindering my judgment again, and he'd been here only a few minutes.

Chad flicked his head in Cyrus's direction, urging me to follow his alpha. He and Darrell wanted to travel in the back to keep an eye out for any demons that might come through the portal.

I forced my legs to move, my breath catching at how heavy they felt. Flying might have been a better option than walking. I'd have to stay near the treetops to watch the demons we had in our custody. "I'm going to get an aerial view."

Since they were in wolf form, they couldn't verbally protest, but I heard a snarl behind me.

Not wanting to delay us further, I flapped my wings and ascended into the sky. I skirted a redbud and a large oak tree, my charcoal feathers brushing some of the yellow and red leaves. I flew more slowly than normal, not wanting to outfly the group on the ground but also unable to go much faster. The sun was higher, its rays warming my skin even as the cool wind blew past me.

I caught up to Cyrus, needing to keep Levi in sight. Even though he'd hurt me beyond anything I'd ever experienced, I couldn't force myself to not care about him. My heart yearned for him as much as my body craved his touch, but my head screamed *no*. The one time I'd let my guard down, he'd almost shattered me.

If I let my guard down again, he might annihilate me.

I'd become just like one of those girls in the gods-forsaken movies Sierra made us watch.

The musky vanilla and lilac scents of Midnight and Annie floated around me, along with the musky floral scents of a few other silver wolves. Cyrus must have ordered a few to stay with Annie as protection in case something went awry.

Annie, Midnight, and three silver wolves in animal form came into view. Midnight could easily pass as Annie's older sister. Her hair was almost the same shade as her daughter's, a color Ronnie loved to describe as brown sugar, and they had nearly identical eyes, except Midnight's were slightly more brown. Midnight also had a good five inches in height on her daughter, but otherwise, they could pass for twins.

"He's here now. Let's go," Midnight said as she took her daughter's hand and tugged her back toward Shadow Ridge.

Cyrus approached as Annie nodded, and she and Midnight headed toward a nearby car. The three silver wolves stayed put, waiting for us.

Once the group had converged, the three wolves ran in front of Cyrus and Levi while Darrell and Chad remained at the back.

Loud chirps came from behind me, and I turned to find several large flocks of birds in a five-mile radius soaring through the sky toward us. Their movements seemed frantic, and my heart pounded.

"We need to move faster," I warned the group. I wasn't sure what else to do. I didn't feel any negative energy, so maybe more demons hadn't come through the portal.

Everyone picked up their pace.

Before long, we were approaching Alex's car, and the lack of an imminent threat confused me. Maybe something else had startled the birds, although they'd flown from such a large radius that it was hard to fathom what it could have been.

I lowered myself to the ground by Alex's SUV. When my feet touched the grass, my legs almost crumpled. I *had* to get some rest. I wasn't sure when I'd last had good-quality sleep.

A lump formed in my throat.

That wasn't true. I'd woken from the best night's rest I'd ever had to an empty bed and Levi connecting with me to say he was leaving me. Though that had only been two days ago, it felt like a lifetime. So much had happened in his absence.

As the others appeared, Alex unlocked the car. Cyrus placed Levi in the front passenger seat, and discomfort wafted through our bond. Not pain, exactly, so maybe he was healing on his own.

"We need to get as far away from here as possible." Levi's father rubbed his hands together as he approached the SUV. "Maybe California. China? Australia?"

He had to be joking.

"That's a horrible idea," Cyrus scoffed. "If they have trackers, it wouldn't take long for them to find you."

His father frowned. "Then what do you propose?"

We didn't need to bicker, especially when our time could be limited. "Shadow Ridge or Shadow Terrace," I said. I wasn't sure which was best. The demons seemed to know about both locations.

"We can't go to either." Levi's father shook his head. "If the angels find out—"

"If you're so worried about the angels finding out, maybe your *son* shouldn't have sneaked into Shadow City and convinced someone to hand over a *demon sword* to him." My patience had run out.

Levi's father's mouth dropped, and he stared at Levi. "You sneaked into Shadow City to retrieve it?"

"Let's go to Shadow Terrace." Cyrus waved his hand, motioning for us to get moving. "Fewer supernaturals travel there, and the houses we're staying in are farther removed from most of the vampire residences...if Alex and Ronnie are okay with that."

"Of course we are," Ronnie answered quickly.

A low grunt of dissent came from Levi's father. "What if the council finds out? We'll be persecuted."

"Which is why we should listen to them, Father," Levi interjected. "The demons aren't ready to start the war, so they won't come there."

Start the war.

What had he been keeping from me?

My chest tightened. I didn't want to know.

Annie clutched her chest and dropped to her knees. "Hurry. They're coming."

CHAPTER TWELVE

THE SITUATION KEPT GETTING WORSE. At least we'd made it back to the SUV and should be able to beat the demons back to Shadow Terrace if we hurried.

Cyrus wrapped an arm around his mate, his body so tense, he could be a statue. He glanced over his shoulder in the direction from which we'd come.

We didn't have time to waste. "Alert Killian and the other silver wolves and tell them demons are here," I said. "We need a few silver wolves to head to Shadow Terrace immediately. They'll have to stay there in case the demons try to intercept them."

When the demons had been desperate to get Levi back, they'd tried to snatch two silver wolves when we'd changed guards. Since only a handful of us could see demons in shadow form and we were staying away from others in Shadow Terrace, the wolves had to come and go from Shadow Ridge.

Annie's eyes glowed faintly. "We're informing them now."

My only solace was that I didn't feel a hint of negativity in the air.

Darrell, Chad, and the three other silver wolves stood in front of the group as a barrier. Silver wolves were born protectors, but like any supernatural race, they weren't invincible, especially with the moon less than half full.

"Guys, I'm so sorry—" Levi started, but I couldn't handle it.

"Don't," I cut him off. "After what you did, you don't get to use valuable time to make yourself feel better."

He closed his eyes.

At least he had the sense to look ashamed.

Ronnie opened one of the back doors and waved inside. "Annie, ride in the car with Alex, Levi, his dad, and Rosemary. I'll help the others keep a lookout."

Alex shook his head and held the keys out to her. "You drive. I'll stay with the others."

All this protective mate crap was getting on my nerves. I understood the impulse—I'd just experienced it with Levi—but we couldn't afford to be irrational. "She wants to stay with them because she can see the shadows. You can't."

Annie chuckled, a stark contradiction to her turbulent demeanor. "There's the Rosemary I first met. Cuts through all the shit to resolve the issue."

I nodded at her. I'd needed to hear that. In some ways, it seemed as if the old Rosemary was gone, and I missed her. Now that Levi was back and alive, I felt more settled. Maybe I would be able to recognize myself once again.

That thought was comforting.

Frowning, Alex clasped the keys. He knew he wouldn't win this argument. "Fine, but if anything seems off, I'm turning around."

My patience came unglued. Levi could easily take a turn for the worse if we got into a battle, and we were wasting time instead of moving. "Let's go so *nothing* happens."

Cyrus sprang into action, leading his mate toward the vehicle. "She's right."

Annie bit her bottom lip. "Wait...Mom can't see the demons, either. If they attack..." She trailed off, her lips pursed, and looked at Midnight.

"I'll be fine," Midnight murmured, but her words lacked conviction.

Levi's father cleared his throat. "If everyone staying behind can see demons in their shadow form, I can go with them to the house. That way, everyone who can't see the demons will be in the vehicle and should make it back to wherever we're going more quickly."

That wasn't a horrible suggestion. If demons caught up to them, it could be problematic, but we had Levi, giving us leverage with his father.

Our group glanced at one another. No one outright rejected the idea.

"Fine, but you stay next to me." Ronnie gestured to her side. "Any suspicious activity will result in your head being removed from your body. Got it?"

Alex scowled but didn't say anything out loud. I could only imagine the conversation they were having telepathically and hoped it stayed that way. Our group was already tense.

With that settled, I got into the seat behind Levi. If something happened, I could get my hands around him more easily to heal him...or kill him.

Midnight scooted into the middle seat, and the rest of the car riders piled in from that side. The silver wolves,

Cyrus, Levi's father, and Ronnie took off toward Shadow Terrace.

As soon as the door clicked, Alex peeled out of the cutout. The tires squealed as he swerved onto the road to Shadow Terrace. Luckily, we'd parked close to the town.

Silver fur flashed through the thinning leaves of the oaks and redbuds. The group was moving quickly and should arrive at the Shadow Terrace houses shortly after us.

A herd of deer ran out of the woods, barreling across the road just as demonic energy charged around me. The car squealed as Alex braked hard to avoid them, then jammed his foot on the gas once more.

A heavy sensation coated my skin like sludge. The closer I was to a truly fallen demon, the more crushing it felt.

Annie grunted and leaned forward, placing her head against the back of Alex's headrest. "They're here."

My heart sank, but we were already crossing the wooden bridge into Shadow Terrace. If the demons came here, they would start a war. This close to Shadow City, Azbogah and the other angels would feel their negative energy as well.

"We should be safe," Alex said, echoing my thought.

Levi groaned and fidgeted in his seat. "They'll be desperate to get me once they realize I'm alive."

"Why?" Midnight asked as she rubbed her daughter's back. Lines of worry were etched into her face.

Taking a deep breath, Annie sat upright. The darker brown in her eyes had taken over, removing any hints of honey. "As long as he's alive, they can't use his sword. Only Levi can."

My mouth dried. Annie didn't look like her typical self.

"What's wrong with you?" I winced, regretting how I'd phrased the question.

Rosey, that was harsh, Levi connected, and my chest warmed from him using our connection. *I think you meant to ask, "Are you okay?"*

My throat burned. If he thought acting like nothing was wrong between us would get him off my bad side, I needed to show him that was *not* an effective strategy, so I focused on my error. My words had come out more harshly than I'd intended, but my intent hadn't been to be cruel.

Some honey color bled back into her irises as she grinned. "It's a good thing I know you, or I'd be offended." She placed her hands on her growing belly.

It was already beyond a small baby bump. A silver wolf's average gestation period was three to four months, which was double that of a regular wolf shifter but half that of an angel. I imagined a demon wolf's gestation period would be the same. She was already almost a month and half into her term, and her pregnancy was extremely obvious.

I rubbed my arms. "I didn't mean—"

She waved. "Don't apologize, and yes, I'm fine. This sensation just keeps getting stronger and stronger every time. It's not painful, but it makes me lightheaded, and it's like something is raking across my skin. It happened before when we were closing the portal by the demon wolf settlement and I got really close."

"That's you sensing the demons. The portal has the essence of Hell flowing out of it." I knew that feeling all too well.

"Makes sense." She ran her fingers through her hair and pulled it away from her face.

Alex's hands tightened on the steering wheel, his

knuckles turning white. "I don't like the sound of desperate demons. Desperation makes people do insane things."

"Right now, they won't risk a war," Levi rasped, pain lacing his voice. "They aren't prepared to take on the angels, so they won't risk breaching their territories. Even if my father and I cross the border, the angels won't sense us. That's why they sent me here—because I'm undecided."

The thought wasn't comforting. I needed time to recover, and our group needed to strategize and find out what had happened to Levi in Hell. And I swore to the gods, Levi would tell us *everything*, or I might need to heal him again after I was done with him. "We don't need to panic. As long as the others get back and no one gets hurt, we have time to determine an effective course of action. Anything we do right now would be reactionary."

"She's right." Midnight nodded and glanced at me. "We're all tired, emotional, and stressed."

"And we don't know the entire story and can't decide on sound tactics," I added sternly. *Since you left me.*

What? Surprise floated into me. *Is that what you're upset about?*

And I'd thought he was smart. I wouldn't even humor him with a response.

The white buildings of Shadow Terrace came into view, their red rooftops reflecting the sun. It was close to noon, and I couldn't believe the day wasn't over. So much had happened, and I was exhausted. Yet another strike against Levi.

I'll take that as a yes. His joy didn't ebb, despite his words. *So...I take it you missed me.*

My hand itched to smack him—not punch, since he was in a delicate condition, but a good smack should suffice.

The road that led to the houses at the edge of Shadow Terrace appeared, and Alex turned left.

Wanting to distract myself from *him*, I focused on my friends who were in danger. "Are the wolves getting close?" They should have been in the territory by now, but no one had said anything. Sometimes, they forgot I wasn't included in any of the pack-link conversations.

"They're running through the woods to the houses," Annie answered, and her body relaxed. "They're over the bridge and into the safe area. They're running a little slower to make sure they keep a solid eye on Levi's father, but they're still making good time." She paused. "And I just realized I don't know that guy's name."

"Bune," Levi answered. "And I understand you don't trust him—"

I laughed loudly, surprising myself. "*Him?*" Despite my anger, some of the weight on my chest lightened. Though I'd expected us to come out of this unscathed with that much of a lead, there were no guarantees, especially with Bune in the mix. Levi had only positive things to say about his father, but I had to see the proof for myself. I couldn't take Levi's word on anything. Besides, if the princes of Hell were using the undecided to carry out their agenda, then Bune could decide to fall at any time.

Now that all of us were out of harm's way, fatigue hit hard. My eyes drooped, and my body sagged. The past two days had been a constant nightmare, and the only reason I wasn't coming completely undone was that Levi was sitting in the seat in front of me.

It infuriated me that being near him eased my heart and mind. He'd caused me all this pain, and being close to him again shouldn't have brought me peace. I wouldn't be one of those women who forgave someone just because they graced her with their presence. I wasn't something he could put on and take off, like armor when going to war. I was a person who deserved respect, consideration, and loyalty.

We pulled up to the houses we'd stayed in a few days ago. Levi, Killian, Ronnie, and Alex had stayed in the one next door to the burned-out home at the very end of the street. Annie, Cyrus, and Sierra had stayed in the house on the other side. I'd split my time between the two houses, trying to gain distance from Levi.

Alex pulled up in front of the house he'd been using. I slowly climbed out of the car, my body feeling as if it weighed triple what it normally did.

Uh...Rosey, Levi connected. *I could use some help.*

I glanced at him involuntarily. He was slowly reaching for the door handle, his face red from exertion.

Pain pounded through my heart, and I sighed in defeat. Despite my anger, I had to help him.

When I opened his door, his expression smoothed over. He must not have been sure about me, but he'd soon learn that this didn't change anything between us. I reached inside and helped him get to his feet.

Discomfort flowed into me, and I had no doubt he was locking down the sensations from his injuries. I hated that I couldn't heal him more. An apology almost left me, but I tamped it down. I hadn't done anything to be sorry for, and I didn't want to give him any reason to think things were fine between us.

I wasn't sure if they ever truly could be.

As Levi stood on shaky legs, Alex, Annie, and Midnight went toward the front door.

I helped Levi walk, my skin tingling as our connection buzzed between us. My heart was desperate to forgive him.

Alex held open the door, and Levi and I passed

everyone and entered first. In the sizable living room, I guided Levi onto the tan leather couch closest to the door. He groaned, and his eyes glistened, but that was all he did. I stepped away and leaned against the beige wall on the other side of the room.

Then I noticed the other three hadn't come inside.

"We're going into the backyard to wait for the others," Annie called out. "I can't calm down until I know Cyrus made it safe and sound."

With that, they shut the door, leaving Levi and me alone.

My mouth dropped open. I wasn't prepared to be alone with him. Maybe we could just...sit here in silence.

He said nothing, and I breathed a little more easily. This might not be so bad. I was way too exhausted to deal with the emotions running through me, and it seemed Levi was, too.

However, the moment Levi's mocha eyes focused on me, I realized I'd been mistaken.

"Rosemary, what the hell is wrong?" Levi asked. A muscle in his jaw twitched.

Oh, no. He didn't get to be frustrated with me. *I* hadn't done anything to hurt *him*.

CHAPTER THIRTEEN

IN THE MOVIES and television shows Sierra had made me watch, I had always thought it was pointless when someone parroted back a question. Once again, however, I found myself understanding where the characters were coming from. "What is *wrong?*" I muttered, and any smart person would have known to be wary.

"Did my words confuse you?" His arms flailed, proving how injured he still was.

My anger toward him softened for a second. Then I caught myself.

Being injured didn't excuse his decisions or his actions.

"Yes, they did." His tone made me think his words had been meant as an insult, but I wasn't sure how they *could* be. "I am genuinely confused how you're clueless about why I'm upset..." No, *upset* didn't convey the magnitude of my feelings. "Actually, why I feel hurt and betrayed."

Two days ago, I wouldn't have been willing to admit that he'd hurt me, but denying my feelings was futile. He could feel my emotions, especially the ones raging within. I couldn't clamp these intense sensations down, even if I'd wanted to. My hands shook from the turmoil inside.

Levi scoffed, his irises darkening to more of a coffee shade. "I warned you I would do things you didn't like, and you seemed to understand that. You can't change your mind after the fact. That's not how this *works*."

He wanted to tell *me* how this worked? My chest heaved. "Doing something I don't like is one thing. Leaving me with *no explanation* is a completely different scenario. Not to mention you took a *fucking* demon sword to Hell with you! And how did you know what to tell Kira to look for if that box has been in Shadow City since before you were born?"

"My hands were tied." His nostrils flared, and I could feel his anger and frustration mixing with mine. "And it was my mother's sword. Before she died, she used to draw the symbol that represents our bloodline for me all the time. I knew it would be on the container—she told me."

I wasn't sure how to respond. If I were Sterlyn or Annie, I'd know the right thing to say to deescalate this situation. Even Sierra and Ronnie would have a sarcastic response to convey the issue while maintaining their position. But me? I had no clue. Anything I said would be rash, and I'd already reacted enough. I was letting my emotions get the better of me, and that was unacceptable.

Our friends could be at risk; they hadn't come back inside. All the issues lying between us would have to wait for another day. "I'm going outside to check on the others." I didn't have it in me to argue. I was spent in every way, and I needed some rest. But I had to make sure everyone was safe first.

Levi's jaw twitched. "We'll have to discuss this."

He was right, but not now. One thing I'd learned from

Mother was that not everything had to be addressed immediately, even if you wanted it to be. Sometimes, a good night's rest and a clear head were essential, or the situation would continue to spiral. Levi had just returned, and even though it had been mere days, it might as well have been years. Having this conversation while I was exhausted and he was physically run-down wouldn't benefit either of us. "Eventually."

I walked to the front door, my stomach lurching. Everything inside me screamed to stay with him and take care of him, and I would, but I needed to go check on the others and clear my head. He was too injured to escape, even if he'd planned to. That wouldn't be the case for long.

Please stay, he connected, tugging at our bond.

When my hand touched the doorknob, I paused. *Unlike you, I'm not leaving. I'm just going outside for a second to see about my friends and your father.*

Something unreadable passed through him, and I didn't want to analyze it. The sensation would either calm or anger me, nothing in between, and neither of those emotions was ideal.

Forcing my hand to turn the knob, I opened the door and stepped outside. My chest tightened. I hated leaving him, but it was just for a moment. I couldn't link with the others, and I needed to ensure they didn't require my help.

The sun warmed my skin despite the slight chill of the autumn breeze. I hurried around the side between this house and the burned one to reach Annie, Midnight, and Alex.

I expected to see Sterlyn's group there, too, but they hadn't arrived. "Is everything okay?" My heart pounded, and my ears rang.

"They ran into a snag." Annie rubbed her arms. "Killian, Sierra, and a few of the silver wolves who are heading over didn't get through the clearing in time. A few demons are already there."

All of this seemed too convenient. "We still need them to come here. We need to regroup and devise a plan."

"You also need rest." Midnight's irises lightened, reminding me even more of Annie's. "I can tell that whatever happened has taken a toll on you."

In other words, I didn't want to look in the mirror.

Alex shook his head. "They're on their way."

Wanting to focus on the most pressing issue, I shrugged off Midnight's concern. "Is Bune giving them a hard time?"

"Not at all," he replied. "But don't worry. Veronica isn't letting her guard down."

I didn't expect her to. We'd all let our guard down around Levi, and look where that had gotten us. Every one of us had learned that lesson. "Good."

Paws padded toward us, and I rolled my neck to loosen my muscles. My body was so tense that I'd be sore tomorrow. A yawn threatened to overcome me, and I clenched my jaw, fighting off the urge.

Annie glanced at the house, now that her mate was closer. "Is he okay in there?"

That was a trick question. "He can't escape, if that's what you mean. I could feel his injury even after I'd healed him from death, but he isn't happy that I left him alone."

She smirked wickedly. "I bet, but I'm glad you aren't succumbing to your mate bond—not that I expected anything less from you."

My fingertips tingled. She truly understood my situation. "I'm not crazy for being torn over whether I should be upset with him?"

"You should *definitely* be upset with him." Alex's near-

British accent stilted his words. "He took a *demon sword* to Hell."

He said that as if I hadn't had any inkling. "I'm well aware."

"It's more than that." Annie frowned, concern etched on her face. "Holding your ground goes against the bond, but I applaud you. If I were in your shoes, I hope I could do the same thing."

Though Annie had grown stronger and more secure, she sometimes doubted her inner strength. She was the most resilient person I'd ever met. She hadn't fallen apart during a time in the past when her erased memories had been haunting her dreams. I wasn't sure how many people could hold up under such trauma.

"Thank you." I rarely apologized, and I expressed true gratitude even less frequently. My heart warmed, dulling a fraction of the pain Levi had caused.

Her eyebrows lifted. "What for?"

"Understanding." Not one angel would understand what I was going through. For as long as I'd been alive, there had been no preordained pairing. Between that and the one-dimensional emotions angels felt, they would likely conclude that I'd lost my mind...and maybe I had. But for Annie to understand made me feel sane.

She opened her mouth to say more, but Cyrus, Ronnie, Bune, and the three silver wolves stepped through the trees. Cyrus's face was set into a deep scowl until he saw Annie. The metamorphosis into a full-blown smile made my stomach burn.

I wished Levi looked at me like that.

Theirs was a healthy relationship. Sure, things had been hard between them when they'd thought they couldn't be together, but once they'd completed their bond, their connection had become healthy and improved over time.

Unlike Levi and me. We'd imploded.

I hung my head as shame filled me. I'd always been happy for my friends—as much as an angel could be—and I wouldn't change that now. Annie, Cyrus, Griffin, Sterlyn, Ronnie, and Alex deserved one another, and my mate struggling with comprehension shouldn't take away from their happiness.

Are you okay? Levi connected.

I hated that he could feel my emotions, especially the ones I was ashamed of. *Everything is okay. The others just arrived, and your father is fine.*

That's a relief, Levi replied, though concern pushed my way. *But I'm still worried about you. Something upset you.*

I'm not doing this. The last thing I needed to do was lie. Everyone outside would know something was amiss, and they already knew my situation with Levi was less than ideal.

Rosey... he started.

I said I don't want to talk about it. We'll be heading inside in a second. I pushed my anger toward him.

His hurt wafted back to me. *Okay.*

Instead of the anger I needed to fuel me, my body weakened. I didn't have the energy to fight with him anymore.

Cyrus hurried over to Annie and pulled her into his arms. One hand went to her belly, embracing their child. My eyes burned at the tenderness.

"That's how mates greet each other," Alex teased, and winked at his wife. "So bring it in, *dear.*"

My attention flicked to Ronnie, who stood in front of Bune with her dagger still in view. No wonder the demon hadn't tried anything. She wouldn't have allowed it.

The five silver wolves surrounded the demon, and Ronnie took off toward Alex.

"In fairness, I was keeping watch on him. We don't need another Levi-level escape," Ronnie said, and she kissed Alex.

She probably had as much anxiety as I did about the artifact building. With the shifters proclaiming they'd seen someone fly away, Mother's feather being found by the broken door, and the fact that at least one item was missing —the demon sword—Azbogah would pin it on my mother. She was the last obstacle he needed to discredit to take full control of the angels, and he was feeling threatened by losing more control over the council voting. I was also sure Ronnie had concerns as well, seeing as she'd taken a demon dagger from the artifact building unintentionally. The dagger had magically appeared in her hands after she'd been released from the artifact building and gotten back to Griffin's condo.

Bune rubbed his hands together. "Where's Levi? Is he okay?"

The concern seemed so sincere, but I didn't want to be manipulated again. I had to remain cautious around these two demons. "He's inside on the couch. I came out here to make sure everyone was safe."

He tapped his heel on the ground. "May I visit with him?"

His words sounded as if he needed my blessing to see his son. Levi had mentioned that Bune had left Shadow City to stay with Levi's mother, who'd fallen. The council wouldn't allow her to visit him, and the fact that he felt like he had to ask permission tugged at my heart. "Yes, I'll take you inside." I was eager to have them both inside of the house before any Shadow Terrace residents or tourists spotted them. We were somewhat isolated here at the end of the road, but not entirely.

"Let's get you inside, too." Cyrus kissed his mate's forehead and turned to the five silver wolves. "Please go into the woods and keep an eye out until we determine our next course of action."

Obediently, Darrell, Chad, and the other three ran back into the trees. Though all supernaturals were now welcome on this side of the river, many vampires still weren't comfortable with the presence of other supernaturals, and we didn't want to raise questions about what the silver wolves were guarding. It was best if they stayed hidden in the forest.

The rest of us headed back inside. My skin crawled in anticipation. I had so many questions, but would Levi and Bune be forthcoming? The princes of Hell had an agenda they were attempting to execute, and beyond getting the demon sword, I wasn't sure what their next move might be. One demon sword couldn't take down Shadow City, so something else had to be in play.

Our group entered the living room, and I moved to the wall underneath the television, not trusting myself to sit. I was afraid that if I did, I wouldn't be able to get back up.

Rushing to Levi, Bune reached out a hand to touch his son but hesitated. "Are you still in a lot of pain?"

Levi chuckled, then groaned, closing his eyes.

I inadvertently stepped toward him as nausea churned my stomach. Somehow, I forced myself to stop. He couldn't notice that his pain affected me, or he could use that against me.

"He needs more healing." Bune faced me. "Can you help him?"

His question pulled at me. I wished I could take all of

Levi's pain and discomfort away, but I couldn't. My magic was completely spent.

"Stop, Father," Levi rasped. "She did all she could, and I refuse to let her hurt herself. I'm much better than I was, and I'm not dying anymore."

His lackadaisical comment hit as intended. I rubbed my forehead, trying to fend off a headache. "You're not going to die. I won't allow it."

"Relax. I know you want the demon sword back." Levi grinned, but it fell flat. "Wouldn't want one of the princes of Hell to get their hands on it."

"Stop being a twatwaffle," Annie chastised as she sat on the couch directly across from him. "You got yourself into this situation, so don't try to lay a guilt trip on her or *any* of us."

Bune stood in front of Levi, blocking the injured demon from Annie's view. His neck corded as he murmured, "He didn't have a choice."

"But he did," Ronnie interjected as she stood at the end of the couch next to her foster sister. "He could've told us what the problem was so we could determine a solution together. We trusted him after the last demon battle."

We were spinning our wheels. "We need to focus on the current threat. What Levi should or shouldn't have done is irrelevant." It hurt to say that because all I wanted to do was demand answers, but that could put us in more jeopardy.

So we're okay? Levi connected, his warmth slamming inside me.

That would be what he took out of that comment. *No, we're not okay. But our personal issues won't get us killed. It's the demons desperate to get hold of you that could harm everyone I care about and innocents.*

Cyrus, hovering behind his mate, placed his hands on

Annie's shoulders. "I agree. The demons will try to lure Levi out, so we need a solid plan. They know we'll want to protect humans, supernaturals, and anything with a pure essence."

"Maybe you should shut down the towns." Midnight tilted her head. "That way, you won't have people coming in and out." She took a seat next to Annie.

Tapping his fingers on his mouth, Alex pursed his lips. "That is a good option, but I'm not sure how we can effectively shut down the town. People would have to travel to the border to barricade the roads, which could lead to their capture, defeating the purpose."

"What about Circe's coven?" I hated to ask, but the coven could help. After Eliza had been hurt and sucked into the portal the witches had been closing, we'd given them some distance. Aurora and Lux had helped barricade Levi in the first house in which we'd kept him, but then they'd taken a step back, uncomfortable with their proximity to Shadow City. Their coven and the Shadow City witch coven had bad blood.

Annie and Ronnie glanced at each other. Out of the group here, those two were affected the most since Eliza had raised them, and Circe was Eliza's daughter. In a way, they were family, but there was a lot of tension between them despite Circe being the one who'd handed an infant Annie over to Eliza. Circe had felt abandoned by her mother, and it was hard for her to see how close Eliza had grown to the two kids she'd taken in.

"That's probably our best option." Annie exhaled.

Bune tensed. "You have a connection with witches you trust?" He glanced at each of us to gauge our reactions.

He was way too eager to know the answer, but if they were going to come here, he'd find out anyway. If they didn't, he'd never know who we'd reached out to. "Why?" I asked.

"Because the witch who helped Levi and me escape— she's in trouble."

"What?" Levi exclaimed. "You got that *witch* to help us? Why didn't you tell me? That's dangerous!"

"She's different from the others." Bune glanced at Levi, lifting both hands. "While you were gone from Hell, they placed me in an adjoining cell with her, and I heard them trying to break her down. She's super powerful—that's how we got out."

Ronnie leaned forward, hope blooming on her face. "What does she look like?"

"Love." Alex winced, hurting for his mate. "She couldn't have made it."

"It's dark down there—it was hard to tell." Bune's forehead creased in either confusion or concentration.

I wished he hadn't brought this up again. It gave the girls false hope.

"But she was always talking about her three daughters and granddaughter." Bune squinted. "And how she needed to get back to them."

"Was her n-na-me...Eliza?" Annie murmured with broken words.

CHAPTER FOURTEEN

THE QUESTION HUNG in the air, and I wished Bune would answer it. I didn't want Ronnie and Annie to get their hopes up.

Cyrus glowered at the demon. "That's a simple question."

"It's *not*, though." Bune sighed and sat down next to Levi. "I don't know her name. All I know is that she hasn't been down there for long. She came through a portal with a group of demons and went undetected until another witch down there recognized her."

"Did she have a wound?" Annie rubbed her belly. "In her stomach or close to that?"

Levi, do something. Even though I was frustrated with him, he could help with this. *We don't need him playing with their emotions.*

He's not. There is a witch down there. I noticed her briefly, but she stayed in the shadows. Levi growled. *My father and I aren't manipulative, despite what you think.*

I sighed. *How I wish that were the truth.*

Standing, Bune paced in the center of the room. That

could be a sign of him growing frustrated from trying to remember or him trying to pull off a lie without actually lying as he chose his words carefully. If he was attempting to fool us with what he believed were good intentions, he wouldn't fall. But that was how the darkness got people: it destroyed their morals slowly over time. One unethical decision made it easier to choose another one, and soon, they were snowballing into another dimension.

Rosey, I wasn't trying to hurt you. Levi's annoyance floated into me. *Why are you giving me such hell?*

Hell. What an appropriate word because he'd actually gone there, and I felt like I'd been there with the amount of heartache he'd caused me. If he thought his frustration would make me forgive him, he'd have better luck trying to grow feathers.

"Oh, my gods," Alex hissed. "You're thinking awfully hard about these answers."

"Give him a second," I said. "He's had to be very careful about what he said for the past millennium, and it's ingrained in him." Angels thought through every possibility before answering when able. If Bune was truly *good* and had gone to Hell for his preordained, then he'd lived in a highly turbulent environment for over one thousand years. Though I wanted to be suspicious of him, I also had to consider the possibility that he was being cautious. Otherwise, I'd continue to let my biases rule me, as Levi had pointed out. Though Levi had hurt me like I'd expected him to, I couldn't deny he had made me see things in a different light.

Ronnie and Annie were good. And if the three young demon wolf boys didn't grow up to be hateful like their fathers, then maybe all demons weren't truly doomed. I couldn't deny that the probability of all demons being bad was extreme, just like all angels weren't always good but justified their actions by thinking they were for the greater good. Most people didn't consider themselves bad except for those who enjoyed inflicting pain.

Midnight's eyebrows lifted, and Alex's head tipped back as they regarded me. I couldn't blame them; it sounded as if I was protecting Bune, and that hadn't been my intent. However, we didn't need to be irrational about how he was responding when there could be sound logic behind it.

Thankfully, Annie's and Ronnie's attention was glued on Bune while Cyrus struggled to hold back his anger.

The older demon glanced at me, and his face smoothed. "That's very true. The truly undecided in Hell get threatened and victimized regularly. We have to choose our words carefully to avoid becoming more of a target."

Warmth spread through my bond with Levi as he connected, *Thank you for backing my father. I know it isn't easy, and I appre—*

I didn't do it for you. Though I didn't want to fight with him, he couldn't misread the situation. *Our group has to keep a level head and not let our emotions get the best of us.* A pang shot through my heart. That could have been misconstrued as an insult, and I hadn't meant it to be.

The heat between us cooled. As suspected, I had hurt him, but there was nothing I could do about it. He was letting his emotions get in the way, and unfortunately, I now understood how easy that could be if I weren't aware. By leaving me, he had shown me I could function despite my emotions, even when I wanted to lie down and cry.

"She didn't have a visible injury, but she did hunch over any time she moved, making me suspect she was in pain." Bune steepled his fingers and closed his eyes as if recalling the image. "She mentioned needing to sacrifice herself for the people she loved."

"That has to be her." Annie jumped to her feet but lurched forward, clutching her stomach.

Cyrus launched himself over the couch and landed behind his mate while Midnight and Ronnie flanked Annie.

"Whoa, guys." Annie chuckled as she straightened. "I'm fine."

"What the *hell* happened?" Cyrus placed his hand over hers. "Are you okay? Is our baby girl all right?"

Annie cupped his face. "Yes. I moved too quickly. It was just a little discomfort, that's all. I wasn't prepared for it."

"That'll happen to you more often now that your stomach is getting bigger." Midnight grinned and tucked a piece of Annie's hair behind her ear. "I remember when I had those ligament pains with you. Best discomfort I've ever experienced."

My heart ached. I hoped that one day, I would be lucky enough to carry the gift of a child. Creating life was a miracle that most angels struggled to achieve, and the ones who did received that blessing only a handful of times at most. Cyrus and Annie would be the perfect parents, and they both wanted to raise a complete and healthy family on their own.

Cyrus exhaled and ran a hand down his face. "You scared the shit out of me."

"It'll only get more intense from here on. Then going through the birth will eclipse every worry you've ever had." Midnight chuckled as she patted Cyrus's shoulder. "You need to buckle up."

His face turned a shade paler like he hadn't thought it entirely through.

"I hate to be inconsiderate," I began. I'd learned that if I started with regret before following through on what I wanted to say, my words were usually more welcome. "But if Eliza is the witch who helped them, what does that mean?" If the princes of Hell had plans for her, we needed to get her and the sword out of Hell before our circumstances worsened.

Bune scratched the back of his neck as he sat on the couch again, this time on the opposite end from his son. He placed his elbows on his knees. "When Kobal left after beating—" He cut himself off and pinched the bridge of his nose. Closing his eyes, he continued, "When Kobal *left* Levi, I was distraught. I knew Levi was trying to make the princes of Hell believe he was on their side to rescue me, but something went wrong, and they brought him to the prison cell so I could watch his punishment."

One thing was clear—Bune cared about his son. There was no acting, and it put me more on edge. He'd do anything to ensure his son's safety, including turning against us to help Levi.

Ronnie blew out a breath.

"Anyway, she offered to help us escape. She used some of the magic she'd been hiding, but she said her power wouldn't last long and that we should find the witches who protect the silver wolves to help retrieve her before it's too late." He rubbed his hands together as if he had a chill.

"Oh—" Ronnie sniffled, and tears trickled down her cheeks. "It *is* her."

My breath caught. Eliza was alive. I'd grown to appreciate the former coven priestess and her blunt nature. She was a powerful witch, and I'd wager that she was stronger than Erin. If we could get her out of Hell, then not only would we have a strong ally back, but Annie would have her foster mother here in time, hopefully, for her child's birth.

The silver wolf alphas needed a powerful witch by their side when the baby was born to help if there were any issues. I could fill that role for Annie when the time came, but she'd rather it be Eliza and hold on to tradition.

"Why didn't you lead with that?" Alex rolled his eyes. "Obviously, that little detail would've cleared things up."

Lifting his chin, Bune glared at Alex and sneered, "I don't know—my son would have died if his preordained mate hadn't found him. Then we were running from demons, and I entered a house full of people who treat my son and me like we're going to kill them in their sleep."

If my feathers had been extended, he would've ruffled them. I didn't like his assumption that I wasn't a worthy adversary, but I bit my tongue. Levi had left while I'd slept, so even though it hurt my pride, I couldn't blame him. I'd messed up, and that was my burden to carry.

The connection between Levi and me reopened, and his discomfort and pain barreled into me. As I'd expected, he'd been holding his pain back, and it must have over-whelmed him. And I hated myself for being upset that he was in discomfort.

"Levi needs rest to heal." I gestured to him.

I'm fine, he interjected.

I chose to ignore him. "And I need time to rejuvenate." With this new information, our outlook was better than it had been moments ago.

Levi remained quiet, which both comforted and annoyed me. The fact that he might care that I was out of sorts eased some of the pain inside my heart, but it also irri-tated me. Why had he started caring now?

"We still haven't discussed Killian, Sierra, and Darrell returning or getting Darrell back to Martha," Cyrus said as he placed his hands behind his back. "I want your thoughts since we'll need your help because of...you know."

The demons.

They had reached us before we'd had time to plan. We should've been more prepared. "Why doesn't Annie or Ronnie call Circe? Once she hears the news, the coven will want to get involved."

Alex nodded. "And there's no point risking exposure to the demons more than once, so maybe we can time the wolves and witches arriving here simultaneously."

"The demons will be prepared for anything since they're here to get Levi and me. But they'll likely be hesitant." Bune pointed to his head. "Most of the truly fallen who can travel on Earth largely undetected aren't the smartest, and the undecided will hesitate. They fear becoming like the fallen, who are obsessive and never content."

I noted he hadn't said *happy*. Maybe demons suffered from limited emotions like angels did, but Levi seemed pretty personable, similar to his father.

Ronnie removed her cell from her pocket. "I'll call Circe now, and we can come up with a plan."

I swayed, my knees weakening. I wasn't sure how much longer I could stand. I'd felt this weak only a handful of times, and each occurrence had involved the group around me. "I shouldn't need too much sleep to function again, so if I'm not up in time to go over the plan, wake me." I refused to let them face the demons alone, especially since the number of individuals who could see them in shadow form was limited.

"Where should I take him?" Bune asked as he leaned over Levi and started to lift him.

Scowling, Levi grunted and pushed his father away. "I

can do—" When he tried to get to his feet, they skidded out from underneath him.

Not hesitating, Bune picked up his son.

"Follow me." My heart hammered as I headed toward the stairs to the second-floor bedrooms.

None of my friends offered to stay with Levi. They must have realized I wouldn't take them up on it because the other half of my soul was severely injured. Even if I wanted to walk away, I couldn't.

It petrified me.

When we entered the hallway, I looked straight ahead into the kitchen with its light beige cabinets and darker tile backsplash to the view beyond the window over the sink. I couldn't see the wolves outside, which calmed my pulse somewhat. On my right, the dining room looked unchanged. The circular table didn't have a speck of dust on it, nor did the six matching wooden chairs surrounding it.

It looked like no one had been in the house since we'd left abruptly a few days ago. The only difference was that the scent of dahlias had grown stronger, reinforcing that fall was upon us.

I turned left and took the oak staircase to the top floor. "This way," I said, feeling the need to speak, which was odd. Normally, I was content with silence.

"I'm right behind you," Bune replied, his voice slightly strained.

At the top of the stairs, the hallway led to three bedrooms: one on the left, another on the right, and one straight ahead, with a hall bathroom in one corner. I turned right, heading into the one Levi and I had shared the last time he was here.

I wasn't prepared for the onslaught of emotions.

The fluffy forest-brown comforter on the queen bed

was still ruffled, the pillows in disarray from where we'd lain side by side, and the white sheets tangled from the night Levi and I had completed our bond. My heart twisted, and my throat closed.

An equally heartbroken emotion wafted back into me. Levi connected, *Rosey, I didn't mean to hurt you.*

Tears burned my eyes as I forced myself to enter the room. My vision clouded as I came dangerously close to crying. I cleared my throat and attempted to sound normal as I said, "Put him on the bed. I'll take the couch."

"You won't lie down with him? It will help you both heal faster." Bune shuffled to the bed and slowly laid his son on the spot closest to the door.

I'd never heard that before, but it made sense. When two souls bonded, they made each other stronger.

"I...I can't." Even though I wanted to. Gods, the urge to hold him was overwhelming, and at the realization that it could help me heal faster, I had to hold my arms hard to my sides so I didn't reach for him.

I wished Bune hadn't said anything.

"Leave her alone, Father," Levi rasped, his voice thick with fatigue. The bond swirled with pain.

My heart fractured a little more.

In the past millennium, I hadn't felt much, but my heart had been whole. In the past two weeks, one man had nearly destroyed it. I was beginning to think we were destined for misery, and I wasn't usually the jaded type.

I walked across the room to the cloth couch positioned underneath the window overlooking Shadow Terrace. Blinking back tears, I quickly laid down with my head on the pillow at the end of the couch and looked up at Bune. I didn't want him to realize how raw I felt.

His father glared. "Why don't you go to another

bedroom or back down with your friends, then? I can stay with him."

That wouldn't happen. I didn't trust either of them, and I was staying right here.

"I want her here, and she won't leave, regardless." Levi yawned. "It'll be fine. She won't kill me. She's threatened to several times, but here I lie. She even healed me from death, and I won't let her live it down."

Even while in pain, he had to tease me, but that meant he would survive. I kept my mouth shut, not wanting to humor him.

"Fine, but if you need me, I'll be listening." Bune stalked toward the door and paused. "Angels and demons have a habit of seeing things as black or white, but there's a lot of gray in the world. Sometimes, people do the best they can, thinking it's their only option."

If he thought I would lie here and be talked down to, he would learn I wasn't that type of angel. "I agree wholeheartedly. I've done things other angels didn't understand, but that's the thing about choices. You must deal with the consequences of your actions, even when they're *gray*."

I expected him to retort and act similarly to Azbogah. Older angels, especially men, didn't like being contradicted, and not only was I a woman, but I was also younger than him. Most would find this disrespectful, but I wouldn't apologize for speaking my mind.

He tipped his head and turned off the lights. "That's very true. Just don't be too hard on him." Then he shut the door.

I felt lightheaded. His agreement had caught me off guard.

Silence descended as Bune's footsteps retreated down

the stairs. I wasn't worried about him trying to escape, not with Levi injured.

I closed my eyes, but all that did was make Levi's sweet peony scent more prominent. The ache to be close to him burned, and I fidgeted, determined to get comfortable.

After a moment, Levi's breathing leveled out, and our connection seemed to grow less turbulent, informing me he was asleep.

Then he cleared his throat and breathed, "Rosey..."

I knew I was in trouble.

CHAPTER FIFTEEN

THE NICKNAME that had annoyed me at the beginning was somehow comforting. Now that he was back, I just wanted to hear his voice. "I already informed you that I don't feel like arguing."

All my fight had vanished. Though my heart still ached and I could feel Levi's injuries, it was nothing compared to the onslaught of emotions I'd experienced when he'd vanished.

I don't want to argue, Levi connected with me.

His words and emotions pulled at me harder when we spoke that way, so I would stick to speaking out loud. "Then what do you want from me?"

"Why are you upset with me? I *told* you I'd have to do things you wouldn't like."

Under normal circumstances, I'd get angry, but I couldn't find the energy. "Doing something I wouldn't like would have been *informing* me of your plans, not just leaving."

"You wouldn't have let me go," he said simply. "What else could I do?"

Though I inherently *knew* he wasn't trying to hurt me, his words were like a gut punch. "How could you *know* that? Don't you think I understand what it means to protect the ones I love? Do you think I'm that heartless that I would've put up a fight to stop you from saving your *father?*"

He inhaled sharply. "Of course you would. I wouldn't allow you to save your father by doing something that reckless."

Laughter overtook me. I'd never understood when mortals laughed at times I expected them to yell or cry, but I finally did. His words were that funny. "You think you could *stop* me? And what does that say about you if you'd prevent me from doing something I needed to? All that would do is transform our relationship into something unhealthy, which I guess doesn't matter. You already accomplished that."

"Are you serious?" Stuck on his back due to his injuries, he turned his face toward me. "You'd have let me go? I don't buy it."

I remembered all the times I'd thought the worst of him because he was a demon, like when I thought he'd used the bond to get access to the sword or that he'd saved Kira only because she had access to the artifact building. I'd thought my poor opinion of him couldn't possibly hurt him because I'd believed I was right. Now I was on the receiving end of his *bias*. "Yet you decided what I would do based on what your decisions would be. You did the same thing you accused me of. You didn't give me a chance to see how I'd react."

His brows furrowed, and he blinked. "But—"

"*And* not only did you think the *worst* of me, but you

also confided more in Kira than you ever did in me." Now that I was talking, it was like a dam crumbling.

"She wasn't judging me," he growled. "What did you *expect*?"

"That you would've been honest with me after we'd completed the *bond*." That was what hurt the most. Though I'd never been happy about him confiding in Kira, I could understand it before we'd bonded, not afterward. "You talked a great game about trusting you, but when I finally did, you let me down." My voice cracked with too much emotion.

But he had to understand. When I'd finally let my guard down despite my mind screaming at me not to, he'd confirmed my fears had been warranted.

He closed his eyes as regret swirled from him into me. *Rosey, that's not what I meant to happen. I just had to save my father, and the demon sword was what the princes of Hell sent me here to collect to release him.*

He'd hidden more from me than I'd realized. Things that would've been helpful to know ahead of time. He'd said if he went back to Hell, they'd injure his father, but that was because he didn't have the demon sword. Yet another way he'd manipulated the truth.

Flames burned inside me as I forced myself to turn my back to Levi. I couldn't look at him. One-dimensional Rose-mary would have scoffed at the action, thinking it was a sign of weakness, but that wasn't the case. My heart *desired* to see Levi, to touch him, to feel his skin against mine once more. Turning my back to him sliced my heart in two, but this was what I had to do to stand strong.

I would never judge someone for doing whatever was necessary to stand strong.

Rose— he started.

"Don't." He kept pushing, and I couldn't continue this conversation. "I talked to you when I didn't feel like it, and you now know where I stand. But know this—I wouldn't have stopped you from saving your father, and if it took the demon sword to do it, I would have been upset. But he's your *family*, and that means something. We could've made a plan together, one that wouldn't have affected my family, but none of that matters now. And I need to sleep."

Hurt wafted through him, and I hated that our relationship had come to this. We were both suffering.

I never meant to hurt you, he connected, his agony as intense as mine.

Staring through the blinds, I noted the sun had begun its descent. By its location, I estimated it was close to one in the afternoon. The beauty of the day was a stark contrast to the dreariness that prevailed inside. "Intent doesn't make things right or better. It only allows the person who hurt another to justify their actions to themselves. Just like when I continually thought the worst of you, hurting you wasn't my *intent*, either."

Silence descended between us, and I was thankful. There was nothing left for us to say.

———

WHIMPERS WOKE me from my slumber. As my eyes opened, I noted that the room was darker than it had been. Not only that, but my traitorous body was facing Levi once more.

I'd hoped to feel better, but my body was still laden with fatigue. I turned my head toward the window to find that sunset was almost upon us, making it close to seven.

Angels didn't require much sleep, so the fact that Levi

and I had slept for about six hours with no improvement was abnormal.

Could fighting our bond while we were weak be the problem?

Levi moaned again, bringing my attention back to him.

His expression twisted as his legs jerked under the covers. He gulped air as the icy tendril of fear and hot flashes of torment mixed inside me.

I jumped to my feet and rushed to the side of the bed. Even if I'd wanted to stop myself, I couldn't, not with him hurting like this.

As I slid into the bed beside him, there was no question I was making a foolish mistake. Yet I couldn't *not* do it. The moment my arms encircled him, the familiar buzz sprang between us, and the pain affixed to our bond ebbed.

A contentment that I hadn't found since before he'd left streamed through me. I felt complete with him in my arms, and I resented feeling that way. Your other half was supposed to make you better, not tear you apart at the seams. How could fate have picked him for me?

He sighed and turned his head toward me. He still couldn't move easily, but his face smoothed, and the corners of his mouth tipped upward.

If I couldn't tell that he was asleep, I'd have thought he was manipulating me, but he wasn't. His heart and breathing remained slow and steady.

The buzzing eased my troubled mind, and my eyes closed of their own accord as sleep overtook me again.

Birds chirped outside, and something warm and rough touched my cheek. My eyes fluttered open to find Levi looking down at me, caressing my face.

My heart warmed, and a smile slipped across my lips.

Did you sleep okay? he asked.

I nodded. This had to be a dream, one I never wanted to wake from. This was what my relationship with Levi would have been like if he hadn't left me. When I woke up, the crushing pain of everything we'd gone through would overtake me again.

At least here, I could be happy for a few moments.

His eyes focused on my lips, and something snapped inside me. I leaned forward and kissed him softly. His familiar taste of spearmint tickled my senses, and I became desperate for more.

Slipping my tongue inside his mouth, I couldn't get enough of him.

Gods, Rosey, he moaned as he eagerly responded to my touch. *I missed you so damn much. Being apart from you was the hardest thing I've ever experienced.*

My body stilled, and I pulled away.

He winced in pain. *Easy. I'm feeling better, but I'm still pretty injured.*

This was *not* a dream. I untangled myself from him and jumped to my feet, despite the urge to maul him. "This can't happen."

His body tensed as he frowned. "What are you talking about? You crawled into bed with me. I thought you finally understood—"

I hated to admit it, but I felt well-rested. Though my magic was still depleted, I was physically recovered...and willing to argue. "There is a difference between *understanding*, Levi, and *forgiving* someone for what they did wrong. I understand you needed to save your father—I even admire it—but the execution was worse than subpar. It was what Sierra would call a hot mess and has put our relationship in the same state."

Oh, dear gods. Not only was I understanding Sierra but quoting her, too. Maybe Hell *had* frozen over.

"We've already gone through this." Levi scowled as he slowly sat upright. His chest heaved from either anger or exertion, or likely a combination of the two. Though his complexion was closer to his normal light gold, he was still pale. "I did what I *had* to do."

What made this situation worse was not that he hadn't apologized. I didn't need that. I just needed him to admit he should have handled things differently and prove to me he would do so going forward. He refused to pretend that maybe he'd handled it poorly, and clearly, he thought poorly of me.

It burned.

Our situation had flipped. Maybe if I hadn't been so hard on him in the beginning, he wouldn't have been hard on me when it counted.

Stop, I scolded myself. He was a grown man and accountable for his actions. What he'd chosen to do wasn't because of something I'd done. I would not blame myself for his shortcomings. He held me accountable, and I would do the same to him.

"I'm glad you feel that way. It's clear you don't care what kind of problems your actions caused here—problems that affect my family—but you care only about yours." My chest ached, stealing my breath. I needed air, even if the sun hadn't risen yet.

He scoffed. "Please, don't be so smug."

Smug. I'd said my family was in danger, and I got called smug.

I marched past the bed toward the door. Four days ago,

I'd refused to leave him alone in this room, afraid he might escape. Today, I had to get away. Besides, if he left, it would be for the best.

My heart jolted, calling me out on my lie. As I reached the door, I glanced back at him.

Where are you going? One of Levi's legs jerked as if he intended to follow me, but he moved haphazardly.

I hated seeing him like this. Even though he'd hurt me, I didn't want him to be in pain. What kind of martyr had I become? *Out.*

But we're talking. He inched closer to the side of the bed. He was moving better but wasn't back to himself.

Needing to leave while I had the willpower, I opened the door and stepped into the hallway. "No, we're not. You're just restating your stance, and there isn't any more to say."

The door to my right opened, and Ronnie stepped into the hallway. She wore hunter green fleece pajama bottoms with a white tank top. Her copper hair stuck up in the back, and she yawned, making it clear she'd been sleeping. "Are you okay?"

"Do I look okay?" I hated that it was easy to see I was upset, which angered me even more.

She tilted her head. "Fair enough. What's wrong?"

"Everything." I stomped toward the stairs, needing to fly. With twilight approaching before the sun began its rise, the humans wouldn't see my ascent. There was a certain freedom in flying that couldn't be replicated by other means, and it comforted my supernatural side.

Alex's voice carried toward me as I made my way down the stairs. "Was that Rosemary being dramatic?"

"Leave her alone," Ronnie chastised. "She's hurting."

I didn't want to hear any more.

When I reached the landing on the first floor, I heard the door open to the room I shared with Levi. As slowly as he was moving, I'd be able to get out of here without seeing him again. I stormed into the living room to find Midnight resting on one couch and Bune on the other. Annie and Cyrus must have been staying next door, and I didn't blame them. With Annie's pregnancy, they needed more privacy.

Bune's eyes popped open and focused on me. He threw off his thin blanket and sat upright, almost falling off the couch from his large size. "Is Levi okay?"

Midnight climbed to her feet, pushing her long hair behind her shoulders.

"That's a trick question." My head spun, and I wanted to scream. Levi's spearmint taste was still in my mouth, and my heart was clamoring for me to go back upstairs. Both sides were fighting each other harder than before we'd completed the bond. It felt like two personalities were living inside me, and I had to find a balance before I imploded. "He didn't tell me why he was going to Hell, and right after we completed our bond, I woke to an empty bed with him telepathically telling me he was leaving me just before he disappeared from Earth. Then he came back and expected things to be fine! You tell me if that logic is *okay*."

He lifted a hand in surrender. "I...I don't know the right answer. I've forgotten how to reason with an upset woman."

"That's definitely not the way," Midnight murmured.

"You don't think I'm *reasonable*?" As I said the word, I realized how unhinged I sounded. The agony slicing into me made it hard to stand, let alone show reason. Somehow, I felt more betrayed, but by myself. I'd *known* better than to crawl into bed with Levi last night.

Bune opened his mouth and paused.

My face heated, and I took a deep breath. "He's fine.

You'd better go up there before he tries to make it down-stairs on his own."

I continued through the living room and was out the door in seconds. The sky was lightening to twilight, and the air smelled crisp from the fall weather. When the door didn't slam shut behind me, I glanced over my shoulder to find Midnight stepping outside.

She took a hesitant step toward me. "Can we talk for a second?"

No was on the tip of my tongue, but I swallowed it down. I closed my eyes, enjoying the early morning fall breeze on my skin. It was chilly and helped me get a grasp on my sanity.

I didn't need to fly away until I'd gotten an update from the others on what the witches had decided. I'd hate to be gone when the group needed me. "Yeah, I just wanted some air."

"I understand." She strolled over and stopped at my side. She stared toward downtown Shadow Terrace, giving me a reprieve from her watchful eyes. "I know it's not the same since Tate wasn't truly my fated mate, but it sure *felt* like he was during our time together, and even now, I struggle with his loss."

"That's horrible. I hate that a witch spelled you two to think you were each other's fated mates." I hadn't consid-ered that she'd be struggling with losing Tate. If the spell hadn't broken, she would have felt heartache. A witch had messed with Tate, Annie's biological father, and Midnight because their pairing was likely to result in the birth of a daughter—which it had. Tate's father had orchestrated the spell to gift Annie to a demon for his own personal gain.

She patted my arm and said, "And I hate that Levi hurt

you. But you're strong, and if I can survive the pain, so can you."

Out of everyone here, she was the one who could best understand me. Eliza could have, too, since she'd lost her counterpart, but she wasn't here. However, I couldn't ignore Levi's pain. "He's hurting, too."

"I know. Unlike Tate and me, Levi cares about you, but he has a lot to learn before the two of you can be happy together." She glanced at her hands.

Her words filled me with hope. It sounded like she thought that the two of us could pull through. "How can you possibly know that? We don't know each other well."

"You're right. We aren't close, but I've been around you for over a month, now." A sad smile crossed her face. "Even in that short time, I've noticed how much you've changed since he came into your life. When I first met you, you were serious, no-nonsense, and had a strong sense of what needed to be done. You're still that but more—"

"An emotional fool?" My heart felt like it was shrinking.

Midnight shook her head. "Not at all. You're extra empathetic and seem to *care* more. He's *changed* you, and now it's his time to grow. I'd always wondered why fate had put Tate and me together, and now things make sense because she didn't. But she did put you two together. I can see it in the way he looks at you."

Could she be right? My chest expanded, but hope was a dangerous emotion.

The front door of the house Annie and Cyrus were staying in opened, and Annie came rushing out. Her face was flushed, and her eyes were so wide, I could see the whites.

"Circe called." Annie took an unsteady breath. "They've made their decision."

CHAPTER SIXTEEN

WITCHES WEREN'T PREDICTABLE. Though there was no doubt that Circe and the coven would want to save Eliza, things weren't simple in their world. There were rules about maintaining the balance of good and evil. Every decision had to be thoroughly thought through to ensure they didn't disrupt that balance, even when their hearts wanted them to make a certain choice.

"Let's go inside and tell everyone at one time. Cyrus is on his way." Annie bounced on her feet as her slightly too small top inched up, exposing her growing belly. Her black sweatpants fit her perfectly from the bottom down, making her stomach resemble a basketball.

Between Annie's flushed appearance and enthusiasm, the witches' decision was easy to predict, but she wanted to deliver the news, and I wouldn't rob her of it, even if that meant going back inside and facing *him*.

The inherent desire for self-preservation nagged at me to stay outside, while my heart panged at the thoughts of going inside and seeing him and staying away. Neither choice would mend a broken heart. But my pragmatic side knew that learning what our plan was and what we were up against was required.

Annie scurried to the front door of the house and barreled inside. She yelled, "Everyone, gather round! We've finally heard from the witches!"

That must have been why no one had woken me last night or this morning. The sun was beginning its ascent.

The neighboring house's door opened, and Cyrus made his way over with a huge yawn. He ran a hand through his messy hair and groaned. "I thought witches enjoyed the night."

Midnight chuckled. "That's when lunar witches feel the most comfortable drawing magic. That doesn't mean that they don't wake up early, especially if they have plans for the day."

"At least we weren't up late." He strolled to the front door of our house and opened it. "Let's find out what they had to say."

My legs walked of their own accord, desperate to be close to Levi. At some point, my body and mind had to get in sync. "Don't pretend you don't already know what they said." I smirked at him.

He shook his head and held the door open for Midnight and me, waving us in. "When they called, she jumped out of bed and left the room. I waited for her to come back, but instead, she linked with me to get my ass over here."

"That's my girl." Midnight beamed as we headed inside.

When I entered, the room had been put back together. Both blankets were missing, and Levi sat next to his father on one couch with Ronnie and Alex across from them on the other.

Annie stood underneath the television with her phone in her hand. She gestured for the three of us to come inside.

"Sterlyn, Griffin, Killian, and Sierra are on speakerphone. I figured it'd be easier to tell everyone at one time instead of breaking up the conversation."

I approved of her efficiency. It got annoying when we had to repeat information several times.

My treasonous eyes glanced at Levi. He sat at the end of the couch farthest from Annie. He frowned, and he must have felt my attention because he glanced back at me. His face was drawn, and our bond coursed with pain on both sides, mixing together and adding more agony to the situation.

Midnight made her way to the couch and sat between the demons.

I warmed to her the more I was around her. She had a pure essence, and this further proved that she understood my struggle. Everything inside me had wanted to take that seat, and she'd eliminated some of my inner turmoil.

Cyrus went to stand next to his mate, and I took a seat beside Ronnie. The only issue was that it was directly across from Levi, making it all too easy to look at him. Still, it was easier to look at him than sit next to him without touching.

"I hung up from Circe just a few minutes ago." The honey in Annie's irises brightened. "They've decided to help, and they'll be here within the next few days."

Sierra's voice chimed through the phone. "Uh...hell, yeah! I need some Lux and Aurora time."

I rolled my eyes. Sierra had a way of seeing things one way and drawing expectations. "They're coming here to get Eliza back, not to hang out with you."

She scoffed. "Please. I'm sure we'll find time to chill with each other."

"I wouldn't expect that," Sterlyn interjected from the line. "Aurora will be focused on saving her grandmother, and the other witches will be hell-bent on getting their former priestess back."

Leaning forward, Alex took his wife's hand and asked, "How many are coming?"

"Circe, Aurora, Herne, Lux, and Aspen will be joining us here." Annie rubbed a finger along her bottom lip. "Cordelia, Eliphas, and Kamila are coming, too, but staying off-site nearby. Once they arrive, they want to head straight to Hell. They don't want to be this close to Shadow City for long in case Erin and her coven feel their presence."

Even though I'd expected the coven to want to rescue Eliza, I was surprised they were going to do it. "Are you sure they will help? Or will they just be here in case things go horrendously wrong? There's a reason they didn't offer their assistance right away, even for Eliza."

Ronnie's brows furrowed. "What do you mean? They probably wanted to discuss the situation with the coven like they always do."

Fidgeting in his seat, Bune scratched his chin. "Witches are all about balance, and they have to consider the consequences of their decisions. They could be coming here in case something shifts to help restore things."

"Oh!" Annie pursed her lips. "That must be why Circe said that if the demons need Eliza for something, bringing her back would benefit us, and they were obligated to help."

"When did they say they would arrive? I don't like being away from you," Killian said gruffly. "We should have more people on that side if the demons want *Levi* and *Bune.*"

Levi laughed loudly as jealousy swirled within him. "Like you would actually be of any help. You can't see them in their shadow form."

Killian breathed raggedly in answer.

Even though my heart belonged to Levi, he felt threatened by my friendship with Killian. At one point, Killian had harbored feelings for me, though I had been oblivious. He'd finally come clean after I'd met Levi. There had been no competition, but Levi and I had been unsettled then, just like we were now. Obviously, Levi still felt threatened, even though we'd completed the bond. *Stop being ridiculous.*

His attention landed on me as he sneered, *Oh, you don't like me talking to your boy toy that way?*

My...boy toy? I didn't understand what that meant, but I had a feeling it was derogatory. Before he could explain, I continued, *It doesn't matter what that means. You already know that Killian and I are friends.*

He'd love to be more than that, and you're mad at me. I'm glad he's stuck over there. Levi lifted his chin.

I wasn't doing this with him. He wanted to fight, and I wouldn't oblige him. "We'll determine a way to get out of this."

Griffin sighed. "I sure hope so. Sterlyn, Kira, and I will head over there later. We need to fill you in on a few more things."

They were being vague in case someone overheard. With witches like Erin and Diana, you always had to be cautious, and unfortunately, I had a feeling their news had to do with the fire at the Wolves' Den and the artifact building break-in. I had questions, but now wasn't the time. They'd tell us more when they could.

"Red's coming." Levi smirked.

My blood boiled. Of course he'd act like this since he'd talked with Killian.

His father's forehead was lined with confusion. "Who is Red?"

"A fox shifter named Kira," I answered, ensuring my

tone stayed level. I couldn't let him get to me—that was what he wanted.

Levi leaned forward and almost fell over, his injured state obvious. "I saved her from some shifters, and she's been the only supporter and ally I've made here."

His words cut like a knife. I bit the inside of my cheek to keep from reacting and crying. I hated that his plan was succeeding, and it caused me pure agony that he wanted to hurt me.

"I wouldn't be too eager," Griffin warned. "Her feelings for you have changed."

"What?" Levi's jaw dropped. "But I told her—"

I'd heard enough. The urge to flee overwhelmed me again. "You *said* a lot, so don't be surprised you've hurt more than just me." I needed to get away before I showed an even more unfavorable side of myself.

Angels were about composure and control, and Levi was taking those two things from me.

I stood, and as I took a few steps toward the door, Levi said, "Rosey." The couch made a noise, and I turned in time to watch him stumble.

My body instinctively moved toward him, desperate to help, but I forced my legs to stop. I couldn't keep helping him, not when he kept hurting me. He had to see that he was pushing me too far.

"What the *hell* was that?" Sierra asked enthusiastically. "Holy shit, I need to get over there. Did Rosemary clock him? Please tell me she did!"

Levi caught his balance, showing he was more healed than I'd thought. His demon magic must have been thrumming inside him, needing to heal him before another threat.

When no one said anything, she shouted, "Punch him again!"

"Gods, Sierra." Alex scoffed and leaned back on the couch, unconcerned. "She didn't punch him. He lost his balance for a second."

"What? I thought demons were more graceful than that." Sierra scoffed. "With what he did to her, she *should* deck him."

"He's still not completely healed from his injuries." Ronnie's lips twitched as if she were preventing a smile from spreading across her face.

Sounding like a hyena, Sierra rolled with laughter. "Hell, yeah. Don't heal him, Rosemary. I love it."

I grimaced. Was that what everyone thought? "I healed him the best I could. He almost died, but I—"

"Girl, no explanation needed. I don't care what the reason is. He needs to suffer," Sierra interrupted. "Nobody hurts my family!"

Bune blew out his cheeks. "Is she insane?"

Three weeks ago, I would have said yes, but not now. "No, she cares about me, which is a lot more than your son can say."

"You think I don't *care* about you?" Levi asked incredulously, moving toward me again.

I wasn't doing this in front of everyone. "Annie. Cyrus. I'm going to stay next door with you two again, if that's okay."

"Of course." Annie's face softened, her eyes full of understanding. "You don't even have to ask. You're family."

"Thanks." I'd never been one to avoid confrontation, but I didn't want to make a scene or act in anger. I'd seen Mother and Azbogah do it with each other plenty. Now I knew why.

As I marched out the door, my wings itched to free themselves from my back, but I held them tight. The sun was rising, and I didn't want to chance a human seeing me. Though a vampire could erase their memory, I didn't want to be the reason it was required. I had enough stacked up against me here lately.

"Son, she needs time," Bune said right before the door closed.

My heart pounded harder, knowing Levi might be following me. I didn't want to stay still, hoping he'd come, then find out he'd listened to his father. That would hurt me further.

When I reached the front door of the house Annie and Cyrus were staying in, the door of the house I'd just vacated opened. "Rosey," Levi called.

Out of my peripheral vision, I noted a silver wolf step closer to the tree line. He stood under an oak tree, letting the shadow and leaves hide him from human eyes.

Even out here, we had an audience, but their watchful gaze was a good thing. They not only needed to keep an eye out for demons that might breach the territory but for the demons inside the house, too. None of them could be trusted.

Ignoring Levi, I walked into the second house, which was an exact replica of the one next door. Even the couches were the same, which was standard for supernaturals. These towns had been built quickly out of necessity, so similar floor plans and décor had made building them easier.

Needing a barrier between us, I hurried upstairs. Before we'd bonded, I'd been staying in the same room here as Levi and I had next door, so that was where I went.

As I shut the bedroom door, the front door downstairs opened, and Levi's clunky steps entered.

Rosey, you're being silly. He hurried after me.

I locked the door. It was hard enough seeing him without touching him. If I touched him, I would lose the resolve I was attempting to sustain around my heart. I couldn't forgive him until he understood why I was so upset.

I sat on the couch under the window and wrapped my arms around myself. I had to admit that developing emotions was both amazing and horrible. Feeling things made me understand mortals more, but it also made me unstable. Like now, when Levi wiggled the doorknob and banged on the door.

"Let me in," he demanded. "We need to talk."

"We said everything we wanted to not even an hour ago." And he'd told me that he'd made the right call, even though he could feel what the decision had done to me.

He sighed, and it sounded as if his forehead thudded against the door. "No, I didn't say everything I wanted to."

"You talked about how *Red* was loyal and had your back in front of everyone moments ago." My throat dried. "I stand corrected. I mean, you did confide in her and not me."

"Rose—"

"Just go. *Red* will be here later, and you can have your true friend back." I was acting jealous, but he'd made me feel like he valued her over me, especially with what he'd said.

He groaned. "I was being an asshole. I'm sorry. But when Killian said he needed to be here, it reminded me of how you two are together."

"We've had this argument already. You know he isn't a threat, and I didn't bring him up in that conversation. You started this by insulting him." I wouldn't take the blame for Levi's insecurities and decisions. "Then you added Kira to the mix, making this entire situation worse. Are you trying to destroy me?" I was feeling vulnerable, but I was so damn tired of pretending to be okay. He knew I wasn't okay through our bond, anyway. "When she comes here, you'll just confide in her instead of me."

He pounded on the door again. "Damn it, Rosey. Everything I've done has been to *protect* you. That's what I'm hardwired to do now even when I know it'll piss you off."

"You confided in Kira to protect me?" I stood and ran my hands through my hair. "Do you think I'm stupid enough to believe you or that I'm that desperate to forgive you?"

"Oh, believe me, I know better than to hope for either of those things." He tapped on the door again. "Just open the door. I want to talk face to face."

"It's best if we take time apart to think things through." I needed to get my head together. Whenever I was near him, I acted out of my mind.

He sighed. "Remember, I tried to do this the nice way."

My blood turned cold. He was going to leave. Though I wanted him to go, I also wanted him to stay. I was a walking, breathing contradiction.

Something at the bottom crack of the door caught my attention, and a shadowy presence floated under it.

He wasn't leaving but forcing his way in.

CHAPTER SEVENTEEN

I HADN'T EXPECTED him to use his shadow form to get in. Though he usually pushed my buttons, he'd never gone this far. The last time we were at a similar place in our relationship, we'd been unbonded and couldn't feel each other's torment.

His shadowy form materialized in front of me, hovering a few feet off the floor. His mocha eyes stared at me, confirming they weren't the red of a fallen. He soon flickered back into his physical appearance, solidifying in front of me. His muscular frame called me to rub all over him like a siren.

What part of "we need time apart from each other" didn't you understand? I ignored the part of me that was thrilled he was here. The part that wanted me to forget why I was upset and run into his arms.

He smirked. *We've had plenty of time apart, and I'm not going anywhere.*

The problem was he could follow through on that threat. Shadows could fit through any tiny opening. I could go anywhere, and he could follow right behind.

Though he shouldn't have been able to get into Shadow City with the magical spells that protected it, he'd attached himself to Griffin's Navigator and got in that way. No one had detected him because he hadn't chosen evil.

I'd handle one problem at a time. "You *caused* the separation. You don't get to decide when we're together and when we're not. I have a say in this as well."

Levi glowered, his nostrils flaring. "I did everything for *you*."

"Saying it over and over doesn't make it true."

He moved closer to me, and I swayed toward him as his peony scent overrode my senses. He rasped, "Does it smell like I'm lying?"

I didn't smell the stench of sulfur, though I almost wish there were. Not because I didn't want him to mean it but because it would at least take away from his allure.

"Don't make things more complicated." I stumbled back. Being close to him made me dizzy, and logic attempted to leave me. I couldn't have him messing with my head on top of my heart.

He countered my move. "I'm not sure I could make things more complicated if I tried. I need you to listen to me."

"I have—"

Placing a finger on my lips, he growled, "No, I haven't been clear. Just give me a minute, and if you still want me to leave, I won't argue."

My lips tingled from his touch, and my tongue wanted to dart out and lick his finger. Instead, I took a solid step back. "Fine. Please proceed."

He winked. "I figured you'd say that."

My heart fluttered despite my anger. "You're running

out of time." No matter what, I had to reinforce to the both of us that I was serious.

He didn't seem bothered. His eyes locked with mine, searching for something.

When someone said another person was looking into their soul, this had to be what they were describing.

The world faded away as he licked his lips. "Do you want to know why I didn't tell you about the sword?"

The air left my lungs in one swoop. Of all the times to bring up *Red*, he'd chosen *now*? But I should be grateful. This would help me stay grounded. "Because Kira treated you like a person and not a demon. You've explained." The words were hard to say because they were true—until they weren't. And the *until they weren't* part was what got me.

"At first, yes, but there was more to it." His irises lightened, and the intensity of his emotions coursed through our bond. "I wasn't willing to risk you."

I snorted and immediately covered my mouth with my hand. I'd never made that obnoxious noise before. "Is that how you're going to manipulate it?"

He rolled his eyes, and my chest panged. He'd never looked annoyed or disgusted with me until this second.

"It's not manipulation." He clenched his fists. "It's the truth. The less you knew about what was going on, the more I could protect you."

"Protect me?" I was more than capable of protecting myself. "I'm a warrior—"

"See, that's my point." He threw his hands in the air. "You would have wanted to fix things or determine a way to go to Hell with me. Things that would put you in harm's way. I did"—he pounded his chest—"what I had to do to keep *you* safe. You're my fucking world, and if something happened to you...I couldn't risk you."

"And you don't think I feel the same way about you?" His reasoning wasn't fair. "But I don't keep things from you. I let you know my thoughts even when you don't like them. Why couldn't you do the same thing for *me*? Instead, you caused the worst pain I've ever experienced in my life."

"I felt the same torment while I was in Hell, trying to get back to you. But you hated my guts, and even though we have this insane connection, you were determined to fight it." His face turned a shade pinker from anger. "If I'd told you even part of the truth, I would've spilled everything to you because I don't *love* Re—"

I fisted my hand, ready to punch him. He was healed enough now that I could land a few solid hits without killing him. I *hated* that he called her that, and it infuriated me that it bothered me, which aggravated me more.

"—Kira." He cleared his throat, remorse wafting toward me. "I don't love *Kira*. I love you, Rosemary. Only you. So I told her a portion of the truth because it didn't bother me. I couldn't do that with you."

I'd desperately needed his sincerity, and I clung to it like a drink of water after a long battle, wanting to lap it all up.

Listening to him hadn't been smart after all.

"Staying silent was hard enough. I wanted to tell you everything, but if I'd told you that I needed the demon sword to ensure the princes of Hell didn't harm my father, you would've informed everyone, and he could be *dead* right now. Even though you have my entire heart, he's my *father*. I couldn't leave him down there to rot and die." He sighed. "The last thing I ever wanted to do was *hurt* you, but I also recognized that I'd be gone for only a short time."

My pragmatic side understood what he was saying. "But—"

"But nothing," he said as he closed the distance between us. He pulled me against his chest, and the buzz of our connection sprang to life. Our souls reached for each other, desperate to connect.

You mean everything to me, and no one... He paused and tilted my chin up so we locked gazes. *Absolutely no one is more important than you. You have my heart for all eternity. Nothing could ever change that. I'm sorry for the pain I caused you.*

If you cause it again, I'll hurt you, I vowed.

"I expect nothing less."

He lowered his mouth to mine, and I couldn't find the willpower to move my head.

When our lips touched, the world righted itself. His spearmint flavor filled my mouth.

He groaned. *Gods, you taste so good.*

My body heated, and there was no turning back.

The scent of his arousal mixed with mine, and our mouths moved together. My hand slipped under his shirt, needing to feel his skin. His abs contracted under my fingers, the muscles rippling. A jolt shot through my hand and up my arm, fueling my need for him.

He grabbed my butt, and a moan escaped me. Our connection warmed with the intensity of our desire for each other. Not only did we need each other, but our connection also demanded that we reaffirm our commitment.

His tongue darted into my mouth, and I matched each stroke. He bent his knees to pick me up, and some sanity filtered back in.

You're hurt. Not even twenty-four hours ago, he'd been near death.

Ignoring my resistance, he threw me on the bed. My hair fanned out around me as my body landed on the soft mattress. The way he'd manhandled me had me damn near purring.

He climbed on next to me and ran a fingertip along my face. He connected, *I'm fine. Believe me.*

I tugged on our bond, searching for pain and discomfort, but I didn't sense anything beyond his love and desperation for me.

Hovering over me, he grabbed the collar of my shirt. I leaned my head back, not sure what he was doing. Suddenly, the material ripped, and cool air hit my skin. I turned my head so I could see him again, and the crazed look on his face was my final undoing.

He needed me, maybe more than I needed him.

My breathing quickened as he slipped a hand behind my back and unfastened my bra. Within seconds, he'd removed the material from my body, and his mouth was devouring my breast.

The warmth rushing through my body increased to an inferno, and his free hand unfastened my jeans, then slipped inside my panties and between my legs.

A guttural hiss escaped him as he touched me. *Dear gods. You're so damn ready for me.* But that didn't stop him from stroking me.

My head lolled back as the friction built, and I squirmed underneath his hold.

He chuckled deeply as his other hand caught my arm, pinning me down as he teased my body.

Levi... I started, but I couldn't remember what I'd been about to say. My head spun as an orgasm rocked my body. I convulsed, but he was relentless, increasing the pressure and making the pleasure reach new heights.

When my body relaxed, he released his hold and asked, *Better?*

Fuck, no, I wasn't. *You tell me.* I flipped him over and ripped his shirt from his body. If we were going to destroy clothing, I was all in. I kissed down his chest, toward his waistline, and unfastened his jeans. In one swift move, I removed all barriers and shimmied out of the rest of my clothes.

You are so damn sexy. He grinned wickedly as he watched me undress.

The orgasm he'd given me hadn't satiated me. Our connection needed the joining of our bodies.

He quickly got to his knees behind me and settled between my legs. I grabbed two pillows to prop myself up as he slid inside me. He snaked a hand around my waist, down between my legs, and rubbed my sweet spot as he thrust inside me.

As we moved in sync, our bond strengthened within us. His love poured into me, and I pushed my emotions back toward him. This was exactly what we needed.

Quickening the pace, he shifted his hips, hitting deeper inside. Every time he filled me, the friction heated. He hovered close to my body, and I reached back and grabbed his hair. I pulled, wanting him to feel my growing passion.

A growl emanated from deep within his chest. His head leaned forward as the pace quickened, and his teeth bit into my shoulder, adding to the ecstasy.

My body tightened as his pleasure slammed into mine. My first orgasm had nothing on this moment with the two of us sharing the gratification together. The sensation was endless, and we rode the high for gods knew how long.

Our bond sizzled, back to the temperature it was supposed to be, and our bodies slowly stilled. He rolled off me and onto his side, pulling me into his arms.

I faced him, nestling into his sweaty chest. There was

no place in the world I'd rather be. Then, somehow, we drifted off to sleep.

A CELL PHONE pinged from somewhere on the floor. My head lifted from Levi's rising chest, and I considered ignoring the interruption.

When it pinged again, I realized it was an incoming call. I needed to answer it. People only called me when they needed something or there was a problem. Though my heart screamed at me to remain still, I forced my head off Levi's chest.

Just ignore it, he connected as his arms tightened around my waist. His hardness pressed against my leg, reminding me we'd fallen asleep completely naked.

My body warmed as I thought about an encore performance.

He chuckled sexily. *I'm always ready for more sex with you.* He rolled me onto my back and slipped in between my legs. He slid inside me, and I forgot what I'd intended to do.

Capturing my nipple in his mouth, he picked up where we'd left off. He grabbed my wrists, lifted them over my head, and restrained me.

This time, he was in complete control, and I loved it.

He must have known we didn't have much time because we didn't start slow. Instead, our bodies were slicked with sweat already, and he swiftly entered me.

I lifted my head and bit his chest, needing to let him know I was mad with desire, too. I didn't like being submissive, but it felt entirely right. He wasn't trying to dominate me, but he wanted to do things his way.

I love you, Rosey. He groaned as he approached ecstasy.

His words sent me completely over the edge. *I love you, Levi.*

Our bodies convulsed as we climaxed together.

I would never tire of him and the things he could do to my body.

The phone rang again, and I could no longer ignore it. *I've got to answer that.*

Please don't. He kissed my lips as he released his hold. *Let's just stay here forever. We have everything we need here —you, me, and crazy hot sex.*

I smiled happily. *We can't ignore the world. No matter how much I want to.* I had too many people counting on me, and he wouldn't leave his father in danger, either.

Not bothering to get dressed, I stood and picked up the phone from the floor. Mother's name flashed across the screen.

My heart sank. I answered, "Hello?"

"Are you okay?" Fear laced her voice.

She rarely ever asked me that, and the question put me on edge. The relaxation I'd gotten from the sexual escapades between Levi and me vanished. "I'm fine. Why?"

"Because I've been calling you for the past thirty minutes, and you're just now answering." Her tone was cold.

I pulled the phone away from my ear and looked at the main screen. I had twenty missed calls. I'd honestly thought Levi and I had been faster than that. My cheeks heated, and thankfully, she couldn't see. "I...I..."

"You're with *him*, aren't you?" she asked simply, and I knew what she meant. "When we stopped by the vampire condominium at her request, Sterlyn mentioned he'd come back."

Wolves staying in the vampire section of Shadow City

sounded odd. But where else could they go? "What's wrong?"

"I just needed to confirm firsthand that my daughter decided to sleep with the enemy once more," she said brokenly. "And I need you to come home."

She wasn't fooling me. She wanted to get me away from Levi. "I can't. Not right now." Just like Levi, I wouldn't abandon my family. "I know you need me there, too, and I should be able to make it back soon. We're outlining a plan, and I'm not being stupid."

"I hope you're right." She sighed. "There are murmurs that Azbogah has picked up more followers. Whatever he's planned is working."

My heart sank. "I'll be there as soon as I can. I promise."

"Okay." She murmured. "And Rosemary, please be careful. I...worry about you."

I grinned. "I know. I worry about you, too, Mother."

She disconnected, and I turned to find a dressed Levi. "What are you doing?"

"I'm hungry, so I figured you are, too. Let's go downstairs and find something to eat." He leaned down and grabbed my jeans and panties off the floor and tossed them to me.

I laughed, the sensation becoming less and less strange. "I thought we had everything we needed in this room."

"We *do*." He winked and headed to the closet, then took out two white cotton shirts tossing one to me. "But we need more energy before round three."

I quickly dressed and kissed his lips. *I'm good with that plan.*

I'm not surprised. He booped my nose. *Thankfully, you saw logic, so we've put fighting behind us.*

You admitting that you were wrong helped, too. Otherwise, we wouldn't have gotten to this point. He had to understand that what he'd done was unacceptable. He had to tell me things and include me in his plans. It wasn't right to alienate me.

He paused, his brows furrowed. *I didn't do anything wrong. What are you talking about?*

My body stilled, and I blinked. He had to be kidding.

CHAPTER EIGHTEEN

HIS WORDS ECHOED in my head. It had to be the punchline, but it sure wasn't funny. I took a step back. "You said you were sorry." I sounded stilted.

"For hurting you." He countered my move, reaching to touch my face with his fingers. "I hate that I caused you pain, but I did what I had to do."

I knocked his hand away and glowered at him. I'd thought we were on the same page and that he'd realized he should've confided in me so we could determine the best solution together—one that didn't cause us distress. Obviously, I'd been so wrong.

I'd heard what I'd wanted to hear. This was something I'd judged so many people for doing. I'd felt superior and criticized their ignorance and how my logic would never allow me to do something so...absurd. But yet, here I stood like a buffoon.

Fate had quite the sense of humor. I hadn't believed it until now. I believed in her Divine plan, but how much more agony did she have in store for me? I'd always thought

I could withstand anything she threw my way, but I'd never expected or experienced *this*.

My soul felt ripped in half again, and the sensation was excruciating.

He glanced at the hand I'd smacked away and grimaced. "What's wrong now?"

Now? White-hot anger scorched me, and I didn't try to hide it, wanting him to feel the burn through our connection. "The same thing that was wrong *before*."

He scoffed and searched the room as if looking for answers. "I thought we were past that." He gestured to the bed. "And that things were better."

"Me, *too*." I was so damn angry, and mostly at myself. This was all my fault, even if I'd have loved to blame him. "But I messed up. I thought you were apologizing for everything, including not talking to me before going back to Hell." Replaying the conversation in my head, I realized he clearly hadn't, and I'd been stupid.

No wonder Mother was so worried about me.

"Rosey—" he started.

The nickname tugged at my heart, and I huffed. I needed it to annoy me like when he'd first said it. "Do *not* call me that."

He laughed humorlessly. "I thought angels were supposed to be rational. That they prided themselves on it."

Pride.

Another dig.

Even if it was true, pride wasn't seen in a positive light. It was different from confidence, and his insult hit *hard*.

The worst part was that he'd meant to hurt me after he'd apologized for doing *this* by leaving.

The irony nearly drowned me.

"You're right." There was no point in denying I'd

mistaken his words, wanting them to mean what I'd needed at that moment to justify my actions. "I made a mistake, and now I need you to go."

His head jerked back as if I'd slapped him. His agony mixed with mine, making it hard to fill my lungs. He murmured, "You don't mean it. I'm not leaving."

Determination fueled me. He had to leave before my heart and our bond started to affect me again. I clung to the anger.

I refused to be treated as if I wasn't an equal in our relationship. I'd seen the other couples fate had blessed, and when they had differing opinions, they worked through them together, even if it was difficult at first.

I could only hope that Levi and I were going through the growing pains of a new relationship. I deserved to be treated with respect, courtesy, *and* love.

Lifting my chin, I channeled everything inside me toward him. He needed to feel that I had no hesitation about my request, or he'd use it to his advantage. "You promised that if I listened to you and still wanted you to go that you would. Will you not keep your word?" My heart pounded in protest. The discomfort bubbled deep in my chest, but I pushed it away.

"That was before we made love." He shook his head. "That changed everything."

I'd thought it had, too, but I'd been wrong. He'd be learning the same thing. "That wasn't a stipulation, and I expect you to follow through on your word—unless you're trying to prove you can't."

His shoulders slumped, and his bottom lip trembled. "This is how you want our relationship to be? I thought we were moving forward together like we're destined."

"This is not even *close* to what I want, but I can't be with someone who disregards me so easily."

"I didn't disregard you. I protected you! And I won't apologize for it." His irises turned a dark coffee color, and he straightened his shoulders. "I did what I had to do."

We were at an impasse. "Protecting me was when you stepped in front of the blade that night and almost died. Leaving without telling me anything wasn't protection. It was abandonment, and while your reasons might have been noble, your execution was poor. Until you understand that, nothing more can happen between us." Saying those words was the hardest thing I'd ever had to do.

"Fine." He nodded and strode past me, making sure we didn't brush against each other, like I meant nothing to him. If I hadn't felt the agony crashing through him, I would've thought he didn't care.

But we couldn't hide our emotions from each other, only partial truths and secrets.

"Let me know when you've come to *your* senses," he said briskly as he opened the door. "You know where you can find me."

I wanted to say something smart or hurtful back, but I didn't want to stoop to his level. I wasn't trying to hurt him but rather to remain who I was—strong, smart, strategic, and a fighter. I wouldn't allow him to discount my worth, not to me or to anyone around.

My mother had taught me that.

As he stomped out the door without glancing back, hurt and rage consumed me. Maybe there was a thin between love and hate after all. I now straddled that line, unsure which side I'd be standing on when all was said and done.

AN HOUR LATER, Annie entered the house alone. I shouldn't have been surprised. I'd been expecting someone to show up and was thankful they'd given me time to process before coming to talk. Annie had worked at a children's group home and once had ambitions to become a lawyer. Reading people was one of her strengths. It had come in handy when she and Cyrus had dealt with Mila, who'd blamed Cyrus for the death of her mate, Cyrus and Sterlyn's uncle, Bart.

I sat on the couch, facing the door. I couldn't get myself to go back into the bedroom. I'd taken the sheets off the bed and thrown them by the front door. There was no laundry room in the house, so I was at a loss as to what to do. However, I'd found an extra set of sheets to make the bed, needing his smell *gone* before it made me yearn for him more.

Annie arched a brow as she stared at the sheets. "I can't tell if things went well or horribly."

She could smell the sex. Wolf shifters had incredible noses, even better than angels.

A strangled laugh escaped me. "It was definitely both." The sex and nap had been amazing, but they had come with a hefty price—losing more of my heart. I hadn't realized that was possible.

"I'm sorry." She sighed and sat across from me on the other couch.

Her kindness lodged a sob in my throat, and I had to swallow it. "Why do people say things like that? You didn't do anything. You didn't force Levi to be a scoundrel. That was all him."

"When people say that, it's more that they're sorry that

someone is going through a hardship." She leaned forward and paused, her belly getting in her way. "And I *am* sorry. I wish I could take your pain away. You are one of the most important people in my life—you're family—and you deserve to be happy."

"Happy." The word no longer sounded foreign on my tongue. I now understood what being happy meant. It was those moments with Levi when everything felt like it was meant to be. Those rare, fleeting moments would be blazed into my memory forever. "I'm not sure that's in fate's Divine plan for me. I'm thinking misery and pain shall be my future."

Annie rubbed her stomach. "I haven't seen this side of you before. You're reminding me of a certain blonde shifter."

Sierra. Her implication was clear—I was being dramatic. "I'm not acting like her. I sincerely mean it. Fate picks favorites, and I'm beginning to think I'm not one of hers. I must have done something to upset her, though I'm not sure what. Either way, I need to prepare myself for the probability of being alone and apart from Levi."

"It won't come to that." Annie dropped her hands to her sides and smiled sadly.

Why were all these people attempting to give me false hope? Remaining realistic was the best alternative. "I can't just dream."

"From what Ronnie and Sterlyn told me, they struggled with their fated mates at first, and so did I." She touched her chest. "I have a hard time believing fate would pair two people and not intend them to be together."

"In the last thousand years, no angels have met their preordained mate. Most angels now believe it's impossible. So why now, with him and me?"

"Who knows? No one has the answers. But what I can tell you is that this man *loves* you. He looks at you as if you're the sun that sustains him. And I see how you look at him—no one can miss it."

My chest constricted as a deep, aching pain pulsed inside. "I'm not trying to be rude." There was the qualifying statement Sierra had trained me to use. Now it was second nature, just like wanting to be with Levi. "But I don't want to hear about how much he cares about me. Love isn't enough when someone discounts you."

"I'm not saying it should be. He was *wrong* to leave you like that, but you two were not only enemies but raised in different dimensions." She crossed her legs as she settled into the couch. "Of course it will be harder for you two to adjust, and it will take time. All you can do is stick to your guns even when you feel like crumbling."

That was what I needed to hear. I'd never needed reassurance before, and I didn't require it now, but it was nice to hear that someone agreed with me. "I plan to because if I don't, he'll always treat me like that."

She bobbed her head and glanced at the sheets, and her eyes glowed faintly. She then reached for the remote and flipped on the television. "How about watching a show?"

Not talking about Levi would be nice. He was already on my mind plenty. "As long as it's nothing romantic."

"Girl, please." She waved me off as she lay back on the couch so she could see the television easily. "I'm talking about death, blood, and revenge."

A small smile slipped onto my face. Annie was becoming one of my closest friends, and her presence and support dulled the pain marginally. "That sounds perfect."

"Then let's begin." She scanned the channels, searching for the right show for the two of us.

THE NEXT DAY and a half went by slowly. I stayed inside the house mostly, afraid that if I went outside, I would be tempted to go next door.

Levi had respected my wishes, and even though I could feel through our bond that he was just as miserable, we didn't communicate. Despite that, the pain wasn't anything close to when he'd left this dimension. Though it wasn't comfortable, we knew the other person still cared.

I tried to keep busy, but I was growing antsier with each passing hour. I needed to get back to Shadow City to assist my parents, but I couldn't until the witches arrived and we had a plan. Though I trusted them to come to a consensus, we were dealing with demons. Bune and Levi *should* help with information, but I knew more than the others and could poke holes in their story if they weren't forthcoming.

In my room, I stood in front of the couch, staring out the window. The sun was descending, and from its location in the sky, I could tell it was around six. Darkness would soon fall, and the moon would appear sleepily in the sky. Circe and the others would be here around twilight, wanting to arrive during the transition time when neither the sun nor moon was strong to ensure that Erin and her coven in Shadow City didn't detect their presence. Sterlyn and Griffin were on their way, not having been able to leave until now. From what Mother had said, they were taking a risk by leaving with all the shifter turmoil, but they knew that retrieving the demon sword was vital to solving at least some of the issues. Killian, Sierra, and a few silver wolves would head over at the same time, using the witches to hide them from the demons.

My stomach fluttered with dread and excitement. Both

sensations centered around seeing a certain tall, dark, and handsome demon, and I had to tamp it down. Getting worked up over him before I'd even seen him was a bad sign.

The silver wolves had been on a rotating watch since we suspected that the demons were watching the border like last time. The first two days, the wolves had alternated between their human and animal forms, but they were itching to shift back. Apparently, staying in their animal forms too long could be dangerous for their minds, so the three of them had been rotating. Darrell and Chad were downstairs in the kitchen with Annie and Cyrus, talking pack business. The third silver wolf, who I'd learned was named Jeremiah, was outside keeping guard. They'd all shift back to their animals soon in case things went awry with the demons.

A familiar engine rumbled, and my time was up. That was the unmistakable sound of Griffin's Navigator. My heart pattered as my stomach dropped.

I'd be seeing Levi in moments.

Not wanting to dally, I made my way downstairs. As I expected, Darrell, Chad, Annie, and Cyrus were waiting in the living room.

Darrell stood closest to the door, notably shorter than the other two men. As usual, his midnight-black hair swooped the side of his face like long bangs, and his blood orange eyes were tense with worry. Though only Cyrus and Sterlyn had silver hair by birth, Darrell had silver streaked into his short beard from age.

Standing next to the beta was Chad. He was five inches shorter than Cyrus and a few inches taller than Darrell. He ran a hand through his short golden-wheat hair and blinked his smoky topaz eyes, which stood out more than usual with the dark circles underneath them.

Both wolf shifters wore the same rumpled clothes from when they'd first arrived here, not bothering to change since they kept shifting into their animal forms so regularly.

"We were about to call for you," Annie said as she pulled the hem of her pink shirt down over her bulging belly. "I'll need maternity clothes soon. Everything is way too small!"

"I know, babe." Cyrus took her hand, tugging her toward the front door. "Sierra is bringing you some bigger clothes."

Annie cringed but followed her mate. "I'm afraid to see what she brings."

I would be, too. For once, I was thankful not to be the pregnant one.

By the time Annie and I went outside, Sterlyn and Griffin were out of their car and heading toward the other house. Their expressions were stern, and Sterlyn's usual friendly smile was nowhere in sight.

Something was definitely wrong.

We all reached the front door at the same time, and Sterlyn nodded stiffly as she opened it and led us inside.

When I entered, I scanned the room, the fighter inside me wanting to know where everyone was located in case something went wrong.

Alex and Ronnie sat on the couch farther from the door, facing us, while Midnight, Levi, and Bune sat on the other one. Even with the back of Levi's head to me, my heart did somersaults.

I didn't need to take note of him, but there wasn't a damn thing I could do.

Levi glanced over his shoulder, our gazes immediately locking.

The world went still while the scab on my heart ripped open. I stood in the entryway, frozen.

Annie walked past me and sat next to Ronnie while Cyrus positioned himself behind the couch with Annie in front of him. Darrell and Chad stood in front of the window behind the two demons.

"Before the witches arrive, I wanted to give you an update about the artifact building," Sterlyn said as she and Griffin trudged to the spot under the television, where they could face us all. "There's a reason Kira isn't here, and no one else knows what we're about to tell you. I need to make sure this stays in this room until we're ready to share the news with the council."

When her eyes locked on me, my head spun. Somehow, my body understood the implications, but my head hadn't caught up.

CHAPTER NINETEEN

BLACK SPOTS DOTTED MY VISION. I finally managed to ask, "What's missing?"

Knowing what we were up against would make things partially better. The unknown was always worse.

Levi stood and moved toward me.

My heart wanted him near, especially now. This had to be more serious than I could imagine for Sterlyn to be pausing. However, if he comforted me, I might crumble, and I wasn't sure how much strength I'd have once we heard the truth.

"What are you talking about?" His focus darted to me, then Sterlyn.

"Three artifacts are gone." Sterlyn bit her bottom lip. "With the one Levi took, that's a total of four."

Maybe not knowing was better, because this was worse than I'd expected. "What kind of artifacts? Could they be angel weapons?" If Azbogah was behind the theft, I expected it to be angel swords.

"Someone would have to go to Hell to get those," Bune

said as he turned his body toward me. "Thanks to Azbogah."

My brain short-circuited. I'd heard his words, but I couldn't comprehend them. "The angel and demon weapons are in Shadow City. That's what Mother told me." They clearly knew, and that was why Levi had sneaked into Shadow City.

"Yes, the demon weapons are, but as for the angel sword and dagger, they're in Hell." Bune scratched his chin. "Levi, haven't you told your mate *anything*?" His nose wrinkled as he observed his son.

I laughed loudly. Out of everyone here, I hadn't expected his father to react like that. "Not a thing. He didn't even tell me he was taking the demon sword to retrieve you, which is another missing artifact to pin on my mother."

Bune shook his head. "No wonder she's fighting your connection."

"Not *helping*, Father." Levi glared at him and turned to me. "What do you mean, *pin on your mother*? How could it be blamed on her?"

A smart retort sat on the tip of my tongue, but I paused. He didn't understand Shadow City, and it was unfair to criticize him for that. Just as I didn't understand Hell, and we needed his and Bune's help to retrieve the sword and Eliza. "We suspect Azbogah was behind the attacks on my mother and Kira," I told him. "The shifters who attacked them purposely mentioned a broken door to the artifact building where one of my mother's feathers was left behind. With an accusation like that, the council wanted to do an inventory to ensure nothing was missing." Though I was attempting to sound composed, emotion laced my voice.

Levi's face tensed.

Sterlyn frowned. "Azbogah needs to rebalance the

council in his favor since Rosemary's parents are siding with us, especially after losing Matthew and Ezra. We think he's working with Erin, and this was their way of getting an inventory taken."

"Is Yelahiah not on the council?" Bune's brows furrowed. "I assumed she'd be one of the angel representatives."

The question was odd. "Yelahiah is my mother, and yes, she's on the council."

Bune climbed to his feet and rubbed his forehead. "But you said *parents*."

"Pahaliah and Yelahiah are my parents." Having to explain who my parents were was peculiar. No one had ever questioned who they were before, but Bune had left Shadow City before I'd been born.

He swayed slightly. "Wait. *Those* two are together? But she and Azbogah..." He trailed off, blinking.

As much as it had shocked him to hear who my parents were, it surprised me that he thought Azbogah and Mother would be together. "Gods, no. They can't stand each other."

"Dude, they're always at each other's throats," Griffin chuckled. "Kinda like these two." Griffin pointed at me and Levi.

My lungs quit working. Levi and I were at odds because we cared about each other but couldn't make things work. That couldn't be what was going on between Azbogah and Mother. She'd have told me when we'd talked back at the condo after the fire at the Elite Wolves' Den.

"It's irrelevant." I needed this conversation to change. We were wasting time. "When will Kira be informing the council of the findings?"

"She's dragging out the rest of the inventory. She insisted on taking inventory of the room where Ronnie found her dagger. That's where the most heavily guarded weapons are, which include all angel and demon artifacts, sharp weapons, and anything else that holds special powers. So she was the one who learned about the missing artifacts. She's taking her time while the rest finish with the warehouse. She's trying to time her final accounting until Levi gets back with the demon sword he *stole* from us." Sterlyn stared Levi down, making it clear how she felt about his betrayal.

Good. He'd see that his actions hadn't only hurt me.

His regret slammed into me as he tugged at our bond, using the connection after a day and a half of silence. *I didn't mean to put all of you in this position.*

How did you not? If you'd talked to me before sneaking off, I could have helped. This time, I couldn't hold back the dig. *I told you that your decision could impact my family, and you blew me off as being dramatic.* The urge to punch him overcame me once again. I almost wished the old sensation of wanting to kill him would come back. That might make this whole complicated mess we called a *preordained pairing* easier.

He winced. *I thought you meant because they're on that stupid city council. I didn't know—*

You assume a lot, don't you? I let my bitterness swirl into the bond. It was so much easier to clutch on to, even when my heart had fractured. *Weren't you taught that assumptions make you a nincompoop?*

"We need to focus on getting the demon sword back from Hell and determining where the other items are within the city," Alex said. He straightened his legs in front of him. "We all know it's not just Yelahiah he's hoping to remove from the council. He's coming for all of us."

"He's a coward." Ronnie scoffed and leaned back in her

seat. "Hiding behind people and getting others to do his dirty work."

That was what kept getting my friends into trouble. They were underestimating him. "He's not a coward—he's making sure his hands don't get dirty." I'd never underestimated him, thanks to my parents. They didn't fear him, but they were always wary of his influence and capabilities. He was intelligent to a fault, and I hadn't been able to predict his next attack, never knowing what he'd do until he'd played his hand.

Annie tilted her head. "How?"

"Azbogah is the same damn angel I knew eons ago." Bune's lip curled. "He wants everyone to see him in a golden light, so he gets others to do the dirty work. No one wants to follow someone who's *tainted*."

Tainted was the term Azbogah used to describe the demons. I'd heard him reference them a handful of times, and he'd called them exactly that. Obviously, Bune had heard it directly from him before he'd left.

"That smug asshole needs to die." Cyrus's nostrils flared. "I can't believe that people fall for his act."

Midnight leaned forward. "Look at how the demon pack operated. Tate had a similar hold on them—it was ingrained over centuries. There's no telling how old that angel is."

"He's easily over five millennia. He was the first angel who didn't get the archangel power, and it has always enraged him." Bune smirked. "From what Marissa told me, the day he realized he hadn't been created with equal power as the rest of them, he attempted to pretend he was just like us. You see, archangels are powerful, and when they were created, so was a weapon that could enhance their magic. They were blessed by fate, like a fate-chosen warrior, and have an enhanced sense of responsibility to protect *all* of Earth. Or at least the demons did until they fell. That's one reason I didn't understand how Yelahiah—one of the very first angels in existence—could have feelings for him. He's selfish and only cares about strengthening himself and the angels' status in this world. However, he was charming, which fooled others into seeing him as more than what he ever truly was."

"Could that be why he's desperate to prove himself?" Darrell pursed his lips. "Think about how Chad and Theo acted when Cyrus showed up to take over. They thought that him becoming acting alpha wasn't fair, especially when they thought they were equally as strong."

"Thanks, man." Chad rolled his eyes, but the corner of his mouth tipped up. "Way to throw me under the bus, but yeah, you've got a point. I lost my mind trying to prove I was stronger, but Annie forced me to see reason."

"You mean *I* did." Cyrus puffed out his chest. "I kicked your ass."

"But Annie made me see *reason*. It wasn't your ass-kicking," Chad said, and winked at her.

Cyrus growled. "Watch it. You two may be friends, but she is *mine*."

"I say the pup needs another lesson." Levi shrugged, encouraging Cyrus's mate side to come out stronger.

Stop. We have serious things to address, I snapped at him. The last thing we needed was two dogs prancing around each other, comparing their size. Both were big and burly, but Cyrus's hair told the end of the story, no challenge required.

Levi stepped toward me. *This is serious. Nobody messes with another man's fated. It's best if your friend remembers that as well.*

His reference was clear—Killian. I'd reassured him multiple times that Killian and I were just friends, and I wouldn't repeat myself. Only a fool would expect a different outcome.

The conversation had been so derailed that Sierra might as well have been here. But before we got back to the missing artifacts, I needed one question answered.

I looked at Bune. "Is that why the princes of Hell sent Levi here to steal his mother's sword?"

"Yes. They knew he would be able to feel the pull of the sword if he got close enough, and he hasn't fallen, so he can walk Earth undetected." Bune's jaw twitched. "I'm glad Levi bonded with it—at least that's a little bit of payback."

It's best to drop it, Levi connected as more pain filled him. *Jealous of her strength and that her bond with my father had been strong enough that he decided to fall to be with her, the princes killed my mother.*

My throat constricted. The princes of Hell had caused so much pain, and I'd probably never learn of all their horrors. *They will pay for everything.* Though I was angry with Levi, I hated that someone important to him had been taken. No wonder he and his father had wanted to leave Hell.

A phone rang, and Annie pulled hers out from her pocket. "It's Circe."

The witches had to be close. I glanced out the window, noting the time was drawing near. My favorite shade of orange would soon fill the sky as twilight descended upon us.

Annie put the call on speaker so we could all hear. "Hello?" she breathed. She was excited, not only about seeing the witches again but at the possibility of rescuing Eliza.

"We're pulling onto the road to your location," Circe said robotically. She had purposely avoided naming the city and town, perhaps because this place held so much pain for them. "Where do we meet the wolves?"

Sterlyn's irises glowed faintly, and I assumed she was linking with Killian. Killian had submitted to both Griffin and Sterlyn as alphas, but they weren't officially a complete pack. Sterlyn had done the same with Griffin to protect the silver wolves. They'd recently begun talking about combining the packs, but they wanted things to settle down first. There was enough tension that combining packs and working through power dynamics among the ranks could escalate the shifter drama within Shadow City.

"They asked for you to meet them at a pullout on the road ten miles from the turnoff," Sterlyn said slightly more loudly than normal, since witch hearing wasn't as strong as the rest of ours. "It'll be on your left coming in. It's at the edge of the Shadow Ridge border, but not where the demons should be watching."

I remembered something crucial about that area. During a previous confrontation, Annie had discovered witch bones there, which we'd assumed meant Erin was watching the area. "That's not smart. You need another location. If the witch bones are still there and Circe and the others get close, it might alert Erin." Witch magic was strong, and though Eliza had gotten close to the bones undetected, several witches might draw attention.

"She's right," Circe replied. "We don't want to risk any of them knowing we're near, not when my focus is on saving my mother."

"Then pull into the town limits by the welcome sign," Griffin interjected. "Killian and his pack will meet you there."

"Very well. Another thing—we're hoping that Cordelia, Eliphas, and Kamila can stay with you. We can use their magic to cloak us, and if there's an issue, they can get to us quickly." Circe sighed. "Though I hate for them to be that close to *the city*, I believe it's the best strategy."

Some of the weight on my shoulders receded. Circe was thinking clearly and not letting her negative feelings toward Shadow City affect her judgment.

"That's perfectly fine," Ronnie assured her.

"I figured you would say that." Circe paused. "We'll be there shortly." She hung up the phone.

Annie groaned. "She's *just* like her mother. Why can't either of them ever say goodbye?"

I admired mortals who were direct. Saying goodbye prolonged the conversation. I had developed the habit of doing it, even before I'd developed these wonderfully horrible *emotions*, purely so Sierra wouldn't complain about me in this manner. It made my life easier.

Midnight chuckled, showing again how much of a good soul she had. She wasn't upset in the slightest at the thought of Eliza coming back. She didn't see the woman as competition, and from what I'd seen, most others wouldn't feel that way. More proof that emotions made people act irrationally.

I, unfortunately, had learned that firsthand.

One thing continued to plague my mind. "What do you mean, the angel weapons are in Hell?" I'd gotten distracted from the conversation about my mother and the artifacts.

Bune squinted. "You don't know?"

My shoulders stiffened. "Would I have asked if I did?" Asking questions you knew the answer to was pointless unless you were trying to determine if someone was lying—an effective strategy, but not for this.

He chuckled. "You are your mother's daughter."

I wasn't sure if that was meant as a compliment or an insult, but it didn't matter. I wanted answers. "Are you trying to not tell us?"

"No. I just find it endearing. My son, preordained to Yelahiah's daughter." He shook his head. "Anyway, to answer your question—yes, the angel weapons are in Hell. All the angel weapons were stored within what was to become Shadow City. When the demons were created, Azbogah hid the angelic artifacts so that the archangels who fell couldn't get to them. He had a witch spell them, which created more tension between the angels and demons. There were more demon archangels than angels, so Azbogah secured the weapons, knowing that the demons would want to take their weapons with them. The weapons fell when their owners did."

How could my parents have kept this information from me? "I can't believe I didn't know this." My gaze landed on Levi. "Why didn't you tell me?"

"It didn't really come up," he replied. "Besides, this is common knowledge in Hell—I didn't consider that you might not be aware." Levi lifted his hands. "I wasn't trying to keep it from you."

I glared at him.

"Okay, maybe I wouldn't have been forthcoming at the beginning, but later, had I known..." He grimaced as he trailed off.

But he hadn't been quick enough. "Because you've been so forthcoming with me, even after we completed the bond."

Ronnie snorted. "She totally has you there."

"If Yelahiah and Azbogah were together then, was she involved with holding the weapons?" Sterlyn lifted her chin, her face unreadable.

I'd been wondering the same thing, but I hadn't had the heart to ask. Emotion was clouding my judgment.

Bune shook his head. "I believe that's why Rosemary doesn't know. Azbogah tended to act alone, especially when he was covering up something that could make him look bad. Granted, I hadn't believed that until now."

My head spun. "How would that make him look bad?" My instinct told me that he wasn't referring to hiding the weapons.

"That's what I mean." Bune lifted a hand. "Az—"

Griffin gasped, and everyone turned to him.

"What's—" Alex started.

Griffin cut him off. "There are demons with Circe and the wolves."

CHAPTER TWENTY

SURPRISE FROZE ME. With Circe and the witches using magic to cloak themselves, I hadn't expected the demons to find them.

Annie and Ronnie rushed to the door, but not all of us had the full story.

"How is that possible?" I hated to waste more time if they needed us, but I needed to understand what we were up against.

Pausing at the door, Ronnie glanced over her shoulder. "Does it matter? We need to help them."

Her tone aggravated me. "Yes, we do. But we need to know details so we can go in prepared." I was all for protecting everyone in this group, even those loosely associated. The witches had helped us in the past, though it had been to their benefit. But assistance was assistance, and we would return the favor.

Darrell moved toward the door like he was ready to step in if needed. Chad followed closely behind.

Sterlyn nodded. "You're right. Apparently, a few demons were in Shadow Ridge undetected. They were watching Killian's pack, keeping enough distance to go unnoticed. When the witches pulled up to Killian and the others, the witches had to remove the cloaking spell temporarily. The demons then revealed themselves and informed them that they have twenty human hostages and don't have a problem killing *or* turning them if we refuse to hand over Bune and Levi."

Turning.

My stomach soured.

Would they try to make a new line of vampires or something else?

If the demons turned humans a millennium later, it could potentially create a whole new species and risk the balance of the world, which would stir the witches to react.

They might be smart, but we'd overcome them. I'd make sure of that.

"Even if we were to follow through, the demons won't make the trade," I said. Maybe there were demons who could be trusted somewhere in this universe, but I was pretty sure the demons keeping human hostages wouldn't meet with the others. The princes of Hell had to send out more neutral demons to remain undetected by the angels within Shadow City.

"Are the witches and Killian's group fighting back?" Alex exhaled loudly. "In Shadow Ridge?"

Griffin's shoulders tensed. "They can't. A human could pass by and see the fight, or other Shadow Ridge residents could get involved, putting more people at risk. Clearly, the demons don't want to fight, either, because they offered our friends a chance to talk to the demon in charge of retrieving Bune and Levi. And they said if the demons didn't return within ten minutes, they would do as they pleased with the humans and find more to torture."

Levi closed his eyes, and his jaw twitched. "They won't share where the hostages are. Our friends must go with them to meet with the demon in charge. They want our friends, the human hostages, and their army to be in battle positions when we inevitably come to the rescue."

Circe wouldn't allow the witches to use their magic this close to Shadow City, fearful that Erin would sense it. This was a complete disaster. "Tell the demons we'll make the trade, and find out the location."

Levi spun toward me, hurt lining his face. "I know you're mad at me, love, but *come on*. Do you realize what will happen if they take me back down there?"

Any other time, I'd poke fun at him, but unlike some people in our group, I knew when it was time for humor and when it wasn't. "We won't actually hand you over, but the demons don't have to know that. We have to make Killian and the others think we *will* in order for the demons to believe them."

"I—" Sterlyn grimaced.

She didn't like to lie to her people, and normally, I'd agree with her. But we were protecting them from a hidden truth. We were ensuring we had leverage so the demons didn't have *all* the control. All we could do was take back a small amount, but as long as the demons didn't outright *expect* it, we should be okay.

Cyrus walked around the couch. "I'll inform Killian that we're handing over Levi and Bune. I don't have a problem being the bad guy." He scowled.

At first, I was puzzled as to why he'd reacted that way. The silver wolves had disliked Cyrus for a while, so he was used to them being unhappy with him. Then I noted Sterlyn's pained expression.

"That's not what I meant," she said sadly.

"And that's not how I meant to come across, either." Cyrus lifted a hand. "I meant I have no problem doing it."

Though I now understood how he'd hurt her feelings, we needed to stay pragmatic and not waste time on menial things. Levi and I were at odds, but the safety of others was more important than our misunderstanding. "We don't have time for sensitivity," I said.

Sterlyn nodded. "No, it should be me. Killian will suspect something otherwise." She glanced at Griffin and the other wolf shifters in the room. "Make sure your story stays consistent with mine."

Crossing his arms, Chad frowned. "I hate doing it, but I understand why we have to."

"Will the demons expect us to tell our friends the truth?" Griffin asked Bune and Levi. "Or are we playing into their hands?"

"They won't expect Leviathan and me to go willingly, but they'll think the silver wolves are too honest to lie and that any angel involved is too arrogant to think they would need to bend the truth." Bune glanced at me. "I'm surprised that Rosemary mentioned it, with her father being who he is and all."

I couldn't decipher whether he was insulting my father, but it didn't matter. Not at this moment. I could deal with the negativity after we'd saved the witches, the wolves, and the humans.

He meant it as a compliment, Levi connected with me. *He was telling me about your father, Pahaliah. Apparently, they were friends prior to...* He trailed off, knowing he didn't need to complete that sentence.

His insinuation was clear—prior to Bune's fall.

Annie laughed abruptly, making my skin crawl.

"What's so funny?" Ronnie asked as she turned to her sister.

A low growl emanated from Cyrus. "The demons took them to the silver wolf pack housing where we were staying when the demon wolves first attacked us."

Of course those soulless creatures would go back to the first place we'd kept Levi. They were taunting us, making sure we were aware that the demon who had escaped the night he'd attempted to set Levi free had come back and shared the location with them. The remote settlement had furnished houses, which made it easier to keep humans captive.

"Then we know where we need to go." Now I was the one moving toward the door.

Someone snagged my arm. My skin tingled.

Levi.

"We don't have a full plan yet. If we're supposed to be handed over, they won't expect Father and me to go willingly. What's the plan?"

Levi didn't remove his hand, and my traitorous body wouldn't put distance between us. It'd been way too long since I'd felt his touch.

"What about the other wolf shifters?" Levi continued, sounding smug. "Are we meeting them there?"

"No," Griffin rasped. "Killian just informed us that a demon is watching the Shadow Ridge wolf neighborhood, and another demon is stationed outside Shadow Terrace, ensuring we don't bring a large number of reinforcements. They had Killian list the number they should expect to leave each location. If more people leave than what the demons approved, they'll turn all the humans."

In theory, if the humans were turned, they would

become something similar to a vampire but worse, since demons had become more tainted with time.

"It's fine." Midnight stood and glanced at each one of us. "I've seen this group in action, and if anyone can take on a horde of demons, I'd bet on us."

Though I was a warrior worthy of that praise, sheer numbers could sometimes defeat even the best. Still, we didn't have many options, and at least we had several fate-blessed warriors in our presence—Sterlyn, Cyrus, Ronnie, and me.

"If we need to limit the number of vehicles, we'll have to take our car"—Sterlyn gestured to Griffin and herself—"and Ronnie and Alex's. It'll be a tight squeeze—"

"I'll fly above the vehicle containing Bune and Levi," I interrupted. "Otherwise, the demons will grow suspicious." Angels flew, and if I deviated from that plan, they would question it.

Alex's brows furrowed. "Wouldn't it be weirder if you weren't in the car with them?"

"She can do more in the air." Bune regarded me. "So she's right. It will look more believable if she flies over us, watching for any sign of us attempting to escape."

A scowl crossed Levi's face. "Should I be worried that you and my father think similarly?" Discomfort wafted between us.

"Son, you didn't have the opportunity to train for battle like I did prior to the fall." Bune waved a hand at me. "And she's Yelahiah's daughter. Being a warrior is in her blood. If you continue to get into situations like this—which I have a feeling will be normal now—you'll begin to think along the same lines."

Sterlyn focused on the task at hand. "Then Darrell, Chad, Bune, and Levi will ride with Griffin and me. That way, Ronnie isn't front and center, since the demons are aware of her."

Alex's shoulders relaxed marginally.

I wanted to warn him that it wouldn't last, but I wisely kept my mouth shut. I didn't need him to get all matey.

I sighed. Sympathy took a lot out of a person. I wasn't sure how my allies had done it the entire time I'd known them. I regretted being so critical of them before.

"I'll be riding with you as well," Cyrus said as he kissed his mate.

Annie's head jerked back. "You aren't going to ride with me in Ronnie and Alex's SUV?"

He bit his bottom lip. "Babe...you're pregnant."

"Not handicapped." Annie placed her hands on her hips and seethed.

We were wasting time. "Annie, he's not saying you aren't a strong wolf but rather that you're carrying very precious cargo that many will covet, especially if the demons figure out that your child will be a combination." I didn't specify a combination of what. Though I *wanted* to trust Levi, I couldn't. He'd proven that not only would he keep things from me, but that he wasn't willing to see things from my perspective. The sad truth was I trusted Bune more than my preordained. Bune had been more forthcoming in his short time here than Levi had during his entire time with us.

You do realize that even though I'm not sure of the combination, I know she's carrying a silver wolf's baby, and she smells faintly of demon. Levi arched a brow. *I'm assuming she's a demon wolf.*

That wasn't my news to share, so I didn't bother to reply.

Annie chuckled as her shoulders sagged. "Rosemary, look at you, being an intermediary."

She had me there. "I didn't mean to interfere." I should've remained quiet. It wasn't my business, but I felt invested in her safety.

"That was meant to be nice." Annie sighed.

"Though it's hard, she's right." Sterlyn stepped beside me, placing a hand on my shoulder. "I agree it would be safer if you and Midnight stayed here. We don't need to risk you going outside the territory line."

Rolling her eyes, Annie scowled. "Fine. I don't like it, and if it weren't for my pregnancy, I'd be there. I don't like staying behind when all of you are at risk. And if you need me—"

"Of course, babe." Cyrus kissed her.

Though I'd have loved to be pregnant, right now, I was thankful I was not. Angels were meant to fight, so even pregnancy wouldn't have been a deterrent for me. But my stomach wasn't as upset now that Annie had agreed to sit out.

"Jeremiah will stay behind and protect Annie and Midnight," Darrell said, bringing us back on topic. "He's on his way inside now."

My wings exploded from my back, the action freeing. I'd kept them pulled in since we'd arrived, not wanting to risk the temptation to take to the sky. Now that they were out, I itched to be in the air with the cool night breeze on my face.

Ronnie opened the front door as Annie kissed Cyrus again.

My heart fractured at them being separated, but it was safest for Annie.

Tucking my wings around me, I marched outside,

heading toward the back. Though the humans were likely out of the area by now, I didn't want to chance any of them seeing me.

I was more than capable of handling things on my own.

Footsteps followed me, and Levi connected, *Hey.*

I didn't break my stride, not wanting him to use the impending battle to manipulate me into succumbing to our bond. I'd already made a mistake by sleeping with him too soon.

His footsteps hurried, but I refused to alter my pace. I didn't want him to think he had any power or influence over me, despite my racing heart. But that treacherous muscle mocked me, excited to have his attention once again.

When he stepped in front of me, I stopped and snapped, "Yes?"

"Be careful," he whispered as he tucked a piece of my hair behind my ear.

The gesture had my eyes burning and a lump swelling in my throat. He didn't get to be sweet when I was still mad at him. That wasn't how this worked.

The walls around my heart shook, ready to shatter. When I'd listened to it last time, Levi had stolen a larger piece of the stupid organ. But I couldn't deny I loved him. "You, too." I wished I could do a flyover of the area, but they'd expect that. I'd have to play along until we couldn't.

I pivoted around him before I couldn't walk away. My legs felt like lead. I didn't want to even pretend we were handing him over, but there wasn't a better alternative.

With each step, my heart ached more.

"Rosey, if things don't end well, just know I *fucking* love you," he murmured.

Somehow, the inflection of his words made them mean so much more. Even though I'd die before I let the demons take him or Bune, tomorrow was never guaranteed. I stopped and faced him again, needing him to know that despite it all, he still *owned* me. "I love you, too. I just wish that were enough."

I spun on my heels and rushed to the woods, passing a wide-eyed Jeremiah. He'd heard the entire exchange, but that wasn't my problem. That was what he got for being a shifter.

As soon as I stepped into the tree line, the fall leaves hid me from the human eye. I spread my wings open, and after making my way farther into the thickening trees, I took to the sky.

Twilight descended, and I hated that I'd missed the sunset. Sunrise and sunset were my favorite times to fly, when the colors of the sky were at their most transformative. Raccoons and flying squirrels scurried below sleepily, just waking to begin their night. An owl hooted in the distance as if warning me to stay away.

The cool November breeze caressed my skin, but it couldn't dampen the fiery pain of heat roiling inside me from that moment with Levi. I had to push it away to focus on the inevitable fight ahead.

I scanned the area for any person I didn't recognize or a shadow form that could be using the darkness to hide. Knowing that not all of them would have red eyes, I searched for anything that could even resemble an iris.

Not seeing anything, I hovered half a mile away from the bridge—the territory line—and waited for the others to reach me. I wanted to ensure that the demons would see me flying close to the car, proving that Levi and Bune were inside.

Soon, the Navigator and Mercedes SUV pulled underneath me, and I flew low and close, following them along the road that led to the silver wolves' former secondary location.

Before long, we were pulling onto the familiar road and approached the houses.

As I surveyed the area, I soon found what I was hunting for—Killian's pack and the witches. And the situation was worse than I'd imagined.

CHAPTER TWENTY-ONE

AT LEAST FIFTY demons in shadow form hovered in the opening of the neighborhood pack housing. They were spread out evenly on both sides of the makeshift road, their red eyes focused on us. They weren't paying attention to the four silver wolves and the eight witches who had formed a circle around Sierra and Killian. Our friends stood underneath the demons on the road that trailed down the center of the neighborhood.

In wolf form, the four silver wolves hunkered close to the ground in front of the circle, closest to us. They were half their largest size due to the half moon. The light of the rising moon reflected off their fur, emphasizing exactly what type of wolves they were.

Circe stood at the very back of the circle. Her rich brown eyes locked on me as a faint breeze lifted pieces of her midnight hair, which had fallen out of her bun, and whipped it against her face. Though her expression was stoic, her normally warm beige complexion seemed pale, informing me of her anxiety. Her location in the group indicated she was ready to use magic.

On her right was her daughter, Aurora, who was only a couple years older than Sterlyn. She wore a sky blue shirt, a color she seemed to favor, and her bronze hair cascaded over her shoulders. She looked at the moon, and the light reflected in her chestnut eyes.

Positioned between Aurora—his daughter—and one of the younger witches, Kamila, Aspen showed his tension through his twitching jaw, the ivory skin of his face stretched thin. His jet-black hair was almost the same shade as the shadows.

Kamila's inky irises flicked to her mother, Cordelia, who stood across the circle from her. Kamila's curly, dark brown hair was a little wild, like she'd been running her fingers through it, and her brown complexion glowed as if the moon were lending power to her.

Every time her daughter glanced at her, Cordelia's scowl deepened, making her look older than her forties. The golden warmth in her brown complexion had vanished, and her very curly midnight hair was bunched together more than usual, hanging above her shoulders. Her charcoal irises took in everything, and there was no doubt she was looking for an escape.

Eliphas placed a hand on Cordelia's shoulder as if to restrain his wife from going to their daughter. He was taller than me, and his slate eyes narrowed as he scanned the air for demons. Though the witches couldn't *see* the demons, they could feel their vile energy and could fight them without needing assistance from an angel descendant.

Waist-long ruby hair blew behind Herne, reminding me of a cape from some stupid show Sierra had made me watch. Herne was the second strongest witch of the coven and stood on the other side of Circe and next to her daughter, Lux. She projected a fierceness I'd admired even before my emotions had come into play. Her onyx eyes met mine, waiting for a sign.

But I had nothing to give yet.

Be careful, Lux mouthed, her arctic-blue eyes wise beyond her nineteen years. Her hair was a darker shade than her mother's, reminding me of the color of a deep, crisp red wine.

She didn't have to tell me that. I knew we were in trouble. The negative energy coating my skin made it hard to flap my wings.

This was how I'd felt when I'd fought the demons at the portal near the demon wolf pack settlement, and after a short time, I would adjust. The vileness would still make me uncomfortable, but I'd be able to move more easily, similar to jumping into cold water. At first, the cold overwhelmed you, but then your body acclimated.

Then I could kill each one of these abominations. Taking these few out wouldn't impact their numbers overall, but there'd be fewer embodiments of evil swirling around the universe.

From the demons I could see, their numbers easily doubled our own, and more could be lurking in the woods. Wherever the humans were, there'd be a few demons with them as well.

Griffin idled in the Navigator, and Alex stopped right behind him.

This was it. The ultimate battle. Now we had to be smarter than the demons.

Wanting to handle them, I landed in front of the Navigator about thirty feet away from the four closest demons.

Stay inside, I connected with Levi.

Displeasure wafted from him. *You expect me to just let you stand out there alone, facing at least fifty demons? Hell, no.*

He was letting his emotions get the best of him, which I understood all too well. We had to remain pragmatic; otherwise, none of us would leave here alive. Though their numbers were greater than ours, we had witches, and powerful ones at that. They should give us an advantage, even if it was temporary.

As soon as you step out, they'll attack. We needed to buy time and see if we could get a better sense of their numbers. If I had to guess, at least twenty-five were hidden, hoping to catch us off guard. That was what I would do.

This gave him pause. *Fine, but Griffin's rolling the window down so we can hear everything. One sign that they're about to do something, and my ass is out there.*

Some of my anger toward him thawed. Damn it.

I can take care of myself. I was a warrior. His words of concern shouldn't have warmed my heart but rather pissed me off. My affection toward him had to be from the adrenaline coursing through me, preparing me for war. It could make your mind do asinine things.

The closest demon to the right tilted its head. "You're here to make a trade, we were told." Her voice was strong and confident. Though she wasn't close to being an archangel, there was something warriorlike about her stance that I could detect even in her shadow form.

Rosemary, you need to be careful, Levi warned, his dread sitting hard on my stomach. *These are some of the demons that normally don't walk on Earth because they're high in the hierarchy.*

But that shouldn't have been possible. *How are they here?*

They aren't necessarily strong power-wise, but they've trained their entire lives for battle, he explained. *They're always preparing for war. She's as inner-circle as you can get without having enough power to alert the angels you're on Earth. The princes of Hell have kept her close, waiting for the time when her skills would be needed.*

And now they were. The princes had sent someone they'd trusted and groomed for a war with the angels.

"I swear, it's like nothing is there," Sierra growled. "Then a damn voice comes out of the *fucking* sky. It's horror movie–level creepy. They're cowards, needing to hide from us. They know they can't take us all in their ugly-ass human forms."

The mouthy blonde was going to start a fight before I was ready. Now would be a good time for Killian to tell her to hush. She needed to learn that sometimes, silence was the best course of action. In tense situations like this, she always became louder and way more obnoxious.

"You'll *experience* a horror show if you don't shut your mouth," the demon closest to me on my left rasped. "We aren't stupid and won't fall for your childish antics. We're most comfortable on Earth in our shadow forms."

Maybe Sierra's loudness wasn't all that bad. At least she'd gotten us more insight into the demons. *Is that true?*

Yes, because in Hell, we stay in our shadow form most of the time. We recognize each other's essence, but the demons that stay on Earth favor their human form to blend in since they spend most of their time here. Levi sighed. *They transition when they need to fly.*

I wasn't sure if *fly* was the right word for it. It was more like inching or gliding, but they did ascend into the sky. However, I bit my tongue so I wouldn't correct him.

I realized I didn't just cater to my friends but to *him,*

too. I'd deal with that later. I had enough to handle and didn't need to keep piling on the offenses. *Then why were you in human form?*

I thought it was so I wouldn't appear as threatening to you, but I'm not sure that was it. He hesitated. *I think it's because I didn't want to show you I was your enemy. It was bad enough that you could sense we were on opposite sides even when I was in human form.*

Like me, he must have felt our preordained connection from the very beginning.

"Where are the humans?" I asked the demons, and arched my brow. They had kept only our friends out here, likely so that the majority of the demons could keep an eye on them. If a smaller number of demons had been watching them, as I assumed were watching the humans, our friends would have had a better chance at getting away. Putting them front and center not only kept them in the demons' sight but could also make us act irrationally.

I refused to play into their hands.

Damn *demons*.

"I'm sure they're around *somewhere*." The demon warrior chuckled. Her red eyes glowed, as she clearly enjoyed the moment and the control she had over the situation. "They're humans, so who cares?" She lifted a shadowy hand. "Oh, *you* do."

The guy on the left snorted. "An angel. Oh, how the mighty have *fallen*."

More hatred spewed from them than from the demons we'd faced before. It seemed personal. *Who are these two?*

Hecate is the female. She's one of the princes' main lovers, and though not an archangel, she was front and center and fell alongside them. She hates angels as much as the princes do, Levi explained. I realized this was the most we'd talked in days, but I couldn't keep freezing him out here. Not speaking to him would put us more at risk. *The man beside her is her brother, Pyro. He wasn't there for the fall, but he and Hecate have always been close. He's her right-hand man.*

She must have trained him. Without the angel and demon swords in hand, strength and training were incredibly important. By stripping both angels and demons of angelic weapons, everyone essentially became equal, which was why, when they won the civil war within Shadow City, the other supernatural races had demanded that the angels give up their weapons. I'd known that—I just hadn't known that the angels' weapons had been sent to Hell.

I kept my face even. I didn't need them to determine what made me tick, but I wanted to keep up the idea that I was the typical angel they'd expected—one like Azbogah. "Are we going to continue with the witless banter or actually discuss items of substance?" I hated jokes obviously meant to provoke. He wanted to anger me and get me to declare that I had not fallen.

But the truth was, I had.

Everything about me had changed. The high moral ground I'd once flown over had been decimated. I'd judged others for *feeling* and not being *logical*, and I'd discredited them because *I didn't* understand.

Levi had been right to call me judgmental. I'd thought the worst of everyone, including my friends when times were rough, wanting them to get past their emotions and carry on.

And now I was right there with them, and despite all the heartache and pain, I wouldn't change a thing.

I'd been cruel, though not intentionally, and I'd discounted their intuition when I should've listened more.

Falling in love and feeling emotions weren't the worst things that could have happened as long as I kept my heart and my sense of right and wrong.

"Didn't you hear me, angel?" Pyro asked, sounding disappointed. "I said, you've *fallen*."

Hecate huffed. "It was marginally funny the first time, but not now. Cut it out."

"It wasn't funny at all the first time," Sierra mumbled. "And I like jokes at people's expense."

"You should be quiet," Kamila murmured, but everyone could hear her.

Hecate turned to Sierra and said, "You should listen to the *witch*. She's obviously smarter than you."

Dear gods. Sierra wouldn't let that go. Not responding would be equivalent to her not breathing air. She'd die. Unfortunately, in this situation, if she kept speaking, it truly could result in her death, and I'd have to step in before that happened.

"There are multiple types of smarts." Sierra flipped her sandy blonde ponytail like it was a weapon. Her gaze searched the area where the demons hovered but never settled anywhere, as she couldn't see them. "The intellectual kind, the street kind, and the witty banter kind—which, for the record, is my specialty. Then there's a version of *smart*"—she used air quotes—"that isn't intelligent. It's where a person goes for the blatant jokes that are just out there, like Annie, bare ass in the back of Alex's SUV, searching for blood bags to feed a dying vampire."

Though I was clueless, I didn't ask questions. However, I was darn certain I'd be learning about the story all the same, assuming we all got out of this alive.

Cyrus's low growl came from the back of the Navigator. "She needs to *stop*."

Closing his dark chocolate eyes, Killian pinched the bridge of his nose and ran his free hand through his short dark hair. He sighed and deadpanned, "Sierra, that's not funny."

Why was he encouraging her? This was definitely not the time to humor her delusions and enable her crazy.

I've missed the snarky mutt, Levi linked, and his humor flowed into me.

Levi had lost his mind as well. *She's going to get herself hurt.*

She's riling them up so they won't think rationally, he replied. *Like Pyro was attempting to do with you. However, he has an ego no one can contend with.*

And I don't? He'd always seized the opportunity to take a cheap shot about my heritage.

Something heavy settled on my heart, and I realized it was from him. *At first, yes. But not now.*

My chest lightened, and I realized his approval meant more to me than I wanted to admit.

"That's my point," Sierra said, bringing me back to the present. "It wasn't funny because Alex was dying, which is similar to how that demon's horrible joke was—equivalent to someone croaking. And here I thought demons would have a good sense of humor."

"You stupid *bitch*," Pyro bellowed.

Sierra threw her hands up. "Now we're down to dog jokes." She glanced at me and darted her eyes to the side. "See, Rosemary. It's not just most angels—it's demons, too."

"Do *not* compare me to them," Pyro seethed.

She winced, then cleared her throat, her cocky appearance slipping right back into place. "You were one of them. Right?"

"I'm going to kill you!" he shouted.

Out of the corner of my eye, I saw three demons fly upward from the finished house Sierra had glanced at, situated a row down from where we stood. Their gazes landed on me, but I pretended not to notice. The one thing I did note was that their eyes weren't red but various shades of brown.

Pyro jerked toward Sierra, and my friend had no clue. She stood there, her forehead lined, which wasn't normal. She *was* nervous, but as Levi had said, she was trying to help us.

Hecate's shadow arm appeared and must have grabbed her brother's because he stopped moving. She spoke loudly, "We are *not* attacking. Remember, we're here to make a trade."

The three demons that had appeared dropped back behind the house. But that had given me an idea of where most of the other demons were. Not all of them, but if there were three undecided, there had to be a few evil demons with them to ensure they stayed in line.

Sierra was smarter than I'd given her credit for. Again, the reminder of how narrow-minded I'd been slammed into me.

I could feel sorry another time. Right now, my mind had to be battle-focused.

It's time. Are you and the others ready? I asked, and nearly choked. With almost everyone I loved about to go into yet another battle where we'd be grossly outnumbered, my lungs stopped working. And Levi's presence made my anxiety worse.

My blood ran cold. I hadn't considered that they would

strike at him first. That had to be why Hecate was here—to ensure the sword was freed of their connection as quickly as possible so a prince of Hell could step in and bond with it.

Wait! I connected, but the door had already opened.

Hecate drew a knife from her side, confirming my fears.

CHAPTER TWENTY-TWO

I COULDN'T BELIEVE I'd been this stupid. We'd walked right into the trap they'd planned, and I hadn't even considered the possibility they'd try to kill Levi at the first opportunity.

Mother *plucker*! Of course they would. That was the exact strategy I would use in their position, and I'd let my emotions about my friends being in danger and wanting to stay away from Levi had distracted me.

This was what I criticized everyone else for, and here I was, having to eat my words.

I flew toward the opened door as Levi placed his foot on the ground, and I slammed the door against his leg.

"What the...?" Levi sounded shocked, and then he pushed against the door. *That* hurts. *What are you doing?*

Better a bruised or broken leg than a knife in your chest. I spun so my back was against the Navigator and spread my wings out wide behind me. *The princes sent one of their most trusted and trained lovers. Why do you think she's here?*

My body tensed more, and it wasn't because of me. It

was Levi's emotions running through me. He linked, *To kill me so they can get the damn sword.*

Hecate lowered her knife, and I didn't need to see her face to visualize her expression. Her red eyes were like flames, portraying her anger.

Now was when I stopped allowing emotions to affect me...or at least, not enough to affect me during battle.

And this *was* a battle, if not a war.

"I think, in good faith, you should allow a few of our people to go first." I channeled the former Rosemary, needing her to reemerge within me. I'd determined Hecate's plan a moment before she could execute it, but this wasn't over.

She'd try again.

Inform the others in any way you can before they attack. I scanned the area again for any threat I could find. I tapped into my magic, pushing it outward. I hadn't wanted to use my power too soon, but this would require only a little. Knowing that they planned to eliminate Levi immediately, we needed all the information as quickly as possible. I only hoped that even using this little bit of magic didn't fry my butt.

The bulk of the negativity was in front of us, as expected. Opening myself up to that much evil had my blood running colder, the demons' magic instinctively fighting against mine. However, I didn't need to concentrate my magic there, but rather all the way around me.

"You've got to be kidding me." Hecate seethed. She kept her knife in her hand, not bothering to hide it. "You're outnumbered, and not only do I have your friends, but *humans*, too. Of course, I bet none of that matters to *you*. Since you're Yelahiah's"—she said Mother's name as though it were a sickness—"*daughter.*"

"How do you know that?" My blood cooled further, and it had nothing to do with my power seeking out demons and everything to do with how much information they knew about us.

She laughed harshly. "Oh, I have my ways. It wouldn't be fun if I told you my secrets, but let me assure you, I'm *ecstatic* that you're here."

"And should I know who you are?" I couldn't hide my curiosity, and I wanted her to focus her anger on me. Her resentment toward Mother rang clear, but I'd never heard of a Hecate in my long existence. If she was someone of importance, I surely would have heard about her. All I knew was what Levi had told me, and I wanted to understand why she felt so antagonistic toward Mother. It seemed to go beyond her being an angel.

Hecate floated closer to me, the demons surrounding us inching after her. She lifted a hand and commanded, "Stay where you are."

Using the distraction, I pushed my magic out further. I could feel negative energy to the right, where the three undecided had come from, and some hidden in the woods. Though I couldn't count numbers, the vileness was nowhere close to the strength pouring from the demon hovering in front of us.

What are you doing, Rosemary? Levi asked. *You're going to anger her, and then she'll focus her rage on you.*

He acted as if I didn't know that. However, they needed to prepare because this standoff wouldn't continue for much longer. *Focus on making a plan with Sterlyn and the others. There are a handful of demons in the middle of the second row on the right side and a few in the woods to our left and right. Let me know when you're ready to act.*

246 JEN L. GREY

Needing to conserve my energy, I quit pushing out my magic.

Are you serious? His anger was almost palpable. *She's ready to hurt someone, and she's focused on you! What are you planning?*

Just make a plan. That's the only way we're getting out alive. They clearly want to eliminate you before we can react and then take out the rest of us. At least we have some bearings on the location of the demons to coordinate an attack. He'd made it clear that we didn't have to tell each other things that the other person wouldn't like. He'd left for Hell, forcing me to think he had left me behind because I wouldn't want him to go. Well, he wouldn't like me focusing Hecate's rage on myself, but I'd rather fight her than let her attack Levi. She was the most trained demon here, and she had a vendetta. I'd trained for this my entire life. He could kiss my fallen feathers, for all I cared.

Hecate floated toward me, hovering only a few feet away. She tilted her head as she examined me, and I wished I could make out her human features.

"I'm Hecate," she said, her eyes narrowed, watching me. She expected a reaction, but I had no idea what. I genuinely hadn't heard her name until today.

"Okay."

Her hand shook so hard that it was visible even in her shadow form, and though I couldn't see her chest, I could hear her breaths heave.

Despite wanting to know why she held a grudge against Mother, I had to appreciate that my lack of knowledge bothered her more than Levi being in the car behind me. I stepped away from the vehicle, wanting to lead her away from him. "I'm at a loss, so why don't you fill me in?"

"Your *mother* and I were close friends, and she betrayed

me in the worst way." Hecate's voice shook with unbridled rage.

What injustice did Hecate think my mother had served her? I wanted to ask, but that might spiral the situation out of control, and I wanted to get the best information and plan we could before a battle happened.

"Sis," Pyro grunted from several feet back. "We need to stick with the plan."

"Fine." She inched back, but her focus didn't waver from me. "You were trying to barter for your friends like you actually care?"

If she thought I was heartless, I could use that. She wouldn't think using my friends against me would work. "Why do you think I'm here if I don't care?" I arched a brow.

She lowered her head, her red eyes glowing. "Because if you're anything like *her*, you're trying to gain your father's approval. Maybe playing nice with the enemy to gain their trust and spill their secrets."

"My father *approves* of me. I don't need to do anything special to earn his favor." What kind of man did she think Pahaliah was? I'd never known anyone to dislike my father except for Azbogah. Most held him in high esteem, making him an effective broker of peace and mediator between all residents of Shadow City.

"Then that proves you're a heartless *bitch*, just like Azbogah." She lifted the knife, her gaze locked on the sharp tip.

She thought my father was Azbogah. No wonder there was so much hatred. "Pahaliah is my father. Not Azbogah."

Laughter erupted from the demons, catching me off guard. My skin crawled, and my chest tightened.

"You have a decent sense of humor for an angel." Pyro

chuckled as his shadow form jerked from his humor. "I can't believe Azbogah approves of you saying that."

I tensed. They'd left Shadow City before my uncle's death. The city had probably closed before Mother and Azbogah truly split from each other.

"It's the truth," Killian said from the inner circle. His gaze darted around, attempting to see whoever was laughing at my expense. "You'd know if she were lying."

"Wow." Hecate shook her head and straightened. "I never thought there would be a world where those two weren't together, but we've wasted enough time. Give me Levi and Bune."

Our time had run out. *Please tell me you've got something in the works.*

When the opportunity presents itself, the three wolves in the center will run to the humans. The fourth will run to the right with Chad and Cyrus, and Sterlyn, Griffin, and Darrell will run to the left. That will leave you, Ronnie, Father, me, and the witches to take on the group in the center.

I didn't like that plan in the least. *You need to take one of the silver wolves' places. Hecate is determined to kill you so a prince can get the sword. You cannot stay close to any well-trained demons.*

I'm not leaving you, he replied. *She's unhinged and has it out for your family.*

I wasn't sure that was much worse than her naturally hating me because I was an angel. That sort of hatred ran deep, and even though I'd always thought I didn't have feelings, I now knew I'd had negative ones even when I'd been one-dimensional.

If he wouldn't be sensible, I'd make a plan of my own.

I straightened my shoulders. "I need a sign of good faith. At least give me a wolf and a witch to prove you plan on making the trade." She wouldn't want to risk the cars driving off. Though the demons were fast, a vehicle could be used as a weapon.

"Fine. If it will make this go quicker, I'll give you the smart-ass shifter and the young brown-haired witch." She watched me, gauging my expression.

She wanted to see me flustered. She was handing over who she considered to be the two weakest members of the group. Aurora was almost as powerful as her mother, so they must have been cloaking her magic.

I rolled my eyes. "Of course *those* two."

"Hey!" Sierra growled from her spot in the center.

Not even two hours ago, I would've dismissed Sierra as a pain, but she'd helped me get a visual on three demons guarding the humans, and now I knew they were undecided. "Let's make the trade." I'd borrowed all the time the demons would allow, and anything more could put our plan at risk. Not only that, but my skin and feathers had somewhat acclimated to the vileness coating me. I'd be able to fight and fly a little more easily now.

"Let the annoying one pass first," Hecate called out.

"She better not be talking about..." Sierra started, but when Hecate snapped her head in her direction, she stopped and quickly walked between the silver wolves. That path had her walking in the middle of the demons.

When she reached me, Hecate floated back, getting in position. "Now hand over those two, and I'll release the second."

My stomach churned. I didn't want to put Levi at risk, but he would be either way. They wouldn't stop hunting him until he was dead.

Though my legs were heavy, I stepped away from the car. I prepared myself as I studied Hecate. Unlike the first time, she didn't lift her knife, but the tip moved marginally. She was attempting to hide that she was getting ready to throw it. She must have figured out that I'd predicted what she'd do, meaning someone else might attack Levi this time.

Maybe she'd been playing me, too, with the information about my mother. The two of us were attempting to wear the other one down for information.

You'd better be careful. I wouldn't allow Levi to die today. If someone asked, I'd pretend it was due to needing him to stay alive to keep the princes from using the sword, and that was true. But the raw truth was that even if the princes couldn't use the sword, I wouldn't allow it to happen. Though he'd hurt me, I loved him with my entire being.

The door opened, and my instinct was to go back and slam it shut, but they wouldn't allow another stunt like that.

Levi's sweet scent swirled around me, and I could feel him at my back. He stepped out of the car, and Pyro hurled a blade that he'd been hiding.

I jumped in front of Levi, wrapping my wings around my body.

"Rosey!" he exclaimed. His terror slammed into me, but I'd been prepared for that. The dagger bounced off my wings as he cried, "No!"

I spun, wrapped my arms around his waist, and took to the sky. He was heavy, but I'd once flown away carrying a dead bear shifter that Sterlyn had killed. Levi was definitely lighter than him.

Bune morphed into his demon form and flew beside me.

"Get them!" Hecate screamed, and raced after us.

What the hell, Rosey! Levi exclaimed as his body grew lighter. *You could've died. What were you thinking?*

Soon, he was in his shadow form, floating in front of me.

Seeing him like this was odd since he stayed in his human form around me most of the time. However, this was part of him, and I was surprised that being with him like this didn't feel wrong.

You refused to leave me, so I took matters into my own hands. My wings protect me from weapons. I'd made the smartest decision at that moment. I glanced behind me to see ten of the fifty demons chasing us.

We would have to fight them, but we needed to gain more distance first. Right now, we were distracting them so that the others could free the humans, and the witches wouldn't hesitate to use their magic...or I hoped they wouldn't, despite our proximity to Shadow City.

A little warning would have been nice, he growled, unhappy with me.

If he was trying to make me feel bad, it wouldn't happen. *I thought we weren't informing each other of plans that the other wouldn't like.*

The rising half moon shone in his mocha eyes, making them appear almost silver. *Are you seriously trying to prove a point in the middle of this?*

I'm not. We didn't have time to argue. *I made a strategic decision. It was nothing personal.*

Not even the crushed-tea-leaf smell of the fall air brought me comfort. The cloudy sky didn't help to conceal me. I wanted to fly faster, but we couldn't leave the demons and my friends too far behind. We needed to get back there quickly to help the others.

Two demons broke away, getting closer to us than the others. We needed to focus on them and not on our lovers' quarrel. "We have a problem," I said out loud so Bune could be part of the conversation.

"We three need to split up so they'll have to as well."

Bune removed two knives from his pocket that he must have received from the wolves on the way over.

"I hate the suggestion, but we don't have much of a choice." Levi glanced behind us. "I should lead them somewhere while you two get situated to attack them."

That was a horrible plan. "Are you both trained to fight?" I hated to oblige his request, but the demons would be more desperate to kill him than me for their dear *princes*.

"Yes, we're both trained." Bune sighed. "But we should stay close in case we need to help each other."

That was a good plan. I couldn't wander too far from Levi. "That works."

Levi's contentment wafted through me. *I like us being on the same team.* Then he spoke out loud, "Do you see the small clearing next to the spring running through there?"

I scanned the ground below us. The trickling stream had a slight embankment on each side. There were more bushes at the edge before the trees thickened again. "Yes."

"Let's stay near that." Levi lowered himself, heading toward the water. "We can split up, but stay within a half-mile radius."

Splitting up was our best option since the demons would have to as well to keep eyes on us.

Bune handed me one of his knives, but I shook my head. "You'll need it. I have my wings."

He nodded, and my heart warmed that he'd offered me his only means of protection. He handed the other knife to Levi.

Be safe, Rosey. Levi groaned next to me. *I love you.*

Heart constricting, I replied, *I love you, too.* He knew, and though I was determined for us to make it out alive, it wasn't guaranteed. I *needed* him to hear how I felt in case I didn't survive.

"Let's go," Bune said.

The three of us flew in different directions, and after a quarter of a mile, I slowed, watching to ensure the other two continued to fly in their designated directions. With my long wings, I didn't have to get as close to behead the demons, so it would be best if more than three followed me.

I lowered myself near the water, staying out in the open.

Even before my feet touched the ground, I heard one yell, "There!"

I glanced skyward to see five of the ten heading straight for me. Two pulled out long swords.

If I showed fear, they'd be more confident. I needed to prove to them I wasn't scared, so I flipped my wings over... and charged right at them.

CHAPTER TWENTY-THREE

THE TWO DEMONS with the swords didn't hesitate as I descended upon them. The three without weapons stopped a few feet behind them, hovering in the air, unsure.

Their actions told me everything...or what they wanted me to think. They weren't confident in their fighting abilities, suggesting the two sword wielders were the best fighters, and once I took them out, the others should be easy.

That was what I hoped.

I'd have to keep an eye on the three of them. I couldn't completely discount them; the wary would either become frantic and run *or* take a cheap shot while I was preoccupied.

A warrior knew to keep their eye on every threat, even the ones that appeared inept in battle.

The demon on the left lifted his sword high and swirled it over his head. He laughed deeply as he lurched toward me.

Swirly Demon had no clue what he was doing, and I was a little disappointed. I'd expected a worthy adversary, and this was what I got.

Not wanting to waste time allowing a demon to grandstand, I barreled toward him, my wings pumping me higher into the sky. Just as I reached the top of the nearest cypress, Swirly and I met.

He swung the sword at my neck, and I stilled my wings and dropped. The sword *whooshed* over my head, and I flew upward again.

Pushing myself hard, I flew in front of him before he regained control of his sword. It took more energy to control a wild weapon than it did to hit your mark, so I had a few seconds before he could reset for another attack.

I flipped my feathers to the sharp side and spun. Swirly's eyes widened a second before my wings beheaded him. Blue blood coated my feathers, and I forced my face to remain neutral. I didn't want anyone to assume that the demon's death bothered me because it didn't. Rather, the thick blue blood made flying more challenging and was disgusting.

Focusing, I watched as his head fell from his body. The rest of his shadow stayed elevated for a moment since his body hadn't caught up. I paused my wings and dropped enough to grasp the blade of the sword. As soon as I grabbed it, his body sagged. Unfortunately, his hold on the handle hadn't slackened, and the weight of his body caused the sharp edge to cut into my fingers.

With my free hand, I peeled the offending shadow hand from the sword, ignoring the pain shooting through my fingers and the stench of my blood.

Levi connected, his alarm running through me. *Rosey, I'm coming.*

Oh, he needed to go pluck himself. *Stay focused on your fight. I'm fine.* The last thing I needed was for him to get hurt. Then we'd both be in a panic, giving the demons more of an edge.

But something is wrong, he argued.

Right when I thought that I wouldn't be able to free the sword before my fingers were severed, I pried the demon's hand from the handle, and his body tumbled to the ground.

Thank the gods.

We're in a battle. Of course I might get hurt. I tried to be understanding, but I wanted to focus solely on my fight. *I'll let you know if I need you. I promise. Just do the same for me.*

With my uninjured hand, I grasped the handle and released the blade. Once my fingers were free, the intense pain was worse than when the blade had sliced into them. My breath caught, and I tried to contain my agony so I wouldn't alarm Levi even more.

Fine, Levi replied eventually. *But I swear, if something happens and you don't tell me—*

I will, I replied.

Something on my left came closer, and moonlight glinted off a blade to my side.

The demon was attempting a sneak attack on me, and if I hadn't had warrior instincts, I would've been dead.

I swung the sword, and the blades clanged loudly in my ears. I pushed against the sword. The demon hadn't expected me to block him. He grunted loudly and retreated far enough that my blade couldn't reach him.

Glancing at my chest, the demon swung his sword at my side. He was holding back, the blade not moving as quickly as when he'd attacked me while I'd been distracted.

He was attempting to trick me, expecting me to panic and protect my flank so he could then pierce me in the stomach or chest. If I didn't block, he'd follow through on my side. Either way, he expected to injure me in some way.

But he was greatly underestimating me. I pretended I was going to block him with my sword. He should've seen my hesitation, but he was too arrogant. He shifted his attack, as I'd expected, and aimed for my chest.

I'd expected that target because he'd glanced there before pretending to go for my side. I flew back to give myself more time to get my sword in front of my chest.

His head tilted back in surprise, and he overcorrected, aiming higher for my neck. My feathers were stuck together from the blood, but I managed to shift them and roll to the right. His knife sliced only air, and I jammed the blade into the shadow's stomach.

A pained wheeze left him as I yanked the sword out of his body.

The only way to kill a fallen demon was by beheading it.

Dark blue blood poured from his stomach, and the demon hissed, "Attack her *now*."

Realizing he could die by my hands, he was calling in reinforcements.

Not wanting to allow the illusion that he could make it out alive, I smirked. "There's no hope for you." Using his friend's sword, I beheaded the demon. His red eyes dimmed as his body and head fell below.

A demon from above muttered, "Uh..." His voice sounded deep and unsure.

Turning toward the three of them, I laughed as I watched them glance at one another. Obviously, not every demon here felt comfortable fighting.

I flew to the cypress beside me and wiped the blade on

the closest branch. I got the excess blood off so it didn't drip as I wielded it, but a few scales of bark stuck to the blade.

Wanting to make the three of them more nervous, I took my time. I wanted to see how they would react, especially if they feared me.

Thankfully, no pain resonated from Levi. Even though I'd grown exasperated with him, if I'd felt something off on his end of our bond, I would've been just as concerned. These abominations were here to kill him, and a momentary distraction was all they needed to succeed.

The demon furthest on the right grew longer—standing, I assumed—and removed a dagger from his pocket, the blade side crooked.

Seeing the weapon made my stomach sick. Straight or jagged blades were awful, but crooked ones hurt worse going in, shredding the area around the wound.

An angel named Eleanor had cut me during training. She'd been one of the few female angels in my training class and had been subpar, at best, compared to me. She'd sneaked in a cheap attack when we'd been picking sparring partners and stabbed me in the side. She'd grinned after-ward, and then I'd taught her a lesson. However, it was one of the most painful injuries I'd received during my entire training.

The other two pulled out their weapons more hesi-tantly. The one on the left produced a short sword that was slightly longer than a dagger, while the one in the middle drew a regular dagger.

The three of them glanced at one another as if trying to coordinate an attack. That was a good strategy, and if Levi, Bune, and I hadn't been outnumbered, I'd have employed the same tactic.

Maybe they weren't as unprepared as I'd thought, just hesitant to fight. I forced a yawn, wanting them to think they didn't affect me at all.

The truth was, I wanted to find Levi. I hated being apart from him, but my strategy of drawing the most demons to me had succeeded. Once I killed these three, I'd search for him and ensure he was safe.

My hand still ached from where the blade had cut me, but I didn't want to use magic to heal myself. There was no telling who I might need to heal later. Every time we fought demons, we wound up with casualties, and I refused to drain myself over a hand that could easily heal on its own. I wasn't risking anything extra for comfort.

The three demons hadn't moved, and they'd given me time to derail myself with thoughts. I wanted them to attack, but we could be here all night if I didn't take matters into my own hands.

I flew toward them, and Small Sword's eyes narrowed a little...like he was smiling.

These three were attempting to fool me into thinking they weren't skilled. My trainer's words echoed in my head: *Never underestimate your opponent, and look for signs of trickery.* I hadn't done that with Eleanor, and I had learned my lesson.

Not wanting to rush and make an error in judgment, I hovered ten feet away. My wings flapped, keeping me in place as I examined each of them again. They wanted me to get close. Regular Dagger was eyeing my left side, while Small Sword's attention kept landing on my neck. Crooked Sword glanced everywhere but at my heart. They were each timing the kill, banking on at least one of them to land.

I couldn't let on that I was privy to their plan. My hand

tightened on the sword as I readied to attack. If I didn't time each move perfectly, I could easily be the next casualty.

Crooked Dagger marginally tipped his dagger toward me, and that had to be their signal.

As expected, the three of them charged forward, going for the suspected targets. I plunged about ten feet, and the three of them stopped short and looked down at me.

I had to move quickly before they attacked in unison.

Flapping my wings hard, I propelled myself upward just as Crooked Dagger pivoted toward me. I slashed at the hand holding the dagger, and the weapon tumbled. A strangled cry left him as he held up his bloody hand.

Regular Dagger floated downward, now only a foot above my head. Using the opportunity, I lifted the sword, slicing into his shadowy legs.

He groaned and jerked away from me, and Short Sword raised his sword over his head, barreling toward me. I spun, shifting my wings to propel myself to the left while slashing Crooked Dagger's throat.

A choking whimper came from Regular Dagger, and Short Sword jerked upward to see what was happening.

That was one of the worst things someone could do. If a warrior was engaged in battle, they should stay focused on their own fight until they were safe.

Short Sword was *definitely* not safe.

Using his distraction, I turned toward him.

His red irises homed in on me as my blade slashed through his neck. The sword was sharp, even after beheading others, and cut through bone without issue.

One second...one moment of distraction was all I'd needed to finish him off.

The wind changed directions, splattering his blood all

over my face and in my eyes. Bile churned in my stomach as the cloying, metallic smell filled my mouth. How vampires could ever crave something like *this* was beyond me. Though they never drank from demons or angels, blood was blood.

I moved several feet to the right, needing to get out of the splatter zone and prevent Regular Blade from attacking me easily. I blinked, but the blood stayed in my eyes, making me want to claw them out.

With my injured hand, I clutched the hem of my shirt, and my hand burned as if it were on fire. Though it hurt, I would take this agony over a fiery explosion and Levi leaving me any day. I could ignore this type of torment for the most part, and I had to get the disgusting blood out of my eyes.

Though I hated to use it, I tapped into my magic, needing to sense the location of the lone demon that was still alive and a threat.

As I wiped my eyes, I felt the negative energy retreating.

Yanking my shirt back into place, my gaze locked on Regular Blade's retreating figure. It bothered me that the buffoon thought I would allow him to flee. No soldier would allow an enemy with every intention of killing their loved ones to escape.

Though it was unangelic, I spat, desperate to get the blood out of my mouth. I'd need a shower, a toothbrush, and an antiseptic as soon as we arrived back at the house. The sooner I killed our nemesis, the quicker I could achieve that goal.

Letting desire fuel me, I sped after the demon. I had to be sure he wasn't leading me into a trap, though I doubted they'd had time to make a contingency plan. However, caution was my friend.

The demon's glowing red eyes glanced over his shoulder, and they widened when he realized I was chasing him and gaining ground. His leg injury was impeding his speed.

Suddenly, discomfort churned inside me, and I immediately knew it wasn't my own.

Levi.

I opened our connection to check on him, realizing I'd scolded him for doing the same thing. If I connected while he was in battle, I'd distract him.

My breathing quickened as desperation pumped blood through my veins. I had to finish this so I could get to Levi. I couldn't leave this *demon* alive—he would again attempt to kill me or someone I loved. He was only running because he was injured and had seen what I was capable of.

Though blood crusted my feathers, I pumped my wings faster. I hated that the blood slowed me down, albeit slightly, but any impairment of my normal abilities infuriated me. Our wings were our greatest weapons and the main reason angels were strong adversaries even when we had no blades or guns.

With only ten feet between us, he groaned from the exertion and blood loss. Blood trailed below him, and even if he hid, I could easily find him.

Growling, he spun toward me. He was desperate and realized this was his last chance to survive.

Never underestimate an individual's drive to live. Desperate people were the most dangerous.

Slashing haphazardly in front of him, he charged me, using a random pattern so I wouldn't know which direction he'd slash next.

He'd missed one crucial piece of the puzzle—I had my wings to protect me.

Turning so my wings faced him, I took the blows as he slashed my feathers, but I had them pulled in tight, forming a protective barrier. When he attempted to stab me a second time, I lifted the sword over my shoulder and stabbed him in the arm holding the dagger.

A stifled scream left him, but I needed him to die.

I had to check on Levi.

As I removed the sword from his arm, I used my wings to behead him. As soon as my wing had sliced all the way through, I focused on Levi and my bond, being sure not to connect with it. The yank would lead me to him.

Following the *tug*, I surveyed the area for threats or anything out of the ordinary.

At this moment, it was like any other November night with a cloudless sky and a cool breeze brushing across me. The smell of fall hung heavy in the air, despite the stench of blood that covered me.

Soon, I was back at the stream where the three of us had split. I continued north, following the *yank*.

The discomfort from our bond strengthened into one of pain.

Something was definitely wrong.

I pushed myself harder, flying over thickening trees. My pulse grew frantic as I desperately searched for the man I loved.

A small break in the trees came into view, and the *tug* strengthened as if I had almost reached him. As I drew closer, I saw a demon holding Levi against a tree trunk on the ground and another demon floating in front of them with a flail. She held the large handle upward, the steel chain connected to a spiked steel ball.

She hit him with the weapon, and pain surged through the bond again.

My blood boiled as I flew faster than I ever had in my life.

Anyone who hurt my mate had to *die*.

CHAPTER TWENTY-FOUR

DESPITE MY SPEED, time slowed. I watched helplessly as the demon struck my mate with the spiky ball once more. She laughed, enjoying the pain she was inflicting. Just like the princes of Hell when they'd beaten Levi to the point of death, they wanted him to die slowly.

Pain slammed into me, and I could only imagine how much more intense it felt on his end. His agony made my lungs contract and fueled me to push harder.

The imbecile hadn't informed me that he was in trouble. If he died because he'd been too stubborn to tell me, I'd find a way to bring him back to life so I could kill him myself.

His attention landed on me. *It's Hecate and Pyro. She wants to kill you, too. You need to go to Sterlyn and get more people to fight alongside you.*

He was a buffoon for thinking I'd leave him behind. I didn't fear my death but rather his. *Not happening. She'll kill you, and I won't allow that to happen.* I couldn't endure losing him. I loved him, for better or worse, and I'd rather have a world where he was alive, even if we weren't together, than one where I could never see his face or hear his voice again.

I was in deep with him, and there was nothing I could or wanted to do about it.

The demon with the flail noted Levi's distraction and turned to me, her eyes glowing brighter. "Oh, look. The angel found us. I can kill you both at the same time," Hecate crooned.

I stopped several feet away, hovering in the air, and fluffed my feathers, wanting her to think I was attempting to intimidate her. Her thinking I was like all the other angels would bode well for me.

A month ago, she could have rightfully assumed I was overconfident like Azbogah and so many others, but that had drastically changed now that I had Levi. He'd opened my eyes to my biases and, albeit grudgingly, to emotions. But I wouldn't change a thing because I never would've felt either the extreme happiness or torment that only a preordained mate could put me through.

"I'm assuming there's a reason he's not dead," I said, devoid of emotion.

She bobbed her head and twirled her weapon. "I was taking my time, letting him feel the pain of betraying his people, and I was hoping you'd find us since you don't want us to gain access to the demon sword."

"I told you we should get on with it," Pyro said gruffly. "Now *she's* here."

Hurting my mate was her form of entertainment. I shouldn't have been surprised, but that informed me she had no clue he was my preordained.

The demon flicked what had to be her wrist; it was hard to tell in her shadow form. "Fine. Go ahead and kill him. The princes still aren't happy with your performance. That should raise your stock in their eyes. And *I'll* take Yelahiah's daughter. It's only fitting that I take her child away from her like she did mine."

My body stiffened. I had no clue what she was rambling about.

"Gladly," Pyro chuckled. "Make sure you get an extra stab in before you kill her for me. Even if Azbogah isn't her father, she's the closest we'll get to him for now."

All this resentment toward Azbogah hinted that there was more going on than I realized. He'd brokered the deal between the demons and angels, but it hadn't been on equal terms. If we were dealing with history repeating itself in regard to the dark angel, I could somewhat understand how the demons felt about him...about us. He was manipulating his own people in Shadow City to gain a say over all things angelic and attempting to eliminate the one thing in his way —Mother. If he'd betrayed the demons and the angels had backed him, the demons had a right to resent *all* of us.

Knowing that time was ticking, I darted past Hecate and swung my sword at Pyro's neck. Pyro loosened his hold on Levi and stepped backward, attempting to get out of range.

He wasn't quicker than my sword.

"Not so fast," Hecate rasped, and her hand grabbed my arm holding the sword. Luckily, I had an ironclad grasp on the handle, and the sword didn't drop. Instead, my wrist snapped, and sharp pain shot into my hand and up my arm.

Hecate had waited too long to restrain me, and Levi rushed at her, commanding, "Let her go."

Her hold didn't slacken, but her head turned toward the incoming threat. The hand holding the weapon moved upward, indicating she planned to use it against Levi. I swung my legs forward, kicking her in the stomach.

"*Ugh*," she grunted, and jerked backward. Since her grasp on me didn't loosen, my body also lurched forward.

Using my wings, I stopped my forward movement, but that pulled her upright as well.

Pyro surged toward Levi. The demon pulled out a sickle, reminding me of a demon I'd fought before.

Fight Pyro, I connected. *I'll take Hecate.* Even if we tried to switch, the woman was intent on killing me.

What? No! Levi ducked an instant before the sickle swished through the air where his head had been.

These demons were truly ruthless. They weren't going for kill strikes but rather painful injuries that would force anyone to hope that death was imminent.

Hecate flung her weapon at me, the chain whirling as the spiky ball sailed at my face. Twisting, I wrapped my wings around my body. The sharp feathers slashed through her skin as the spiky ball bounced off.

Levi's panic quickened my heartbeat. We were too focused on each other.

We have to focus on one opponent each, or we'll both die. The best way to make it out of this is to trust the other to hold their own in a fight. That was hard for me to do. I didn't truly know Levi's training, but these two were clearly trained and enjoyed doling out pain. They were the worst kind of fighters anyone could go up against.

Most angels didn't mind fighting, but we didn't seek it out. We battled out of necessity, for a cause, not for enjoyment. These demons had a cause, but that wasn't the only reason they were here. They enjoyed torture.

Hecate moaned as we crumpled to the ground. She released her hold on my wrist and attempted to untangle herself from my feathers. Her blue blood trickled below us, and I dug my feathers in deeper, wanting to ruin her arm as much as possible. My next goal would be to destroy her other arm if I couldn't sever her neck easily.

Fine, but only if we vow to be honest with each other if we need help, Levi connected. His displeasure washed over me, weighing down my body.

Though my gut said to disagree, he was right. That was how a healthy partnership should be. I couldn't continue to expect to do it all if I wanted him to feel valued. We both had to give. *Promise.*

Me, too. He sighed and took off toward Pyro, wincing from his injury as he removed his knife from its scabbard.

My limbs lightened. He hadn't lost his weapon. Though a larger weapon would have been more convenient, his knife was better than nothing.

Hecate kicked between my legs, taking a cheap shot. I'd been expecting it, and at this speed, we were getting dangerously close to the ground. I opened my wings, letting her drop as I flapped hard, shooting toward the treetops.

Dirt flew from her feet hitting the ground, but before her entire body could slam down, she inched back up toward me.

I gritted my teeth. I'd hoped that her body would make impact, leaving her stunned. She would still be hurt, but not to the degree I'd desired.

Taking the slight reprieve, I glanced over to find Levi blocking a blow from Pyro's scythe. He used his free hand to punch the demon in the face, making me feel more confident in his fighting abilities. Other than him taking that fatal hit for me, I'd never seen him in action until now.

Focusing back on Hecate, I prepared myself for the onslaught. She probably fought similarly to me and wasn't used to anyone else having the upper hand. Her irises were so bright red that they were almost blinding. Clearly, her rage and hatred amplified the color.

She swirled her flail over her head and screamed. Though anyone else would have found her intimidating, I was certain that wasn't her intent. That was just how angry she was.

Anger was both good and bad. The adrenaline would give her an edge against pain, but it could make her more irrational. This was why emotions had to be kept in check when at war. Personal vendettas could easily get someone killed.

I scanned my surroundings and moved in front of a large oak. Some of the orange, red, and yellow leaves had fallen, making it easier to access the trunk.

My plan was in place, but I had to wait for the right time.

"I will kill you," Hecate seethed as she stilled about six feet away, "and leave at least one of your *friends* alive so they can take you back to the city. I'll watch from afar as they travel into the town, knowing that Yelahiah will feel what I've felt for a millennium."

She spoke as if Mother had killed her child, but Mother wouldn't do something like that, even under Azbogah's influence, unless the child wasn't innocent. If she had killed Hecate's child, it had been for a just reason.

Hecate released her flail, and the spiked ball hurtled toward me on its chain. I stilled my wings, dropping a few feet. The weapon struck the tree trunk and got stuck, which had been my plan all along. I wouldn't allow her to retrieve it.

Flying back up, I slammed into her, pushing her away from her weapon. She sailed backward a few feet before she could stop, then laughed harshly. "You've been trained well."

Some would see her words as a compliment, but I knew better. She was stating a fact, not meaning anything beyond the words themselves. "As have you." If I'd been almost any other angel, she would've taken me before now. But I was one of the few fate-blessed warriors, and the purple of my eyes told that truth.

"We could use someone like you in Hell," Hecate offered. "And we could even allow Levi to live if you joined our side."

Of every possibility, I hadn't expected an offer like that. I laughed but kept my entire focus on her. Did she actually think I would contemplate that offer? "I think you already know my answer."

"I'd think twice. It could save many lives, including your friends back in the neighborhood." She floated in front of me, her head tilting.

And demons said angels were arrogant. "I don't need to make a deal with you because we *will* make it out alive. Though I may not agree with everything the angels stand for, I won't turn my back on my people, humanity, or the people we were *created* to protect."

She cackled. "Is that what you think you're doing?"

I'd had enough. She was stalling, though I wasn't sure why. I *wanted* to know what she was talking about, and she was counting on it.

I soared toward her, aiming my sword at her neck. This was it, the moment she finally died.

She dropped a few feet, but I'd expected that and added a split-second adjustment to my attack.

Then she lifted her arms, holding a sai in each hand. She used one of the long metal prongs to halt my weapon and move it so that my blade caught between the two curved side prongs.

I gritted my teeth. I hadn't expected that. Before she could use the other weapon, I swirled my body and jerked the sword hard. Hecate lost her grip on one sai, and I quickly grabbed it and placed the weapon in my belt loop.

"Argh!" Hecate screamed, and soared toward me.

She swung the weapon, aiming straight for my heart. She was done playing games.

Swinging my sword, I blocked her blow, and with my injured hand, I punched her in the face. She flipped onto her back, then slammed her feet into my chest.

My back smashed into a branch of the oak tree, its limbs cutting my arms and face. Hecate raced toward me, and I couldn't fly out of the branches in time. Flipping my legs over my head, I detangled myself while Hecate slashed at the air where my feet had been.

I swung around the trunk, picking up air as I flew higher into the sky.

Countering my move, she came from the opposite direction around the trunk, her sai aimed at my eye.

Letting instinct take over, I spun, using my wings as a weapon. That was what I was most comfortable with, after all. The sai scraped the feathers, but I felt a cold hand clutch my leg.

No! I tried kicking her off with my other leg, but before my foot could connect, she jammed the long prong of the sai into my calf.

Agony ripped through my muscle, and I bit the inside of my cheek to keep from making a sound. I wouldn't give her the satisfaction.

I'd done the one thing I'd been taught not to do: I'd

grown overconfident. I'd been certain I was going to kill her, and she'd gotten the upper hand.

More frustrated with myself than with her, I kicked her in the face with my uninjured leg. Her head jerked back, and she dropped before gathering herself. I took the reprieve to get myself together.

Bending down, I grabbed the handle of the sai lodged into my leg. My hand screamed from where the blade had cut me earlier, but I had to get the prong out of my calf. The longer it stayed in, the more damage it would do, though I could tell it had missed any major arteries.

I yanked the weapon from my leg. My vision blurred, and the my mouth watered as both the raw burn of my hand and the sharp, tormenting pain in my calf made vomit inch up my throat.

Blood dripped from my leg and hand. I'd made the injury to my fingers and hand worse, but I didn't have any other option. These wounds would heal later.

Knowing that I'd promised Levi to tell him if something horrible happened, I linked before he reached out to me. *I'm fine. I just got stabbed. Nothing major.* I winced. I should've left the getting-stabbed part out; that could make him react poorly. I still wasn't used to the whole emotional side of this bond, and realizing I didn't word things correctly before the other person had time to react made it worse. I added quickly, *In the leg. I'm fine, and I'll be killing her now.*

At first, there was no response, and I *nearly* contemplated that maybe our link had broken. I glanced at him in time to watch him stab Pyro in the arm.

Glancing back at me, Levi grimaced as his irises darkened to coffee. *I don't even know how to react to that, love. You act like getting stabbed isn't a big deal.* Even though his words were light, I could feel the turmoil he was attempting to hide.

My resentment toward him weakened some. Though he didn't want to, he was respecting my wishes. *I've had worse.* And that was the truth. He hadn't seen the state I'd been in on the day of the fire. Apparently, he had felt it, though, like I'd felt him being tortured.

Not helping, Rosey. He shook his head and focused back on Pyro as the demon swung his scythe at his stomach. Levi dodged.

Hecate moved in my direction, and I watched her. Since their weapons were hidden by their shadows until they used them, I had no clue how many more she might have on her. That was one bad part about the shadow form, not being able to see what tools they had at their disposal.

She moved like she was thinking about running, but I knew better than to fall for it. She had a scheme in mind. I had both sai now, so if she had no other weapons on her, the likeliest item she would attempt to retrieve was her flail... and the way she moved was meant to draw me away from the tree the flail was lodged in.

This time, I wouldn't let my guard down.

Needing her to believe I was falling for her ploy, I jerked toward her, flicking my gaze behind her as if I planned to attack when she moved further out. I prepared my mind and body to shift backward as soon as she showed any sign of going for the flail.

I floated another two feet closer and prepared myself. I had to act fast if I didn't want her to know I was on to her. I yanked my body as if to attack, and just as I expected, she sailed underneath me.

Shifting my weight, I spun around and swung the sword hard, using my wings in case she tried to escape.

That time, she was the one caught off guard. Her eyes widened as my blade sliced through her neck. As I watched her head fall, my throat closed. I wanted to know what Hecate had meant about my mother.

Her death didn't mean I couldn't find answers. There had to be a way.

A sickening crunch sounded below, followed by discomfort through the bond. I twisted around, dreading what I might find.

CHAPTER TWENTY-FIVE

ACROSS THE SMALL CLEARING, Levi had Pyro pinned against a cypress tree fifteen feet in the air. Our preordained bond allowed me to sense which one was Levi, just like I could feel the maliciousness wafting from Pyro.

I prepared myself for Levi's pain to hit, but nothing more than mild discomfort flowed through our bond. I wanted to ask if he was okay, but I didn't want to distract him.

A low cry emanated from Pyro, and his shadow wrist was unnaturally bent. However, the cry didn't appear to be from physical pain as he glared at me with more than hatred.

He knew I'd killed his sister.

He glanced down to where Hecate had fallen, confirming my suspicions. His negative energy increased tenfold, and the heaviness to which I'd acclimated thickened around me.

Despite that, I couldn't thank the gods enough that Pyro had gotten injured and not Levi.

It had to remain that way. Unfortunately, from when

Levi had left me, I knew firsthand that heartbreak was a deadly motivator.

I took a moment to shake off my battle with Hecate. There was no telling what was happening with our friends, and we needed to check on Bune since two demons had gone after him. Hopefully, Bune would be able to alert us if he needed backup.

Head clear, I soared toward Levi and Pyro. We had to end this once and for all.

Levi swung for Pyro's head, but Pyro raised his broken hand, blocking the shot. Despite Levi's fist striking the broken wrist, Pyro didn't grunt or moan. He continued to fight, making me think his adrenaline and heartbreak had overridden his senses.

"I was planning to kill Levi first to make the princes of Hell happy, but they won't know if I make killing *you* a priority," Pyro snarled.

Even though they were perhaps twenty yards away, they might as well have been miles. Though I moved quickly, I couldn't reach them fast enough to help Levi. In horror, I observed Pyro using his unbroken hand, which held the scythe, to swipe at my mate.

Levi! I linked. Desperation clung to my thought, even through our telepathic link. Before I could finish my train of thought, Levi reached across his body, blocking the scythe with his knife.

Seconds before I reached them, Levi kicked Pyro in the stomach, and the demon crumpled forward.

Pyro had righted himself, and he swung his scythe at Levi's side. My mate lurched back, and my blood turned cold as the weapon *whoosh*ed in front of Levi's chest.

He'd barely gotten out of reach. From what I'd gathered, vampires took after demons in the sense that a vampire who had chosen evil or turned their back on humanity could only be killed by decapitation. However, if a demon hadn't chosen that route, they could be killed like the rest of us, with a blow to the heart or by bleeding out. *Levi* could be killed with a blow to the heart.

Before Levi could straighten, Pyro snarled and charged at him. He plowed into Levi, barreling him toward the ground.

It felt like forever had passed, but I finally reached them. I slammed into Pyro's side and wrapped my arms around his torso, yanking him off my mate. Levi dropped a few more inches but leveled out before impact as Pyro swiped at me with his scythe. I shifted my wings, covering my left side. The sharp tip of his weapon hit my feathers, but they didn't budge, protecting me from injury.

"Do *not* hurt her!" Levi bellowed as he rushed toward us.

My feathers blocked it. I'm fine. Are you okay? I felt discomfort when you broke Pyro's hand.

I removed the sai from my belt loop and stabbed Pyro in the stomach.

Pyro growled in my ear and reached for the sai with his broken wrist. Though he didn't feel the pain, he couldn't get a good grasp on the handle since his hand couldn't move well.

Hissing, Pyro took his scythe and swung it at my neck.

To protect my neck at the angle I was holding on to him, I had to release the demon, as he'd intended.

It was just the way I moved when I punched him. It bothered the injury in my stomach, Levi assured me. *Just concentrate on kicking his ass.*

Under any other circumstances, I'd have found it amusing that he was the one to chastise me, but not when we were under this sort of threat. He was right. I'd seen that he was fine. I shouldn't be bothering him with questions he could answer later.

Damn emotions.

Inching away, Pyro used my temporary distraction to put his scythe under his arm and reached to remove the sai from his stomach.

At least he now had a broken wrist, and his stomach was more injured than Levi's. Giving him no time to recover, I pushed myself hard toward him. I'd figured that Hecate and Pyro were the strongest warriors among these demons, but I'd thought they'd stay behind and we'd be fighting them upon our return. Clearly, they'd wanted to eliminate Levi as quickly as possible and not wait for our return to save our friends. That, and Hecate had wanted to kill me, almost obsessively.

Pyro removed the sai from his stomach as I approached. I held out my sword, prepared to behead the menace. As I swung the weapon, Pyro laughed and tossed the sai toward my chest.

I pulled in my wings, dropping a foot and leaning to the right. The weapon sailed past my head, and the sharp point drenched with blue blood nicked the edge of my ear.

Pain twinged through my ear, but the cut was superficial. I blew out a breath. I'd barely dodged a lethal blow, proving my assumption about them.

Rushing toward Pyro, Levi moved faster than I'd ever seen. He came up behind the demon. I couldn't make out his face, but the anger coursing through our bond was palpable.

My stomach dropped as I feared that Pyro would pretend not to see him and attack when he got close enough. *Don't!* I shouted, though Pyro's entire focus was locked on me.

Without hesitation, Levi slammed his knife into the side of Pyro's neck. The demon's eyes widened, and he spun toward my mate.

He couldn't behead Pyro, which meant we weren't out of harm's way yet.

I had to help Levi.

I surged forward, using every ounce of strength I had to reach them in time.

"Stupid undecided," Pyro spat, and moved to slash Levi with the scythe.

My mate jerked back, but it was futile. Before the tip could lodge in his heart, I kicked Pyro hard in the side, yanking him to the right.

Miraculously, the scythe stabbed Levi in the upper arm and not the chest.

The agony I'd expected to feel earlier slammed through me, but I didn't pause my assault. I punched Pyro in the face, and he dropped all his weapons to the ground. I didn't need to give him a break, so I linked with Levi as I kicked the demon in his injured stomach, *Take my sword and behead him. The blade is longer and sharper than that knife.*

Yeah, I tried to cut through his neck, and it was like stabbing the tree, Levi replied as he appeared beside me.

Pyro grabbed my ankle and lifted my leg, throwing me off balance. Levi flashed to me, taking my sword as he turned toward our enemy.

"I'll *kill* you both," Pyro groaned as he released his hold, ready to attack my mate.

That wasn't happening. I'd already caught my balance and spun, kicking Pyro under the chin and moving head into position for Levi to take the killing blow easily. *Now!*

Growling, Levi sliced Pyro's head from his body. Just like his sister, his body hovered in the air for another moment while his head tumbled. Even in death, they remained shadows.

I flapped my wings lazily, enough to keep me still. My heart pounded so hard, and each beat echoed in my ears. That had been more intense than most of the battles I'd fought, but we'd come out alive.

Pyro's body dropped, and Levi pulled me into his arms. I'd always thought that if we touched in his shadow form, it would bother me, but it didn't. More of my demon biases that I needed to overcome.

I breathed in his sweet rose-peony smell. His smell went perfectly with the scent of fall, and I could never imagine a more tantalizing combination. Not even the red blood that trickled from where the scythe had cut him and from his stomach could get me to remove myself from his arms.

Are you okay? He pulled back, his mocha eyes scanning me.

My mind screamed that I should still be upset, that the issues we had between us hadn't been resolved, but I couldn't seem to care. I was sure they would all come back, but right now, he was alive despite his injuries, and I needed to feel his touch.

I'm fine. You're the one bleeding. I pulled away, not wanting to hurt him more. I couldn't see his features, so he could easily hide if holding me was causing him more discomfort. I tried to survey him, but I couldn't make out anything other than where the blood trickled from his body.

He touched my face, and his cool shadow form caused my skin to buzz from our connection. He vowed, "I'm fine. I promise."

Though I wanted to stay here, just him and me, we had

loved ones who needed our assistance. No stench indicated he was lying, giving me no reason not to trust him. "Okay, then we need to find Bune first, and then the others."

He exhaled. "You're right. It's just, seeing you fight Hecate—" He stopped as his worry and love crashed into me and warmed my heart.

I understood all too well. "You don't have to say more."

A shout rang through the woods, and it wasn't more than two miles away.

Bune.

Father! Levi connected, and soared toward the noise.

His father was in a fight. We needed to help him.

I flew quickly behind Levi, pumping my wings hard as our connection opened to each other. My magic collided with his and somehow combined, and I was able to fly faster.

The moon rose higher, lighting the area. Thankfully, it was waxing, and the silver wolves were gaining strength. A silver moon would have been ideal while we were outnumbered by the enemy.

Soon, we reached the spring again, the water trickling and the stars and light shining off it reminding me of an hourglass.

Something dark caught the corner of my eye—the moonlight shining upon two shadowy forms. My body tensed. *There.* I turned toward the two figures engaged in battle.

Following my lead, Levi hurried behind me. Annoyance flared inside him, but he didn't say a word.

I had a feeling he didn't like me leading the charge, but he was wise enough to keep his thoughts to himself. I had to give him credit for that. *Go to the right, and I'll go left. It looks like it's your father and one demon. We can take the demon by surprise before he notices us.* That would be ideal, but I'd learned that things rarely went according to plan. However, it was still better to have some sort of strategy.

Fine, but please make sure you kill the right one, Levi linked, only half joking.

I couldn't tell the two shadows apart from afar, so it was a valid concern. *You and your father don't emanate malice. As long as I pay attention to that and eye color, your father will be safe.* I would ensure that I beheaded the appropriate person.

Some concern ebbed from inside him. *I trust you.*

His words warmed my heart, but now wasn't the time for feeling all warm and...gooey.

Here, take the sword. Levi held the weapon toward me.

I shook my head. *I have my wings, and I'm used to beheading demons with them. You need the sword. Your knife didn't cut it.*

Warmth shook in our bond, almost like laughter. *That was cute.*

What? I wasn't sure what he was getting at. His knife literally hadn't cut through the demon's neck. I didn't know what he was insinuating.

Your pun, he explained slowly.

I hadn't used a pun, so I was confused. *I have no idea what you're talking about, but we need to help your father.*

Didn't cut— You know what? Forget it. You're right.

Glad to have that strange conversation behind us, I flew right as he veered left. I stayed wide of the figures, not wanting the enemy shadow to pick up on me.

I should've known better. Just like I could feel this negative energy, they must have been able to sense my positive energy.

The one shadow figure stalled and glanced directly at me. Its red eyes glowed, marking it as our enemy.

Bune took the interruption and lodged his knife into the demon's neck, but as he went to behead the demon, his hand slipped off the handle.

Grabbing at its neck, the demon clutched the handle and removed the blade. "You dare strike me? I was told not to kill you, but now I have justification for plucking you like an angel."

I wasn't sure if the analogy worked, but his intent was clear.

The demon had lifted the knife, aiming for Bune's chest, when Levi darted in from a nearby tree. The demon's head jerked in my mate's direction, but he didn't have time to react. He screeched like a banshee, and Levi cut through his neck, providing us with blissful silence.

I rubbed my ears, wishing the ear-piercing ringing of the scream would vanish. "Why do demons scream like that?"

Bune's hand disappeared at his chest, and I could only guess he was touching it. He said, "It's an effective diversion. People who aren't used to hearing it or aren't trained for battle want to cover their ears instead of attack."

"It *is* effective. I'm well trained, and it pains me." In some ways, I'd rather have my ear nicked again than listen to that moaning. When they screamed like that, they kind of reminded me of Sierra.

Turning around, Levi canvassed the area. "How many demons did you fight?"

"That was the third one I killed. How about you two?" Bune asked.

"Seven between the two of us," I said. That meant all ten were dead, and we could head back to help my friends.

Levi spun toward me. "Wait, you killed *six*?"

He sounded surprised. Lifting my chin, I placed my hands on my waist and winced from my injured fingers. Just fate's little way of reminding me not to be prideful and keeping me grounded. "Yes. Do you not believe me?" I lost some conviction on the last two words.

"No, I do." He sighed. "You're just so amazing that sometimes it's hard to believe you're my preordained."

"I agree." Fate putting the two of us together was comical, but he was truly meant for me...if only he'd learn to trust me with his secrets.

Levi arched a brow. "You agree that you're amazing, or that it's hard to believe that fate chose us to share a soul?"

"I wouldn't necessarily use the word *amazing*. I'm a proficient fighter, but your sentiment is the same as mine." *Amazing* was something someone with an ego needed to be told, and though it was nice to hear, I didn't require words of affirmation like that.

His father grinned. "She reminds me of her mother with that confidence."

Even though the three of us were safe for now, that didn't mean the others were. "I have to go protect my friends and the silver wolves."

"We're family now." Bune gestured toward the neighborhood pack house. "So we'll go protect your friends together."

Family. Though I'd grown up with parents, I'd never used that term before. But I liked it, and I didn't even want to argue that it wasn't fitting. "Let's go."

Something unreadable passed through our bond on Levi's side, but I didn't want to analyze it.

Our battle wouldn't be over until everyone I cared about was safe.

I soared back toward the pack house with Bune and

Levi flanking me. I felt...protected. Not that my friends wouldn't give their lives for me, but this was different.

Almost...sacred.

My mate and his father. Something I'd never experienced before.

As we reached the pack housing, I saw Sterlyn with her back to a demon like she didn't even know it was behind her. The group of people behind her weren't warning her.

When the demon lifted its hands, my stomach churned.

CHAPTER TWENTY-SIX

"STERLYN!" I tapped into Levi's magic, borrowing another boost to get to my far-distant cousin quicker. Even with that power, I still wouldn't reach her in time.

But I had to try. Doing nothing wasn't an option.

She turned to me, her lavender-silver eyes glowing, and searched the area for a threat.

When the demon didn't continue his attack, my stomach fluttered. I noted the group surrounding her: Circe, Griffin, Alex, Ronnie, Killian, and Sierra. They all stood tense and aware, but they weren't in battle stances.

Circe lifted a hand. "It's okay. He's spelled and contained."

I landed beside her and faced the demon. I wasn't sure why they'd allowed this menace to live. "I can kill him."

"Whoa!" The demon lifted his shadow hands. "Listen, I'm no threat."

No threat? Okay, maybe some demons were funny after all. I laughed.

"New Rosemary is a tad bit creepy," Sierra whispered loudly.

Killian sighed. "I agree with Rosemary. We should kill him. In fact, we should kill *all* the demons." He obviously had chosen to ignore Sierra's comment and focus on the matter at hand.

That was one reason why he and I got along so well.

Levi and Bune reached us, and as soon as their feet touched the ground, they changed into their human forms. Now I realized they did that to make us feel more comfortable since they were used to being in their shadow forms.

"He's not a risk," Levi said, and turned his back to the captive as he scanned our surroundings. "Where are the others so I can help them?"

"The fight is over, and we were about to do a location spell to find the three of you," Ronnie said as she gestured to me. "But here you are."

My stomach dropped. I hoped I'd done enough to protect the silver wolves and my other friends. However, this group wouldn't be standing around with a captive if something had happened to the rest of our allies.

I could hear the murmur of voices. "How many did we lose?" The silver wolves were almost extinct, and every death was more tragic than the last. Their only hope was that any child born of a silver wolf would be full-blooded silver. Angel magic didn't dilute as other supernatural magics did over generations, but silver wolves also had low childbirth rates, and most couples had only one child.

"None." Sterlyn's shoulders sagged with relief. "But only because of the witches. If it weren't for them, the outcome would've been different."

Witches were super powerful, but as with each supernatural race, there was always a cost to magic. Silver and demon wolf magic were tied to the phases of the moon, witches drained quickly, especially when their full coven wasn't performing with them, angels took a long time to regain their magic if not under Heaven's lights, and the list went on and on. The perfect balance was when you had a diverse group like the one we'd created, although people outside our group considered us more of a threat.

Griffin placed his hands in the pockets of his khakis. "It also helped that the two smartest demons in charge went after you three."

"You three splitting up from us wasn't part of the plan, so the third demon in charge wasn't prepared to lead," Alex said as he took Ronnie's hand. "Between that and Ronnie's ability to switch into her demon form and blend in with the undecided, we got an edge."

That was the thing about strategy. Any hesitation could shift the momentum, and in this situation, it had shifted in our favor. That was one of our group's best attributes: we could think on our feet and follow each other's lead. I hadn't considered using Ronnie's shadow form to our advantage, but that trickery would have worked. The demons would have been so focused on the other individuals that they wouldn't have noticed her as easily, unlike Bune and Levi, their main targets.

Either way, we needed to eliminate all threats. I spun toward the undecided demon, and he shuffled back. However, it was like he slammed into a wall behind him, despite the closest redbud being fifteen feet away. There was nothing to stop him, but whatever magical barrier Circe had placed around him was keeping him contained.

His dark eyes reminded me of black diamonds with flecks of crystals inside them.

The princes of Hell must have leverage over him; otherwise, he wouldn't be here.

"Which proves why we can't err in our judgment,

either." I had shifted my wings to the side, ready to eliminate the threat, when Levi grabbed my arm and stepped between me and the demon, stopping the movement of my wings...barely.

If he'd done it a second later, I would've killed him instead. I clenched my teeth. "What is *wrong* with you?"

"Me?" Levi touched his chest. "They've detained him, but you're just going to waltz over and kill him without a second thought?"

Killian growled, "Maybe you should just kill both demons. No harm, no foul."

The thought of Levi dying pushed me over the edge, especially with the turmoil between us and his injuries. "Too *far*." I almost called him *mutt*, but Killian didn't deserve that. My emotions were getting the best of me, and if I'd been in Killian's spot, I probably would've said something similar or taken matters into my own wings.

"Why don't you mind your own business, *pup*?" Levi popped the Ps, emphasizing his disdain. "I was speaking to my *mate*, not you."

The demon behind him gasped. "Whoa. Mate. Is that why you didn't want to leave the other night?"

My body tensed as I soaked in the meaning. "Wait. Is *he* the one who broke you out of the house that night the demons attacked us?" I already knew the answer, but I wanted to see if he would try to bend the truth without outright lying. The demons had attacked me and the silver wolves who'd been on guard when Levi had been our prisoner here. Aurora and Lux had spelled him inside a house, but a demon had used our fight to lure everyone away so he could help Levi escape. Realizing what had happened, I'd rushed back here and discovered Ronnie chasing after *this* demon, who'd broken the spell barrier at the house. But Levi had remained behind.

Levi glared over his shoulder. "Zagan, you aren't *helping*."

His attempt to ignore my question had my blood pumping. *You'd better choose your next words carefully. My patience is almost gone.*

Love, you never have been the most patient. He pinched the bridge of his nose.

And he deflected again. *"Love" me one more time, and I'll make you scream.*

A wicked glint reflected in his eyes. *Is that a promise?*

Yes, it's a promise. I'll hurt you so badly, you'll be asking me to stop. Why was he amused? I had wings, and though I might not be able to kill him, I could cause him a lot of pain.

He winked. *I doubt I'd ever want you to stop. Sex with you—*

I gaped at him in disbelief. *I'm not talking about sex.* He was purposely irritating me, and I was allowing it to work. I inhaled deeply to center myself. "Is *he* the one who attempted to break you out that night?" I reiterated, pushing my agitation and frustration through the bond. He would *feel* that I was at my wits' end.

Wisely, he dropped his arrogant smirk. "Yes, because the princes of Hell thought I'd been gone too long. However, I didn't leave, if you remember correctly."

"Oh, I do." A small part of me wished he had. Then we wouldn't have completed the bond, and maybe this whole disaster wouldn't have happened.

But the raw, honest truth was that *this* would've happened regardless. Maybe centuries later, but destiny had a way of making things come full circle, which included Levi and me completing the bond. I just wished it would also include us figuring out a way to be together. "You still needed to get the sword."

"That wasn't the only reason, and you know it." His irises lightened, and my heart skipped a beat.

Bune positioned himself behind Levi and the demon and said, "Zagan is a *good* demon. He just doesn't have any family and is doing what he thinks he has to do to survive."

Red flags waved all around me. "The princes don't have any leverage over him, and he's still doing this?"

"How the hell is he still undecided, then?" Griffin's brows furrowed. "That sounds like he's chosen to me."

"Where is he supposed to go?" Levi challenged. "He's not welcome here, and any demon who comes across him that *has* decided—which is most of the demons on Earth— would attack him for not conforming. It's not like he has many options."

Ronnie chewed her bottom lip and shivered. "Levi has a point. I despised living in group homes, but it was better than going to new foster homes. Sometimes, the evil you know is better than what could be waiting someplace else. I knew how to survive in a group home."

Yet another item I'd never considered before. All my life, I'd been taught that *all* demons were bad, but with Levi, I'd learned that wasn't true. And now demons were informing us that undecided demons were stuck because they didn't feel safe to leave *or* stay.

"We have more *important* things to attend to than this demon." Circe waved her hand in Zagan's direction. "I don't give a damn what we do with him. We need to stay somewhere overnight and recharge after exerting so much magic. In the morning, we can head out and leave Cordelia, Eliphas, and Kamila behind to help with what- ever you decide his fate to be. Either way, we need to get away from all the magic so nothing can prohibit us from doing what we planned, and then our coven can head back home."

She was remaining vague so as not to alert Zagan to the details of our plans, which I appreciated. The witches had the same level of trust in the demons as Killian and I did, so I wasn't surprised. Either way, Circe planned on retrieving her mother and heading home as soon as possible.

Thankfully, she also planned on resting, so that would give Levi time to recoup. Despite not having discussed it, I knew he planned on going back to Hell with the witches. After all, he was the only one who could handle the sword he'd left there. Though I didn't like the idea of him leaving, especially since the princes of Hell were determined to kill him, there wasn't a better option.

A ginormous part of my heart wished I could go with them, but the princes would be alerted to my presence as soon as I walked through the portal. I also needed to stay put in case my parents needed me. Just as Levi couldn't abandon his father, I couldn't leave my parents behind.

Circe bounced on her feet with nervous energy. She was petrified that the coven in Shadow City would know they were back. She suspected that the Shadow City coven had assisted Saga and Dick Harding in capturing infant Aurora to force Eliza into kidnapping Cyrus when he and Sterlyn were born. The last thing we needed was for the Shadow City witches to descend, so I agreed with handling things delicately.

Sterlyn's eyes glowed. "Alex, Cyrus is requesting your assistance. The humans are beside themselves, and they need help calming them down. The witches aren't having much luck since the humans don't want to be messed with."

Her political savviness peeked through once again. If I

hadn't known exactly what she was insinuating, I would have been none the wiser.

What are they talking about? Levi asked, and stepped closer to me. His hand brushed my arm, and I didn't have the strength to step aside.

There was no reason not to tell him everything. He was part of our group, even if we were at an impasse when it came to our relationship. *The witches won't influence anyone good if they aren't welcomed. Vampires don't have an issue manipulating the mind, even when a person might protest. Alex doesn't enjoy doing it, but he understands that sometimes, it's necessary to keep our existence a secret.* Alex had even messed with Annie's mind at Ronnie's behest after her traumatic experience of being an evil rogue vampire's blood bag before we'd realized she was a supernatural.

We have to do whatever is necessary to survive. Surely the witches know that. There was no judgment in Levi's response.

It's easy for them to decline when they know a vampire will step in to prevent the information from leaking out. It's about balance with them, and they know there's an alternative to forcing their magic on someone unwilling. The witches' whole motto was to harm no one.

"I'll help, too," Ronnie offered as she took her mate's hand. "They tend to forget I can do the mind-massaging now."

Sierra shook her head. "You should be *offended* that they didn't ask for your help. But don't worry. I *am* enough for the both of us."

Jaw twitching, Killian side-eyed the mouthy blonde. "Now isn't the time."

"There is never time for that," Alex scoffed as he

hurried toward the house where I'd spotted the three undecided guards before.

Stomach knotting, I spun to Zagan. "Where are the other two undecideds?" Maybe he'd been distracting us so that his comrades could bring in reinforcements.

His eyes widened. "What?"

I hated that I couldn't see his expression. His shadow form was truly problematic. "Don't play games, and tell me the truth. I know you're using your demon form to hide things from us."

"We killed the other two." Circe crossed her arms. "They attacked us—he didn't. That's the only reason he's still alive."

My lungs started working again. Maybe we had a little more time before more demons came. We needed to get our people to Hell and back again before the princes suspected that something had gone wrong. Luckily, angels and demons didn't have pack links like animal shifters did and weren't alerted when one of their own died. That would've caused a lot more problems. "Are we sure that none got away?"

"Yes. We'd just finished interrogating Zagan about that exact thing when you arrived." Sterlyn tilted her head as she stared at the demon. "He doesn't appear to be lying and says he's sure that no one followed him."

Bune stepped toward Zagan and said, "He can be trusted. He's like a son to me and a brother to Levi. I took him in when his parents passed, shortly after Marissa died."

Marissa? I'd never heard that name before.

Levi frowned, and my heart twisted from the pain radiating from him. *My mother.*

I wanted to ask more about his mother's and Zagan's

parents' deaths, but now wasn't the time. Maybe when we got back to the Terrace.

"As a sign of good faith, why don't you change into your human form to make these people feel comfortable?" Bune arched a brow at Zagan.

"Yeah, that would be nice, seeing as not all of us can *see* him." Sierra blinked like she expected him to magically appear in front of her. She was staring to the left of him, making it obvious that she wasn't sure where he stood.

A loud huff escaped Zagan, but instead of protesting, he surprised me by flickering into full view.

His tan clay-colored skin glistened under the moonlight, and his shoulder-length raven hair hung over his face. He was shirtless, so his athletic body was on display for everyone.

"Holy shit!" Sierra gasped, and she wiped the corner of her mouth, checking for drool. "He's *just* as hot as Levi. The phrase *hot as sin* makes perfect sense now."

Zagan glanced at her with a cocky smirk and a head-shake, like he was both conceited and surprised at the same time.

I moved, blocking Levi from Sierra's view. Even though I agreed Levi was delectable, I didn't want her commenting on it. He was *mine.*

I love your jealous streak. Levi chuckled behind me.

Jealous. I hated that word. *Not jealous. Just possessive, but don't get any ideas. We still have issues.*

But possessive means I haven't totally screwed up and there's hope.

His warmth exploded in my chest. Anything I said would encourage him, but I didn't want to discourage him, either. I *wanted* to be with him. *Let's not get ahead of ourselves.*

Herne hurried over with Aurora and Lux on her heels. The older woman said, "We need to go. Alex wants us out of here before he and Ronnie finish. He's afraid that if the humans see us, it could cause some of their memories to resurface."

The human mind was very manipulatable, but if the humans saw something triggering, some of the memories could come back. We needed a clean break.

The other witches and wolves headed over, leaving Ronnie and Alex alone with the humans. I turned in their direction and noticed a couple I'd seen the other day when I'd been on my way to Shadow City. They'd been coming back from the blood bank, and the man had been doting on his wife then, just as he was now. He had his arm wrapped around her, and she buried her face in his chest.

Their love seemed so pure. Maybe even humans had soulmates. They didn't deserve a life haunted by horrible memories.

"Put Zagan in the Navigator," Sterlyn instructed, and glanced at Cyrus, Darrell, and Chad. "You all sit around him and make sure he doesn't try to escape. If he tries, kill him."

"Here," Levi said as he held out the sword to Cyrus. "I know he won't betray us, but you don't. This sword will make killing him easy."

Zagan's jaw dropped. "What the hell, Levi?"

My heart skipped a beat at Levi's action. He had made it clear he was on our side. I placed my uninjured hand on my hip. "If you don't try to escape, then you shouldn't have a problem."

"Levi is right." Bune reached to clap Zagan on the back, but his hand couldn't move beyond the barrier. "We trust you, but they don't. We need to give them assurances."

Circe twirled her hand. "The barriers are gone. I'll ride in the Navigator, too, in case he tries something. Herne, drive the van, and let's roll. I want to get out of here."

Our group dispersed, and I took to the air, needing an escape of my own.

This time, Bune and Levi shifted into their demon forms and flew beside me. After fighting with them today and seeing how much the princes of Hell wanted them dead, I didn't have any reason not to trust them. The last thing either one of them wanted was for demons, angels, shifters, and witches to be hunting them.

They had enough enemies.

We flew back to Shadow Terrace in silence. Levi didn't even talk to me through our bond.

My heart panged. I'd hoped he'd try to mend things between us before he went back to Hell, especially since he'd commented that maybe he hadn't blown his chance after all.

Trying to concentrate on the cool air and clouds, I still couldn't find peace. But as I saw some raccoons scurrying and owls gliding below, hunting for their nightly meal, some of my anxiety eased. They didn't come out when demons were here, and though I didn't sense anything malicious, noting that the animals were at ease brought me comfort.

When we approached the Terrace, I began to descend. "We need to fly near the treetops in case humans are on the outskirts of town," Though they should all be heading to the blood bank, it was still best to err on the side of caution. Hikers could get lost, and though it didn't happen often, all it took was one person to see something and run before we could alter their mind.

The two of them followed me, and we landed at the edge of the tree line by our temporary housing. Levi and

Bune changed back to human form, most likely to prevent Jeremiah from thinking that demons were attacking, especially since we'd beaten the others back.

I marched toward the back door, not wanting to dawdle outside and give Levi the perception that I desperately wanted to talk to him.

You couldn't force people to change when they didn't want to or weren't ready. I'd seen people try and fail too many times.

A strong hand wrapped around my arm and gently tugged me around. My skin buzzed, and my heart leaped as Levi said, "Father, do you mind going inside and giving Rosemary and me a moment alone?"

"I'd be glad to," Bune said. When he walked past me, he paused and murmured in my ear, "Just hear him out, please."

Jeremiah ran from the trees behind us in his wolf form. He pawed at the ground, and there was no question what he was asking. I answered the question: "You can go, too. I can keep watch."

He happily trotted toward the house.

Stomach churning, I took in a shaky breath and tried to ignore the tingle between his flesh and mine. I'd thought that Levi would want to make up with me, but Bune made it sound like that wasn't the case. I'd face whatever he wanted to say head-on. I wouldn't shy away from conflict. Even if he shredded what was left of my heart.

CHAPTER TWENTY-SEVEN

DESPITE MY LUNGS filling with air, dizziness overcame me. My mouth dried like I desperately needed a glass of water, but I refused to budge. Whatever he had to say, I wanted to hear it.

"I'll tell Annie and Midnight that the two of you will be inside shortly," Bune called over his shoulder as he walked between the burned-out house at the very end of the street and the one our friends were waiting in.

Levi's eyes locked on me, and I shivered. The intensity of his gaze stole my breath, and black dots spotted my vision.

I tried to shut down the bond on my side. I'd never passed out from anticipation before, but Levi was a first for many things. However, he didn't need to know the extent of my emotions for him.

A laugh bubbled from me. I truly was a buffoon if I believed he didn't know.

He pursed his lips as his concern wafted through me.

Oh, dear gods. I'd always looked at others this way, like

someone might have lost their sanity. I'd never been on the receiving end before, and it burned.

Needing clarity, I stepped back, removing my arm from his grasp. His touch wasn't making things better. I crossed my arms, waiting for him to speak.

His face fell. "You aren't making this easy on me."

"I'm not sure what you mean." I was standing here, waiting for him to discuss whatever was on his mind. If I wanted to be difficult, I would ignore him and march inside. "I'm here."

He ran a hand down his face. "I know, but you're giving me standoffish vibes."

"Of course I'm standing." I dropped my hands and glanced at my legs. "I didn't realize you wanted me to sit." I guessed I could do that, too, if it would hurry up the conversation. I moved to sit down, but he caught my wrist.

He closed his eyes. "That's not what I meant."

"Then what *did* you mean?" I wished he would get to the point. My armpits were sweating, which *never* happened, even when I was exerting immense physical energy. Unfortunately, it had everything to do with this man in front of me and wanting to know what he had to say.

He still hadn't opened his eyes, and I wanted to scream. If he was trying to be cruel and torture me, he was succeeding. I wanted him to tell me whatever was on his mind so I could go inside and lick my wounds. With the way he was prolonging this, there was no way it could be good.

I couldn't continue to stay here and wait for the words he was holding hostage. That wasn't right, and I was done being agreeable. "You know what? It's fine. You don't have to say anything. There are so many things against us having a relationship anyway, and it's probably best we stopped dragging this out." The words had rubbed my throat even rawer, but they'd needed to be said. I'd made it easier for us by tossing them out there. Now we could move on with whatever our lives would look like without each other. "But you still need to retrieve the demon sword. Not just for our safety but for Bune's, Zagan's, and your own." If the demons killed Levi, they'd have the sword and potentially reign with even more terror.

His face twisted in pain, and my body flushed.

Not able to be around him any longer, I spun to go, but he kept his grip on my wrist.

"Damn it, Rosey," he growled. "You're so damn difficult."

He was calling *me* difficult? "Excuse me for cutting to the chase and saying what you're struggling to get across. There's no reason to keep grappling with our pain and emotions. We keep doing this back-and-forth thing, and it has to end. I was making it *easier* on you by saying what you clearly can't."

"That's the thing!" He took a step toward me, his sweet scent overwhelming my senses. With his free hand, he tilted my head up so he could stare straight into my eyes. "You're so smart, and most of the time, you figure things out before anyone else. You have this amazing mind that can usually see the big picture, but you have one fatal flaw."

He'd complimented me, then turned around and insulted me. This was the whole back-and-forth scenario I'd just alluded to, but I couldn't turn and walk away. I wanted —no, *needed* to know what he thought my flaw was. "And that would be?" I stepped back so his finger slipped from under my chin, but I kept my head elevated. I didn't want him to think he was the reason I kept my head held high.

Dropping his hand, he snickered without humor. "You're *jaded*." He groaned. "You expect the worst outcome and for everyone who isn't in your inner circle to disappoint you."

"That's not jaded. That's realistic." *Expect the worst.* That was something I always strove to do. That way, I was prepared, and if things improved, it was easier to pivot. "You don't go into battle expecting beautiful trumpets to play and peace to magically happen. You go in expecting disappointment, heartache, and destruction."

"I agree, but the difference is that *everything* isn't a battle." He fisted his hands. "Our relationship isn't easy, I can attest to that, but it's not a *fucking* war. And *I'm* not going anywhere."

He had lost his mind. "You have to go to Hell—you're the only one who can retrieve the sword."

Dropping his head into his hands, he made the oddest noise I'd ever heard. The sound was a combination between a growl, a laugh, and a scream. Then he rasped, "That's not what I meant." He stood straight, his eyes lightening as he closed the distance between us. "You're literal, so let me be clear."

The air sawed at my lungs as I tried to breathe. Whatever he said next would define everything between us.

"You're it for me, Rosey, and I'm all in." He cupped my cheek and continued, "I'm done fighting this, and tonight, you opened my eyes to what we will be when we stop fighting each other and start fighting *for* one another."

A painfully sweet warmth spread through me, but I tried to keep my head on straight. I couldn't lose my senses just because he was saying kind words to me. His actions didn't back them up, and that was the true testament to a healthy relationship. "I want this, too, but you leaving—"

"I was wrong to do that to you," he interrupted. "I know I

said that I was right and there was no other choice, but tonight, when you risked your life to save mine without even a *warning*..." He heaved a breath. "I understood what you meant. I should've told you everything, especially after we'd cemented our bond. But I thought I was doing the right thing. It took being on the other end of the situation to realize how it felt, and you didn't even leave my ass. I can't believe the amount of pain I put you through, but I'm willing to make it up to you...*forever*, if you let me. What I did was wrong, and I'm so sorry."

My heart grew so full, I was pretty sure I might explode. "If you're just saying this, just..." I trailed off, unsure how to finish the sentence. There were so many possibilities that could result from him throwing words around carelessly, but the emotions that wafted from him backed up his proclamation.

"If I were lying, you'd know." He placed his forehead against mine. "You'd smell the lie, hear the change in my heartbeat, and even feel it through our bond. I'm all yours... if you'll still have me."

My throat constricted, and I couldn't speak. Because he was being sincere and laying everything on the line for me, there was no way I could ever turn him away. He was what my heart and soul wanted. Even my head wasn't screaming warnings anymore, which was peculiar. "Okay," I murmured.

He lifted his head slightly, a smile slowly spreading across his face. "Really? You're in like I'm in? Like we're truly doing this?"

The corners of my mouth tipped upward. "As long as you keep your word, but this is your *last* chance." I couldn't keep opening up my heart, only for him to tear it apart. Each time, the pain got worse, but I had to try one last time so I didn't have regrets. Eternity was a long time to live with what-ifs.

"I won't need a fourth, but I need you not to expect the worst from me. If you do, then we don't stand a chance. I deserve what you give your friends—the benefit of the doubt until you get a chance to hear me out." He licked his bottom lip. "Can you give me that?"

The question rocked me. He was right. I did expect the worst from him. In fairness, he'd proven me right every time, but that probably added to why he hadn't come clean with me in the first place. A relationship had to be a partnership, and I couldn't pretend Levi was the only reason we'd been struggling. If he was going to try for me, he deserved the same in return. "I promise."

"Thank gods," he murmured, and kissed me.

His lips were soft and firm—in other words, perfect. I responded in earnest, not wanting to deny the attraction and devotion between us any longer. After all, I'd just promised him that I wouldn't be jaded.

Opening my mouth, I welcomed his tongue, craving his spearmint taste. It'd been only a few days since we'd last kissed, but it might as well have been a lifetime with all the turmoil between us. His leaving for Hell tomorrow wouldn't help matters, either. It was like every time we took a step forward, something happened to get between us. But this time, we wouldn't allow his departure to take us several steps back.

I love you, he linked as his hands slipped around my waist.

Those words were my final undoing. *I love you, too.* I wanted to procreate with him, but the others would be here any second. Though our bond was important, our survival was slightly more urgent. Not only that, but he was injured, and the last thing I wanted to do was hurt him more.

Even though we didn't have time, I could show him I desired him. Wrapping my arms around his neck, I pressed my body against his and paused. *Did I hurt you?* I'd forgotten about his stomach injury.

He groaned as his fingers slipped under my shirt, pushing into my skin and pulling me against him. *There is nothing in the world that would make me not want you plastered against my body right now.*

My skin heated. I'd always liked sex on the rougher side; it was a way to feel things the only way I knew how. With Levi, I didn't need that, but he still had the perfect balance: not too sweet, but still tender, with just the right amount of grit.

Griffin's car engine purred as it neared us, the effect like someone drenching us with cold water. I didn't want to untangle myself from Levi, but we needed to determine our next steps to ensure his survival and keep my mother from being blamed for missing artifacts.

As I pulled away, Levi grumbled, "Of course they'd show up now. They couldn't give us an hour or two."

"Oh, don't worry. *This* will be happening tonight." I moved my hand down and stroked him through his jeans, enjoying that he wanted me as desperately as I wanted him. "And I'll need more than two hours."

"Good," he said as he pulled me back against him. *Because I don't think I'll ever get enough of you.*

He'd better not.

Knowing we required a moment to cool down, I kissed him one last time and begrudgingly removed myself from his body. "We need a breather."

"That's one way of putting it." The scent of his arousal hung thick.

The car pulled up in front of the house, and I took his hand and led him in that direction so we could greet everyone. My body was on fire, wanting to reaffirm our bond now that we were finally on the same page, but it would have to wait a little while longer.

Just as we reached the front of the house, the others got out of the Navigator and van. Alex and Ronnie were still missing, but they would be here shortly, I assumed.

Sierra's gaze shot to our joined hands, and she placed a hand on her chest. "Thank gods you two finally worked things out. It just took a battle and almost dying, yet again, to get you there, but hopefully, this last one does the trick. I'm not sure how many more breakups we can take."

Of course she'd have a snarky comment to commensurate the moment. However, not even that could remove the smile from my face or dampen my joy.

But the scowl on Killian's face didn't go unnoticed.

"Fate always forces her hand," Herne interjected.

Circe eyed the houses. "I take it this is the one in which Annie is waiting for us. With you shifters, I can't always count on lights being on when someone's home."

"Yes, but it'll be a tight squeeze inside," Sterlyn said as she turned to the silver wolves and nodded toward the woods. "Darrell, why don't you go home to Martha, and Chad, you should go get some rest at your own home. Jeremiah is heading out now to go back with you as well, and Kodi and Hugo are coming here to relieve you three as we speak. We'll be okay in the interim."

The front door opened as if on cue, and Jeremiah joined us outside. He took a step toward the woods and paused. "I can stay until—"

"Go," Cyrus said as he climbed out of the back seat, staying close to Zagan. "You need time with your mate after being apart for a few days, and Chad, you need a break after how often you two had to take charge."

The three silver wolves glanced at each other, likely communicating via their pack link. Then they headed toward the woods as Darrell called over his shoulder, "Let us know when you need us again." He disappeared, rushing back toward Shadow Ridge.

Cyrus's eyes glowed. "Go inside, demon, and don't try anything stupid."

With a deep-set frown, Zagan moved toward the house. Wisely, he didn't say a word.

Giggles came from Aurora and Lux, who were watching the demon walk into the house. Their faces were flushed, and it wasn't hard to tell they found the demon attractive. If it weren't for Levi, I might have found Zagan appealing, but my sights were locked only on my preordained.

Eliphas and Aspen remained at the back of the group, surveying the area. Cordelia and Kamila were rigid, making it clear that the only two witches not on guard were Aurora and Lux, the youngest of the group.

"Come on." Griffin walked to the front door, acting more like a diplomat than ever. "Let's get inside so we can discuss tomorrow."

I let everyone go in front of us, wanting the opportunity to examine the area one last time before going indoors. Though the threat had been temporarily eliminated, with no one on guard, I needed to do one final inspection.

Levi's hand tightened on mine. *Is something wrong?*

Nothing seemed out of the ordinary. A flying squirrel jumped from branch to branch near us. *Nope, just letting*

314 JEN L. GREY

the others go first. Seeing the squirrel helped me feel more at ease.

I pulled my wings inside my back, and we stepped inside.

To say the living room was cramped would have been an understatement.

Circe flipped a hand toward Zagan and said, "There. The barrier spell is complete. He can't leave the house without outside assistance or one of us removing the magic."

Not needing any additional encouragement, Cyrus hurried to the couch furthest from the door and stood behind Annie, who sat in the middle seat. He touched her shoulder, needing to be close.

Fidgeting, Midnight sat on Annie's right side. She nodded at the witches as Bune came to stand behind her, trying to make room for everyone else.

"Oh, goddess," Lux gasped from against the wall behind the couch closest to the front door. "Annie, you're so pregnant. I can't believe how big you got in such a short time."

Sierra snorted and looped her arm through Aurora's, dragging the young witch to the opposite couch. She sat across from Midnight, putting Aurora across from Annie, and said, "That sounds like something Rosemary would say."

I'd never understand mortals. It was okay for Lux to say something like that, but if it had been me, Sierra would've scolded me.

"Wolves and angels don't have long pregnancies." Annie beamed as she rubbed her belly. "Which I'm thankful for."

"I can't wait to meet our little girl," Cyrus cooed, and I didn't even grimace at the sweetness.

Herne followed Lux behind the couch, with Circe and Aspen filing in behind her.

Everyone was finally settled once Kamila sat next to Aurora and Cordelia sat across from her. Eliphas stood behind his wife, and Killian leaned against the wall across the room.

Sterlyn, Griffin, Levi, and I stood in front of the wall the television was mounted on while Zagan pouted in the corner of the room furthest from the front door.

Yawning, Circe covered her mouth with her hand. "Do we know if Ronnie and Alex are okay?"

"They called a few minutes ago." Annie leaned back in her seat. "They've got vampires coming to help the humans to their cars so they can head home immediately. Alex and Ronnie don't want to risk them staying around and triggering a memory."

"How is that different from humans getting their memories erased at the blood banks?" Kamila crossed her legs. "If they were going to have memories triggered, wouldn't all humans have that problem from staying in town after donating?"

That question proved how little the witches were around other supernatural races. "The blood bank donations aren't traumatic. The vampires brainwash the humans into donating, which is a common practice among humans. What they make them forget is the coercion and the odd time of night the donation occurred. What *these* humans experienced was truly traumatic."

"And memories like that aren't easy to forget." Annie rubbed her arms. "Believe me. I thought I was going insane when I went through something similar."

It was surreal how well Annie had adapted to remembering she'd suffered a similar terror and had almost killed

Ronnie while under the mind control of a rogue vampire. Once we'd learned she was a supernatural, it had made sense that she'd resisted the compulsion to kill her foster sister.

Sterlyn sighed. "Most likely, the memory was triggered because it involved Ronnie. It's hard to get distance when it's family."

Cordelia patted Annie's arm. The older witch murmured, "It all worked out as it should."

Destiny had a funny way of ensuring its plan was followed.

"As the witches pointed out, tomorrow will be a long night, and we all need time to recharge and heal." Levi tugged me toward the front door. "Rosemary and I will stay at the other house, and I'd like to tend to my wounds and rest since twilight tomorrow will be here before we know it." *And I need to get you naked several times before then.*

Oh, you'll only need to get me naked once. My clothes aren't going back on until you need to leave for your journey. My heart twinged at the thought, but it had to be done. There was no way around it.

He grinned naughtily. *Now that sounds like Heaven.*

"The eight of us can sleep down here," Circe offered. "I know we're trying to stay under the radar, and we have no issues sleeping on the couches and floor. We'd like to stick together."

"There are extra sheets, comforters, and pillows in the linen closet upstairs in the master bedroom," Annie offered. "I know because they're stocked like that in the house next door."

"Then it makes sense if the majority of us stay here to keep an eye on Bune, too." Sterlyn gestured at each person she named. "Annie, Cyrus, Killian, Sierra, Rosemary, and

Levi should stay next door while the rest of us stay here. I want to be here when Ronnie and Alex get back, and the rest of us can make do here for the night."

What she meant was that she wanted Annie to have a little distance if something happened, and Killian and Sierra couldn't see demons. She probably didn't want to argue with Levi since he was going to Hell to retrieve the sword and needed to be at full strength. Her logic made sense, but I wished there was another way.

"Enough talking." Circe arched a brow at her coven members. "It's time to rest."

I hated to leave them, but they were right. I hoped to have a sex-filled twenty-four hoursI with Levi, and we would have plenty of it, but we needed rest as well. *Come on, let's go to bed.* I moved toward the door but hesitated. "Let us know if you need us. I can be here in seconds."

"Don't worry. We will." Griffin wrapped an arm around his mate's shoulders. "Believe me, I always want you fighting in our corner."

Levi tugged me to the door, eager to be alone. As we stepped outside, leaving the others behind, someone stopped the door from closing.

Familiar milk chocolate eyes appeared as Killian joined us outside. "I want to talk to you for a minute."

A low growl emanated from Levi as his anger poured into me.

I wasn't up for the two of them arguing again. It was time I put them in their place.

CHAPTER TWENTY-EIGHT

I STEPPED in front of Levi, blocking him from Killian, and connected, *Why are you so threatened by him? You know how I feel and that you're it for me. He's just my friend.*

Levi's annoyance flared. *I know how you both feel, and he still wants you.*

Though I wasn't egotistical, I'd been able to view myself pragmatically for a millennium. *I'm a strong warrior and not ugly. It's not odd that he might feel more than friendly toward me, despite being a wolf. Are you insinuating I'm not worthy of being desired?*

What? No. His disbelief crashed through me. His lungs deflated. *You're hot, but you're mine. He needs to stop inserting himself between us. Don't try to turn this around on me.*

For all we knew, Killian could want to talk about his time while he and our group had been held captive. *And you say I assume the worst of others.* I threw his words back at him, wanting him to realize that he struggled with the same thing I did.

I turned my attention back to Killian, who was staring at

where my hand was joined with Levi's. I really needed him to prove Levi wrong, but it looked as if he might accomplish the opposite. I tried not to let my frustration bleed through, but I was tired and wanted to spend alone time with Levi. "Yes?"

Killian shook his head as if snapping back to reality. "Yeah, sorry. I just wanted to say that the demons holding us captive confirmed it was Eliza."

My heart raced. We'd determined it was her, but it was nice to have confirmation. "What did they say?"

He shut the door and got closer, dropping his voice to a murmur. "They said they got one of the witches responsible for closing the portal, and they thanked us for handing her over so easily. Apparently, they need a witch who hasn't chosen evil to perform whatever spell they need so they can leave Hell undetected."

Levi pivoted around me so he could be part of the conversation. "It's a good thing we're going to retrieve Eliza *and* the sword."

Of course the demons needed Eliza, probably due to a balance between good and evil that kept them from traveling to Earth since their negative surge would alert the angels to their presence. Maybe they needed the witch to hide their energy. "When are you going to tell the coven what their plan for Eliza is?"

"They already know, but I didn't want them to overhear me informing you and upset them again when we all need rest. They used a lot of magic tonight, and we need them at their strongest. We'll talk more about it tomorrow." Killian grimaced.

That worked better. Everyone would be thinking more rationally then.

Killian wanted to protect those he cared about, and

those witches had made it into his heart. I said, "They might have some insight on what the demons are planning if they know Eliza is involved."

"And we should have a long conversation, going over all scenarios," Levi declared. "It should be at least an hour, if not two, minimum." *We should be able to get through one round without an audience that way.*

One round? That was a peculiar thing to say, but then my brain caught up. He meant sex. *We should get through at least three or four rounds in that time.* If we did things properly, orgasms would come quickly. We didn't need an hour to build up to one. That would be a waste of time.

Not with what I have planned for us. He turned his head and winked at me.

"Yeah, I'm sure it will take all that." Killian blew a raspberry. "I'd better head back in so you two can get some...rest. You had a hard night."

Oh, it's about to get hard, all right. Levi waggled his eyebrows at me. "Yeah, thanks, man."

He tugged on my hand, heading to the house next door.

The front door opened, but Killian's footsteps paused. "Oh, and if you hurt her again, I'll kick your ass. I don't care if I can't see you in your demon-ass form or not. I'll find a way to kill you. No one hurts my family like that, especially more than once."

"Family, huh?" Levi asked as he stopped and looked over his shoulder at Killian. "I can get behind family and your threat. I was a dumbass, and I won't make that mistake again. She means more to me than anything in the entire universe."

The animosity didn't waft off Levi like it had when Killian had first stepped outside. Maybe they'd made some sort of progress after all. I might have gotten emotional, but that didn't mean I suddenly understood men. Some mysteries would never be solvable, and that was one of them.

"Good, because killing you would hurt her, and I don't want to cause her pain." Killian smiled sadly. "I want her to be happy. That's what matters to me."

My eyes burned, and warmth swirled in my chest. Killian was an amazing person, one of the best I'd ever known. The self-absorbed playboy façade had been an act to cover up the loss of his parents and little sister, and then Sterlyn had shown up and grounded both him and Griffin. He was now becoming the man and alpha he was meant to be, and I hoped he found a worthy fated mate to stand at his side. "And I want the same for you."

His shoulders slumped, and he glanced at the cobblestone ground. "I know. You two have a good night. I'll give you at least an hour before the rest of us come over."

Levi's scowl dropped, and he picked up his pace again. *We don't have one second to lose.*

Laughter bubbled inside my chest. Despite growing more accustomed to emotions, this one was by far the strangest of them all. It wasn't unpleasant, but I felt the most out of control, like I couldn't contain it even if I'd wanted to.

As soon as we entered the house, Levi swept me off my feet. A slight yelp escaped me as he sped toward the stairs.

His eagerness shifted something inside me, and my body warmed in expectation. When we reached the top of the stairs, he placed me on my feet, and we rushed into the room I'd been sleeping in. He said over his shoulder, "Warm up the shower and grab us some towels. I'll bring the clothes."

I hadn't expected to take a shower, but now that he

mentioned it, we were both bloody and sweaty from battle. Not to mention the first time we'd consummated our bond had been while bathing with each other, so maybe he wanted a do-over. I wasn't appalled by that in the slightest.

Inside the bathroom, I peeled off my clothes and shoes. My feet padded across the cool red oak tile, and I made my way past the white marble sink and toilet. When I reached the tub, I leaned inside to turn on the shower.

As the water warmed, I bent underneath the counter-top, grabbed two clean towels from the drawer, and placed them on the edge closest to the tub.

Though Levi didn't make a noise when he entered the bathroom, the air charged around me, alerting me to his presence. I spun around to find him drinking in the sight of me.

He clutched burnt orange yoga pants and a white shirt in one hand and a pair of men's black pajama bottoms in the other. "Gods, Rosey. You're so damn gorgeous." He tossed the clothes on the other end of the counter and slammed and locked the door before eagerly walking toward me.

However, my attention focused on the blood spatter on the dark shirt he wore. It was harder to see now that it was dried, but I still detected the thick scent of his blood.

Before we reconnected, I needed to heal him. I didn't want him to hurt himself worse with our fun, and he needed to be healed for his trip to Hell tomorrow.

"Here, let me heal you quickly before we climb in." I tapped into my magic, and my hand glowed as I reached for his stomach.

He caught my wrist and chuckled, "Slow down, Rosey. We aren't in a race."

I never said we were. There were times when I felt like I was talking to Sterlyn and her friends instead of him. He was just as old as I was, but his vernacular was way more modern, likely due to new demons being created and the weaker ones being able to roam Earth. Still, I didn't like feeling confused most of the time. I needed to head back to Shadow Ridge University for more modern classes and complain less when Sierra made me watch those dreadful things she called romantic comedies. *I just want sex.*

His smile grew so wide that dimples appeared on both cheeks. *Oh, we'll get to that, but we'll take our time.*

I did *not* want to take our time. I wanted hard, fast, and as debilitating as possible before the others made their way here and we had to be quieter. *I don't want to be able to walk without discomfort tomorrow.*

Hissing, he gritted his teeth. "I never imagined hearing you say that would be so fucking hot, and one day, we'll do that. I'll make it so you can't even walk the next day, if that's what you want, but not tonight."

Inhaling deeply, I kept my mouth and mind quiet. I wanted to complain, but if he wanted slow and boring, I would oblige. He was going to Hell tomorrow, after all.

You're pouting. He laughed as he slowly removed his shirt, grunting slightly from the pain.

Nausea rolled in my stomach when I saw how bad his abdomen was. Despite his supernatural healing, large gashes still marked his stomach where the spiked ball from the flail had hit him several times. They were so deep that they hadn't scabbed over, and blood still oozed from the wounds.

The air warmed, and not just from my desire; the water was hot, and steam filled the room. He kicked off his tennis shoes and removed his jeans and boxers.

Unable to help myself, I ogled him. All of him. Every

lickable...delectable...inch. A little bit of sanity left my mind, his injury the only thing keeping me grounded.

I had to remedy that.

"That has to hurt." I didn't like him being in pain. I'd rather take the brunt of it and spare him any more discomfort.

With his other hand, he flipped over my hand and nodded at my fingers. "Your injury is just as bad, if not worse. What were you doing? Holding a damn blade?"

"It was a strategic move. I needed the sword, and the demon had the handle. I knew I was delivering a killing blow that would get the weapon." Even though my wings were great, having an extra sharp object was ideal, especially because I didn't have to account for the aerodynamics of my wings.

His jaw dropped. "You seriously grabbed the sword's blade? You could be missing appendages right now!"

I wouldn't have allowed it to get that far. He was ruining the mood, so I pulled my hand away and turned to the shower. *Let's get clean so I can heal you and work off our frustrations.*

When he didn't argue, I wanted to pump my fist in victory. I would get my way after all.

I stepped into the water and let it run over my body. The almost scalding temperature felt good on my tense muscles, and I turned, allowing it to hit my back where my wings connected.

He slid into the shower after me and wrapped his arms around my waist. I tipped my head up, looking into his eyes, and he cupped my cheek. Warmth spread between us as he asked, *Are you okay?*

Better than okay. Being with him was right. Fighting

and being apart wasn't natural. *This* was how we were meant to be.

Running his fingers through my tresses, he tipped my head back so water wet my hair. Just like the first time, he wanted to take care of me. Knowing better than to argue, I enjoyed the view as he turned, got the shampoo, and lathered it into my hair.

My hand darted to his stomach, desperate to heal him, but he stepped back and rasped, "Let me take care of you first. I'm fine."

I cut my eyes at him, but since discomfort wasn't charging through the bond, I let it go. It wasn't hurting him too badly; otherwise, he wouldn't have been able to hide it.

After he'd cleaned my hair and body, he massaged my scalp and back, relaxing me further. I'd never had someone take care of me like this, and if it had been anyone else, I wouldn't have allowed it. With Levi, I felt safe to let down my guard.

After he gently washed my injured hand and lowered my arm, he slapped my ass and commanded, *Move, so I can get clean.*

Grabbing his shoulders, I switched places with him. *You washed me. I get to take care of you now.*

His mocha eyes lightened to an almost milk shade. *I'm all for that.*

I grabbed the sides of his face and tilted his head back.

He winced, which made my jaw clench. I said, "Let me heal you." This was getting beyond ridiculous, especially if his stomach was causing his agony.

"That isn't the problem." He mashed his lips together, but I could still feel his humor through our bond. "You just tilted my head too far back is all."

My cheeks burned. Clearly, gentle and caring was not

my specialty. *I'm sorry.* I dropped my hands, not liking the odd sensation within. I wanted to hide my face in embarrassment.

Don't be. He took my uninjured hand and leaned back so his hair got wet. *I love what you're doing. Don't stop. Please.*

I moved to get the shampoo and realized there was something I had to do first before I could work his body. I tapped into my core and let the magic fill my injured hand, healing it. I hated to waste magic on myself, but I wanted to be able to take care of him.

Within minutes, the skin healed itself, and he shook his head. *It's amazing to watch you do that.*

Obviously, the demons had lost that handy ability when they'd fallen, which made sense, since they'd lost their wings as well.

Now it was my turn to wash him.

A guttural growl emanated from him as I washed his body thoroughly, helping me gain confidence. I left his stomach for last since he complained every time I tried to use my magic on him.

More gently, I placed my hand on his injury and tapped into my magic. This time, he didn't gripe, and I pushed my magic inside him. His cool essence swirled around mine, the two temperatures colliding. However, this felt different, as if neither of us was holding back.

Our magic intertwined, and I pushed more of mine into him. It took at least twice as much magic to heal him than any other supernatural race. Though I could feel the magic depleting, something yanked inside me—a more desperate need for him filling my soul.

He groaned, *Our souls need us to combine. It's like they know we're done fighting the bond.*

That was the perfect description. I needed him, but it was different from all the other times. Before, we'd been frantic, as if our souls were trying to force us to connect. Tonight, it was need, but one of a deeper sort of connection...of true love.

He kissed me, and I opened my mouth to him willingly.

His tongue slipped inside, and I kept channeling more of my magic into him. His injury was almost healed. As our magics intertwined inside us, our mouths danced together.

I wasn't sure how much time had passed, but Levi finally pulled away, leaving me breathless.

"Let's go to the bedroom," he murmured as he kissed my cheek and turned the water off.

Wait. No. Let's have sex here first. Now that his injury was healed, I dropped my hand lower.

Moving backward, he caught my wrist and snickered, "In the bedroom, Rosey."

His command both turned me on and infuriated me. However, my body was too desperate for release for me to argue. The two of us slipped from the shower and dried off. I snatched the clothes from the countertop and rushed into the bedroom without putting them on. I wouldn't have been surprised if he said we should get dressed and have a cup of tea downstairs before we made love.

I was getting my release *now*, whether he liked it or not.

He followed close behind me, and when he locked us into the bedroom, I threw the clothes on the ground, then took him in my hand and stroked.

Gods, I love how you take charge and let me know exactly what you want. He moved his hips in rhythm with my hand but had me inching backward toward the bed.

When the back of my legs touched the mattress, he

hovered over me, making me sit down as I continued working his body.

Lie back, Rosey. He slid next to me on the bed. When we settled, he quickened my pace on him as he slipped his hands between my legs and rubbed.

The friction increased immediately, and I moved to sit up, but he kept his hold on me. *Let's take it slow*, he linked.

As he circled my sensitive area harder, I soared on the building pleasure. Ecstasy took over. My body convulsed, but he didn't slow his pace. Instead, he kept going harder.

I lost track of time as orgasm after orgasm rippled through my body. When he'd said we'd take it slow, I hadn't thought he'd have me panting from pleasure. I was so sensitive that each touch had me almost tipping over the edge again.

But it still wasn't enough.

Levi, please. I wasn't above begging. *I need you.*

A cocky smirk slid across his face as he rolled on top of me and positioned himself between my legs. *That's what I was waiting for, and thank gods. I wasn't sure how much longer I could last.*

He slipped inside me, moving slowly, and leaned over me, kissing me.

We moved in sync, our souls truly connecting. I'd never had anyone treat me with so much care and love.

Slow was not boring. It was mind-numbing in its own right. I wrapped my legs around his waist, and he moaned as he hit deeper inside me.

Our pace picked up slightly, and I dug my nails into his back, wanting to brand him in any way to make him mine.

His pleasure floated into me as our bodies neared the edge.

I love you more than life itself, he vowed, and lifted his head to stare me in the eye. *I will never hurt you like that again. All I want from here on out is to make you smile and make you feel loved.*

I feel the same way. I pushed my emotions toward him, not wanting him to doubt me, either. *I love you so much, it hurts to breathe.*

Our pleasure mixed together as an orgasm rocked us at the same time. It was the most intense pleasure I'd ever experienced, and we rode the emotions while holding the other's gaze, sealing the vow we'd just made to each other.

When our bodies calmed, he pulled me into his arms.

And as I fell asleep, I didn't worry about him leaving.

———

THE NEXT DAY, we spent our time in bed. Surprisingly, no one bothered us, and we didn't even leave to eat a meal.

We talked, had more sex, and napped, and I tried not to think about what would be happening within hours.

However, a knock on the door eventually came, and my heart dropped.

Killian cleared his throat. "I hate to interrupt, but we need to discuss some things."

It was official. Our time was over, and the next threat was here.

CHAPTER TWENTY-NINE

MY HEART SHUDDERED, but there was nothing we could do about it. Levi and I had purposely avoided the topic of him leaving, but the time was almost upon us.

Levi huffed as his arms tightened around me. *Can we just ignore him? Maybe he'll go away if we stay really silent. He might think we aren't here.*

Sex is thick in the air. There was no way Killian would ever believe we were gone. *And we both know that putting this off will make the princes of Hell realize that something went wrong here on Earth.*

He kissed the top of my head and slowly disentangled himself from me.

The urge to wrap my legs around him and convince him to stay coursed through me, but I'd just scolded him for having those same thoughts.

The longer he and Bune remained on Earth, the more precarious the situation in Hell could become. They needed to get down there and retrieve the sword and Eliza while the demons still thought Hecate and the others were scheming to kill Levi.

"Are we meeting next door?" I climbed to my feet and grabbed the clothes I'd tossed hastily after our shower last night.

Feet shuffled on the other side of the door, and Killian answered, "Yes. We've been trying to call you, and you haven't been answering. So I came over to get you, which you both owe me for. Sierra wanted to be the one."

"Thanks for that." Sierra would've been teasing us and making inappropriate comments that would have annoyed me. Better Killian than her.

After tossing Levi's boxers and shorts at him, I slipped on my burnt orange yoga pants. "We'll be there in a few minutes."

Levi followed my lead, a frown on his face.

Neither one of us wanted to face what would happen next. We were finally on the same page, wanting to make our relationship work, and he was heading into a dangerous situation without me—again.

"Sounds good." Killian fidgeted uncomfortably. "But if you don't hurry over, I'll send Sierra next."

"That won't be necessary." That was the last thing I desired.

I don't know why you give the feisty girl a hard time. Levi pulled the shirt over his head, his abs contracting.

If we hadn't just had sex at least a dozen times, I wouldn't have been able to keep my hands off him. As it was, just seeing him like this made me ready to roll into bed with him again, so it was fortunate I had extensive expertise with self-restraint, or Sierra *would* be coming over here. *I don't. She enjoys picking on everyone else. I'd rather not hear her talk about the scent of our sex and how she'd like to find someone like you to drape over her body.*

I might hurt her if she made any sexual comments about

my preordained. She'd made it clear several times that she found him hot, and that was bad enough.

Don't worry, love. He winked and took a few steps closer. *There is only one person who will ever be draped over my body from here on out. You have nothing to worry about.*

I yanked the white shirt over my yoga pants and shifted my weight to one side. *Oh, I know. If anyone even gets too close to you, the both of you will be dead.*

He chuckled, but when my expression didn't change, his smug expression disappeared. He scratched the back of his neck and rubbed his arms as he said, "Sometimes, you scare the hell out of me because I don't think you're kidding."

"Oh, I wasn't." All the times that Sterlyn, Griffin, Annie, Cyrus, Alex, and Ronnie had gotten all growly and possessive, I'd thought they were being ridiculous. My view hadn't necessarily changed, but even entertaining the idea of someone else getting close to Levi made my stomach sour.

"Good." He took my hand and led me toward the front door.

Every step closer we got to the others made my belly roil more. I hated the idea of him leaving, especially without me. *I wish I could go.*

I'll be honest, I'm glad you can't. His hand tightened on mine as we reached the bottom of the stairwell. *I'd rather you stay here—*

"You'd better watch your next words." I planted my feet firmly on the floor and yanked on his hand to turn him around. "I'm a warrior, and I refuse to be coddled."

"Believe me, I know," he said, and caressed my cheek. "But that doesn't mean I can't be happy you're safe."

He had me there. I'd just rather he stay here and be safe as well.

When I didn't argue, he kissed my lips and led me through the living room and out the front door.

The sun was setting, and twilight would be upon us in the next ten minutes. Being with him, I'd lost track of time, which never happened to me.

I know where the sword is being stored and where Eliza is being held. He squeezed my hand comfortingly as we reached the door to the other house. *We won't have to be in Hell for long.*

The worst part is that we won't be able to communicate. At least if the sword had been here, we could have connected, as long as I stayed close by. He was going to a different dimension, and our connection would be faint. I'd only know if something went horribly wrong, like last time. *But I'll be fine. I just need you to concentrate so you can return to me.*

When we walked up to the house next door, silence greeted us. Was anyone inside? The witches must have cast a spell to make it appear as if they weren't here.

He opened the front door. *I swear, my entire focus will be on accomplishing everything quickly so I can make it back to you.*

His determination flowed into me, and I didn't have any questions about his sincerity.

"They're here," Circe said from where she stood next to the window, like she had the night before, with Aspen on her right and Lux on her left. "We need to prepare to move."

Alex and Ronnie stood with Killian against the wall across from the television, with Sterlyn and Griffin by the television. Everyone else was in the same spot as before.

The only difference was that Zagan had a shirt on, which made me feel a little more comfortable. He stood in the corner with his arms crossed and a deep scowl on his face.

I didn't bother wasting time on him. "Is there anything we need to do before you leave?" I hated being out of the loop, but spending time with Levi had been more important.

Herne shook her head. "We need to go while we're still undetected. If the demons figure things out, even while we're in Hell, it will make things more difficult."

"Are we sure it's wise to send a bunch of witches down there when they already want to use Eliza?" The last thing I wanted was for Levi to go down there unprotected, but I also didn't want to give the demons more witches and make their work that much easier.

Sierra's mouth dropped. "Do you want to hand over your mate to the demons?"

"Of course not." I resented that she'd even asked the question. "But we all need to be on the same page. Maybe it would be better if I went down there with him instead of you five."

Turning to me, Levi lifted a hand. "They'd sense you as soon as you stepped through the portal. The witches and I can blend in with people who are already down there. An angel would be like a beacon, informing everyone that we'd arrived."

"We can hide Levi and Bune, as well as ourselves, down there." Circe rubbed her hands together. "Like Levi said, if our energy blends in and we cloak ourselves, we should be able to move around undetected."

Should.

That was the problem.

"They're right," Sterlyn said, and touched my arm. "I

know it's hard, especially since he's your mate. I would feel the same if I were in your shoes, but I'm telling you as a friend that this is the best strategy we have."

She was right. I was being irrational because I didn't want him to go.

"If something goes wrong, they can reach out to us." Cordelia stood from her spot next to Annie. "And the rest of us can go to Hell and help them. Hopefully, it won't come to that, but if they get into trouble, they can use these to communicate with us." She held up a pyrite pendulum charm. The gold-like rock sparkled in the light.

My chest relaxed a little, and breathing became easier. All I'd needed was confirmation that they had a backup plan, and if it came to it, that I'd be going with the witches down there. "Okay."

"Maybe I should go with them." Ronnie pursed her lips. "I could be helpful."

Alex growled, and red bled into his irises, making it clear he didn't like that suggestion.

"You need to stay here in case something happens and the council is called to meet." Griffin wrapped an arm around Sterlyn. "It's likely that something will happen, and if you're gone, it would raise questions."

"He's right," I said. Though I'd love for more people to go with them, we couldn't be careless back home.

Aspen moved toward the front door. "We need to go if we want twilight to help cover us."

This was it. The time had come for them to leave. "We should go with you to the portal."

"No, it's best if you stay away. If you get too close, it could alert the other side to our presence," Bune interjected.

Is that *why you prevented me from chasing after that*

demon the first day we met? Had Levi been protecting me from our first meeting, or was that wishful thinking?

He tugged me against his side and answered, *Yes. Demons could have come across at any time and flown back to alert others that an angel was close by. Since the group had left, I was worried that one would come to check in and gain reinforcements.*

"And they're paying attention down there, since they know where the portal opened." Zagan put his hands in his pockets and shrugged. "So it *is* best if you don't get close. They have witches in Hell since Hecate was sent here."

I was outnumbered and needed to listen. They had relevant points, and I didn't understand how Hell worked.

"Be safe, young grasshopper," Sierra said as she hugged Aurora. "Remember me while you're there, and channel whatever I would do."

"Don't." Killian shook his head. "Please don't. You'll wind up getting into trouble."

Lux chuckled. "Don't worry. I'll be her voice of reason."

"That's not very reassuring," Aurora teased.

Aspen, Circe, Lux, Aurora, Herne, and Bune drew closer to us as they moved toward the door, but I needed another moment with Levi. I didn't care if I caused a scene.

I faced him, placing my forehead against his. *You'd better stay safe and come back to me.*

Nothing in either world could keep me away. He cupped my cheek and stared deep into my eyes. *Rosey, you're my life, and I will come back to you. There's no way I can't. I love you that much.*

A deep throb penetrated my chest, and my throat dried as I blinked back tears. I could easily fall apart, but that wouldn't be fair to him. He needed me to be strong so he could go to Hell and focus without worrying about me.

I love you, too. And if something happens, I will come and fight for you. I pushed all the love I felt for him toward him, and I kissed him, wanting him to feel my love emotionally and physically.

His tongue slipped into my mouth, and I answered in earnest. This might be the last time I kissed him for a while, and I refused to hold anything back.

"Uh...Kill? Is this how pornos start?" Sierra murmured. "I've never seen one, but they're practically swallowing each other. This has to be how they start."

And just like that, she ruined the mood. *This is why she annoys me.*

Killian coughed like he'd choked. "Why are you asking me?"

She called Killian out. I'm here for it. Levi pulled back from me, his mocha eyes glinting with humor.

What an odd thing to say. *Of course you're here. You're not even twenty feet from her.*

"Oh, please." Sierra crossed her arms. "Like we don't know what you do. You've been so hard up—"

Alex stepped in front of Killian and said, "*And* it's time for them to go. Let's not allow Sierra to take us down the road of this particular topic."

Even though I had no problem with people who chose to watch porn, I agreed that I didn't want to think of Killian that way.

I forced myself to take a step back, putting a little distance between us. I'd keep finding an excuse to kiss Levi and keep him here otherwise.

Eliphas placed his hands on Cordelia's shoulders. "Be safe. We're here if you need us."

If I thought I'd experienced the hardest thing I'd ever gone through in my life before, I'd been so wrong. Watching

Levi walk out the door and into danger while I stayed behind almost killed me. Though all seven of them had proven to be worthy warriors, I liked being part of the battle. If something happened, I was there to assist and determine a solution with them. This time, I was completely removed from the situation, and it burned.

A sob built inside my chest, but I swallowed it. I couldn't break down, especially now. He could feel my emotions, and I couldn't let them get the best of me.

The room was silent.

Even though no one else had a mate who had left, their absence sat heavily on our hearts. Not only that, but getting Eliza back would happen only if their mission was successful.

"Levi and Bune know their way around down there, and they're strong," Zagan said awkwardly from the corner of the room. "If anyone can pull this off, it's them."

For the first time, I hoped a demon was right.

THE NEXT THIRTY minutes crept by. Sierra had put on a stupid show, but I couldn't pay attention enough to know anything about it. As usual, it was some guy and girl fighting their relationship, reminding me of Levi and me.

Sterlyn, Griffin, Alex, and Ronnie were outside, talking with the silver wolves on watch. I was too upset to concentrate, so I stayed inside and pretended to watch television while I latched on to my bond with Levi.

We're at the portal and heading in. Levi's voice popped into my mind. *I'll be back soon.*

Be safe. My heart threatened to shatter, but I inhaled deeply, trying to remain calm.

The moment he stepped through the portal, Annie and I knew. Annie gasped, her hand touching her chest as the warmth of the bond cooled to lukewarm.

I'd been expecting it, but that didn't stop the panic from churning within. "They're g-gone." My voice broke at the end.

"Now we wait for them to come home with Eliza." Annie sighed as she leaned her head on Cyrus's shoulder.

And the sword, but I wisely kept that part quiet. Both Ronnie and Annie were more concerned about their foster mom.

"I don't understand what we're watching." Zagan exhaled. "Why would those two be fighting their connection like this?"

"It's just one of those love dramas." Kamila crossed her legs. "Mom and I watch movies like this every Friday night."

"We do, but Eliphas goes to bed and reads biographies," Cordelia said. She patted her husband's shoulder.

Eliphas looked back from where he sat on the floor in front of her and shook his head. "I'd rather read something that truly happened than watch a made-up drama."

I could agree with that, especially since I didn't want to sit here and watch two people in love. My mind was centered on Levi.

The front door opened, and Sterlyn barreled through. Her gaze landed on me. "Rosemary, it's your mom. She needs you *now*."

CHAPTER THIRTY

A LUMP FORMED in my throat. I'd meant to get my phone after Levi had left, but I'd forgotten. "What has Azbogah done?" There was no doubt in my mind who'd caused this crisis.

"It's..." Sterlyn pinched the bridge of her nose. "They have the list of missing artifacts and will be alerting the council soon."

Mother plucker. I leaped to my feet, needing to get to Shadow City as quickly as possible.

"Wait...that's a good thing," Sierra paused the television show. "They'll go and see she doesn't have them."

If only our world worked that simply. "If they're going to the house to look for them, Azbogah is certain they won't come up emptyhanded." He'd make sure something was there. I headed to the door. "She must have been calling me." And I had let her down. She'd done so much for me, and here I was, not there when she needed me.

"She doesn't know that the inventory is complete, so she won't be warned in time to recheck the house. We didn't want to do anything to alert Azbogah or any other council members that we'd been notified. Kira gave us a heads-up via the burner phone we gave her." Sterlyn stepped aside. "You need to go. We'll be right behind you."

"*Burner* phone?" I had my own cell phone, of course, but I'd never heard it called hot.

I was on my feet, ready to go out the door. However, I needed to know what that was in case somebody said something about it.

"It's an unregistered cell phone so no one but the person who has it knows about it." Sierra rolled her eyes, but her voice was tense with consternation. "We need to discuss your terminology later. If you're supposed to be blending in with the rest of the world, you need to work on your modern knowledge, but at least you aren't calling it a mobile cellular anymore."

I didn't know what that last part meant, but her message was clear. I was old, despite looking young, and I needed to refocus on my studies at the university. But that would be later, when Levi was back and my mother was free of any unsavory accusations.

I'd gotten what I needed. Kira hadn't utilized a witch or anyone else. Griffin or Sterlyn had given her the mobile... cell phone. That meant no one else should be alerted outside of the artifact police force and our group.

Time was of the essence, so I rushed past Sterlyn and out the door. Then I slowed down. Even though I was desperate to take off, I had to give the illusion of composure. I couldn't draw the attention of any nearby humans or vampires.

Griffin reached Sterlyn's side as my feet hit the cobblestone road. Alex and Ronnie had just gotten into their SUV, and Alex turned over the engine.

"We'll follow you there," Griffin vowed, his eyes lightening as he placed a hand over his heart.

Ever since he'd asked me to risk my life for his mother, he'd softened more toward me. We'd become somewhat friends because of Sterlyn, but it felt like we were moving beyond that...or my emotions were allowing me to see things differently. Either way, I realized he planned to save my mother, just as I had saved his. "Just don't act too out of sorts." Even though my heart pounded and sweat pooled under my arms, I needed to remind them to stay rational. "Otherwise, they'll realize we know something."

"In other words, don't drive like a bat out of hell?" He arched a brow.

That sentence was nonsensical.

"If that means don't drive quickly, then yes. We need to keep them oblivious to the fact that we've been alerted so I can scour the house and find anything that might've been planted. If anything is there, I hope I'll have time to dispose of it." And the sooner I could get there, the likelier I'd be able to accomplish my goal.

Griffin nodded. "We'll ask Kira to hold them up as best she can."

Though I'd never been fond of Kira, she'd proven herself to be an ally, and I had to remember that. I couldn't let my jealousy over how Levi had befriended her jade me to the facts. I'd been allowing that to happen, and I refused to let it continue. "Yes, but don't let her cause trouble for herself." Afraid I might retract what I'd said, I pivoted toward the back of the house, moving quickly toward the tree line.

"I'll get Sterlyn to call her right now." His eyes glowed faintly, indicating that the two of them were using their pack link to communicate.

If a vampire saw me take flight where a human could see, it would get back to the council, even if Alex and Ronnie tried to intervene. Though the vampires inside Shadow City had never left the gates, the Shadow Terrace vampires provided blood for the city daily. Therefore, the vampires talked to one another, and things got back to the council that way.

Two silver wolves in wolf form were stationed at the corners at the back of the house. They stayed deep enough in the thickening tree lines so no humans would notice them and where the vampires would have to be actively searching to see them.

As soon as I was deep enough in the woods, I stepped behind two large oak trees positioned together. My wings exploded from my back, and I ascended into the sky. With the dark now over us and the height of the trees, I should be able to make it to the skyline without detection, and if a human saw me, they'd think I was a large bird.

Pawing at the ground, the silver wolf whimpered with worry. He could feel the tension rolling off me.

Great, I wasn't doing a good job of disguising my anxiety. The threat to my mother and the fact that I couldn't feel Levi as strongly had me on edge. "There's no attack happening," I reassured him, though he had probably already linked with Sterlyn and Cyrus.

A few raccoons scurried toward the town, desperate for food. Some tension eased from my body. At least that was a sign there weren't any evil demons close by. The fact that we hadn't been able to detect them earlier was a whole different situation, but Annie hadn't felt the flare of the portal from her demon connection until Levi and the others had gone through.

We should be safe for now.

Both the Navigator and the Mercedes were driving off as I reached the top of the trees. As I pushed myself higher into the clouds, I watched them travel slowly toward the city.

Good, they were taking my advice.

Knowing I couldn't be seen this high up, I pushed myself faster, soaring over the town. I could see ant-sized people walking around between the flames of the flickering gas lights.

Within seconds, I was halfway across the Shadow Terrace bridge. The cool early November breeze caressed my skin, but it didn't bring me comfort. Between Mother being at risk and Levi being gone, not even the chill could ease the boiling blood pumping inside me.

Now that I was within the magical spell that hid the bridge and Shadow City from human eyes, I lowered myself so the vampire guards could see my arrival. Sometimes, I wished the dome wasn't covered in glass so I could just fly inside, but that was the cost of protection.

After learning everything I had, I couldn't determine if it protected the residents from outside threats or from learning the truth about our corrupt council. The more supernaturals I met outside of our town and city, the more corruption and hidden truths I saw within.

Forcing myself to take deep, calming breaths, I focused on my bond with Levi. Even though it was significantly cooler than it had been an hour ago, I clung to the lukewarm sensation. Levi was not dead or harmed.

I straightened my shoulders and kept my chin high as my feet touched the cement of the bridge. The golden wires that ran from the towers swung gently in the air, making a slight creaking noise that seemed almost too natural...too human.

A loud cranking noise churned, and the bottom of the wooden gate creaked open. I took a few steps forward, eager to slip underneath. If I hadn't been worried about seeming anxious, I'd have been on my belly, inching underneath the door right now. But that would have looked very suspicious, and that was the last thing I needed. Nervous energy rolled through me, and the urge to bounce on my feet was nearly uncontrollable.

Calm down, Rosemary, I chastised myself. This wasn't the first time I'd dealt with a precarious situation. But I hadn't dealt with something like this with all my emotions at the surface. This anxiety and worry was a whole new experience, and I again found myself empathizing with the others in similar situations.

When the door was to my waist, I couldn't wait any longer. I forced myself to not walk too quickly, but I ducked underneath and took flight once again. I didn't bother speaking to the vampire at the guard shack, and guilt edged over me.

These strange emotions were worse than before. I had no clue what was bothering me, but my stomach roiled.

With the moon ascending, more vampires were out. Even though the ones who lived in the city hadn't lost their humanity and were safe in direct sunlight, vampires favored the night. Darkness was their friend, likely due to their pale complexion. Even vampires with dark brown skin had a pale sheen.

I flew higher, all their combined cloying scents making my stomach churn.

The dome lights flickered around me. The smoke from the fire had cleared, and the lights were back to normal. Though they weren't as bright as during the day, they still contained a charge that helped replenish my magic. Healing both myself and Levi had taken some energy out of me, but I'd be back to normal in minutes.

I headed toward the capitol building, having to pass by it to reach the angel section of the city. I flew faster than normal, but not at a speed that would be considered unusual. If anyone noticed me, it would look as if I were focused on a task, not a true mission.

The biggest problem that kept circling in my mind was what I would do if there were artifacts in the house. I couldn't take them back to the artifact building—someone would see me with them—but I couldn't allow them to stay in the house and have Mother take the fall for something she didn't do.

Though not ideal, the best place to stash them would be near the woods that abutted the angels' housing. I'd hate to risk shifters getting their hands on them, but if we could clear this matter up quickly, we could strategize how to return the artifacts after things settled down.

I sailed over the capitol building, noting that the lights were off, and headed toward the woods. The council and police force were clearly not at the capitol, leaving two options: they were still at the artifact building...or they were already at my house.

I hung west more than necessary to see if I could glimpse activity at the artifact building. If they were still there, I had a chance of stashing the items before they reached our high-rise.

The large storage building was located between the edge of downtown and the woods. It was the lowest trafficked area of the city. Most people gathered either in the middle of the city or in the shifter woods, wanting to roam free. As I reached the more isolated area, my shoulders went slack. Azbogah, Mother, Father, Erin, Grady, Diana, and Breena were marching toward the building's front door.

Kira must have called the council to inform them the inventory was complete, and they were arriving to discuss what was missing. If I could find the items, I could remove them without my parents getting involved.

Though I'd learned not to hide things from them, their lack of knowledge would bode well for them if they were questioned. The more plausible deniability, the better.

Maybe, for once, things would go in our favor without too much of a cost.

Now that I'd reached the woods, I didn't hold back. I flew over the cypresses, redbuds, and oaks that still showed the healthy green colors of summer foliage. Though Shadow City was located in southeast Tennessee, the temperature was controlled here, and it was comfortable and warm all year long.

The all-glass angel high-rise came into view, and my eyes focused on the top balcony that led into our unit. The moon had just risen in the sky, alerting me that I was running out of time.

Moon magic ran through my blood, similar to how justice ran through it from my mother, but it felt as if the moon were mocking me.

Damn emotions.

Blood raced through my veins, and the pounding of my heart echoed in my ears. Every moment brought Azbogah and the authorities closer to arriving here.

Most angels were probably in their homes, reading up on battle strategies, playing chess, or engaging in whatever other mind-stimulating activity they enjoyed most. As I reached our building, I spotted three men who had trained me hovering in the air, sparring with swords. They attacked each other with a vengeance, each determined to prove his superiority.

If only *that* was what I had to worry about.

As I passed by, I waved at them, trying to look relaxed.

On our balcony, I pulled my house key from my pocket. As expected, the sliding glass door was locked, but that didn't mean anything. The cops had keys to every house in the city in case of emergencies, so Azbogah could have easily gotten his hands on ours.

Not bothering to turn on the lights, I tiptoed through the house. Part of me expected to find something planted in the middle of the room, easy to spot, but that would be unbelievable. The stolen item had to be somewhere hidden.

My first instinct was to look for a large object, but that would defeat a discreet plan and would be noticed...eventually. Whatever was planted was probably small and easy to hide.

Circling the large room, I looked at the bareness of it all. Two couches were the only furniture we had in here. The cushions...

My chest tightened as I rushed to the couches and removed each cushion, looking for a small cutout that could hide something easily. Each seam was in place, however, and I even ran my hands along the tops and bottoms to feel for any lumps.

Nothing.

I gritted my teeth. The kitchen was all glass, and the table and chairs couldn't hide anything.

Where else could contraband have been placed?

If I were a manipulative person who wanted no doubt about who had stolen the artifacts, where would I put them?

I wished Levi were here to help me figure this out. He was right—I had a hard time seeing gray. All I saw was right and wrong. Thinking like a criminal was forcing me to go outside my comfort zone.

Then it hit me like a bolt of lightning.

Their bedroom. It had to be on my mother's side of the mattress because she could possibly find it if it were in her pillow.

With renewed determination, I ran to their room on the right side of the house.

It was almost the same as mine, but the bed was a foot longer. Glass formed the bed frame, and the fluffy gray comforter could almost pass for a cloud. I raced to the right side where Mother slept—it would be easy for a stranger to determine her side, for her lotus scent was heaviest there.

I slipped my hand between the mattress and the bed frame and ran it along the edge. Near the halfway point, I stilled.

I'd found it.

Sliding to my knees, I lifted the mattress as warmth spread across my chest. I'd thought it would take longer to locate whatever this was, so I wouldn't protest.

A section of the glass was cut out. Whoever had done this was skilled with manipulating glass, but that wasn't what was most surprising. There wasn't just one artifact but three: a bulky golden ring, a skull key with a lock in the shape of a spinal cord, and a single red ruby.

Even more surprising, there was a hand-drawn picture of Mother and Azbogah wrapped in a lover's embrace from their time together. But now wasn't the time to focus on that.

A power that I'd never sensed before wafted from each artifact, though the ring had a similar signature to Mother's.

Something to address another day.

I grabbed all three items, and the key shocked my fingertips as I placed it in my hand. Startled, I almost dropped it, but I clutched the artifacts.

That was odd, but I didn't have time to dwell on it.

I left the picture that would haunt me for the rest of my existence and held the artifacts tightly as I put the mattress back in place. I'd rather Mother never know what I'd found.

Knowing time was running out, I barreled toward the sliding door. At least these smaller items would be easy to hide in the woods. I just needed to get out of the house.

But as I slid open the door, my gaze landed on Mother, Father, Azbogah, and Ingram. They were fifty yards away, and their attention instantly focused on me, and then on my clutched fist.

No.

If I could make it outside the city gate, I might have a chance to hide these items before anyone could prove they'd been here.

Not bothering to shut the door, I took to the sky and rushed toward the gate.

"Rosemary!" Mother yelled frantically, but that wouldn't stop me.

Ingram's tawny wings looked almost as dark as Azbogah's in the night sky. He called, "Munkar, Phul, and Ishim, stop Rosemary!"

The three angels who were battling in midair turned their attention up to me. Munkar's dark brows pulled together, but Ishim gasped, "Do you feel the power coming off her?"

"She has the missing artifacts!" Azbogah bellowed. "Get her!"

"Missing artifacts?" Phul parroted, then swung his sword at me.

I ducked at the last second, leaving his sword *whoosh*ing

through air. He wasn't trying to kill me but rather distract me while the others surrounded me.

I tried to dodge and fly on. These three angels were warriors and older than me, and I respected them. They'd helped train me. I didn't want to hurt them. They were following orders, though they didn't understand what was at stake.

I dropped and hoped I'd done enough to slip away. They were strong, but I was lighter and faster.

"Not so fast," Ishim rasped as he appeared right in front of me.

He reached to grab my waist, and I kicked him in the face. His head jerked back, but he kept his hands outward, still trying to grasp me.

I twisted and swooped close to the ground. With the other two above me, going up wasn't an option.

Munkar dropped in just overhead. I could feel his hunkering presence, and I had to get away before it was too late.

When I flapped my wings to gain speed, something solid hit me in the back of the skull. Pain shot through my skull, and the world went fuzzy. I shook my head and tried to focus. I didn't have a choice. I had to get away.

Locking my focus on a tree, I flew toward it. If I could keep it centered as the world twirled, I'd maintain some sort of bearing. But my wings were growing sluggish, indicating that the hit had likely given me a concussion.

Large arms encircled my waist, trapping me, and Ingram's mossy scent filled my nose. He growled, "Did you really think you could get away?"

No, but I'd had to try. Though I wouldn't admit that to him.

Azbogah, Father, and Mother appeared in front of me.

Mother's eyes darkened to hunter green and widened as her attention locked on my hand. Father's normally calm essence was tense, and his jaw twitched, putting me more on edge and making the world spin faster.

"Open your hand," Azbogah commanded.

There was nothing else I could do. They'd caught me, and I had nowhere to fly and hide. So I did as he'd asked. At least these items would be returned to the artifact building.

I straightened my shoulders the best I could, ignoring Ingram's chest pressed against my back, and held out my right hand, slowly opening my palm.

The three items lay precariously on my hand, and the energy burst around me. It was strange—I hadn't noticed the power surrounding me until now.

"Rosemary," Mother gasped as she glanced at me, then at Azbogah. She scowled, and her face hardened.

I wasn't sure if that expression was directed at me, Azbogah, or both of us.

Father's jaw dropped, and he didn't come to my side. Instead, he remained a bystander, watching everything unfold.

Somehow, that hurt worse.

Agony flashed through my chest, but I had to believe they were acting this way because they had no choice but to play along. Neither of my parents would turn their back on me. I'd done this to *protect* them...to protect *her*.

I wasn't sure if they actually thought the worst or if they believed I might be capable of this because I'd bonded with a demon. Either way, their actions burned.

A quote Sierra always chanted when she was angry crossed my mind: *Hell hath no fury like a woman scorned*.

Azbogah and his followers had no clue who they were messing with. Not only would I persevere and get out of this, even if it killed me, but Levi and my friends would stand beside me, and Azbogah would feel the fury of a demon he'd done wrong.

"Take her to the prison," Azbogah commanded flatly.

A deep chuckle vibrated in Ingram's chest as he murmured in my ear, "Ironic that mine is the last male touch you will ever feel."

My blood boiled, and the edges of my vision were spotted. I threw my head back, connecting with Ingram's nose. A loud crack filled the air, and his arms loosened.

I'd hit my target, and I spun around, ready to take him on.

If I was going to prison, I might as well make it worthwhile.

This plan had been a gross miscalculation. I'd been so hopeful that I could execute it without issue, but this was the worst situation I'd ever faced. Now I could only pray I found a way out of this...and that Levi forgave me.

ABOUT THE AUTHOR

Jen L. Grey is a *USA Today* Bestselling Author who writes Paranormal Romance, Urban Fantasy, and Fantasy genres.

Jen lives in Tennessee with her husband, two daughters, and two miniature Australian Shepherds. Before she began writing, she was an avid reader and enjoyed being involved in the indie community. Her love for books eventually led her to writing. For more information, please visit her website and sign up for her newsletter.

Check out my future projects and book signing events at my website.
www.jenlgrey.com

ALSO BY JEN L. GREY

Shadow City: Silver Wolf Trilogy

Broken Mate

Rising Darkness

Silver Moon

Shadow City: Royal Vampire Trilogy

Cursed Mate

Shadow Bitten

Demon Blood

Shadow City: Demon Wolf Trilogy

Ruined Mate

Shattered Curse

Fated Souls

Shadow City: Dark Angel Trilogy

Fallen Mate

Demon Marked

Dark Prince

The Wolf Born Trilogy

Hidden Mate

Blood Secrets

Awakened Magic

Cursed

The Artifact Reaper Series

Reaper: The Beginning

Reaper of Earth

Reaper of Wings

Reaper of Flames

Reaper of Water

Stones of Amaria (Shared World)

Kingdom of Storms

Kingdom of Shadows

Kingdom of Ruins

Kingdom of Fire

The Pearson Prophecy

Dawning Ascent

Enlightened Ascent

Reigning Ascent

Stand Alones

Death's Angel

Rising Alpha